MEANS

OF

ESCAPE

There is always a way!

A Chance and Choices Adventure
Book Four

Lisa Gay

Lisa Gay

Chance and Choices

ISBN-13: 978-1-945858- 08-6
ISBN -10: 1-945858-08-7

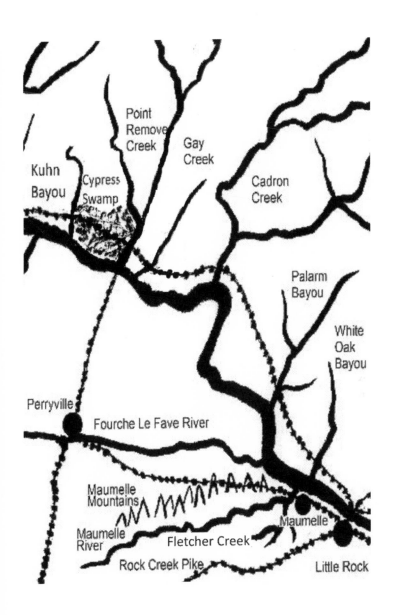

Those Involved in these incidents:

Place of Origin – Harmony
Ann Williams – the oldest sister – Noah's wife
Stephanie Yates – the middle sister – Eli's wife
Sally Williams – the youngest sister
Eli Yates – Stephanie's husband
Chris Williams- Ann, Stephanie, and Sally's father
Emma Williams - Ann, Stephanie, and Sally's mother
Eyanosa – Noah's horse
Dusty – horse previously owned by the Williams

Place of Origin – Indian Territory
Noah Swift Hawk – Ann's husband

Place of Origin – Unknown
Hank Butterfield – Butterfield Gang member / Roy's brother
Roy Butterfield - Butterfield Gang member
Gus - Butterfield Gang member
Ben - Butterfield Gang member
Russell French – Traveling Resupply Business co-owner & first owner of the injured mules
Arnold Buzzmann - Traveling Resupply Business co-owner & second owner of the injured mules

Place of Origin – Pine Bluff
Roscoe Bacon – founder of Bacon's Trading Post
James Bacon – Eli's alias as Roscoe's nephew
Nancy Bacon – Sally alias as Roscoe's niece

Roscoe's donkeys:
Little Jenny – miniature donkey
Little Jack – miniature donkey
Big Jenny
Shaggy
Spot
Blanco
Chocolate
Smiley
Honey
Quick Silver

Roscoe's mules:
King
Ace
Rose
Hector
Molly
Jumper
Blue
Chief
Diamond
Stubborn - (Redeemed)

Roscoe's goats:
Snowflake
Bella
Fancy
Billy

Place of Origin – Little Rock

Daniel Hall – Judge of State of Arkansas

Pearl Hall – Judge Hall's wife

Ansel Hall- Judge Hall's son

John Peabody – Peabody Inn owner

Mr. Hillcrest – Hillcrest Inn owner

Clark – owner of the general store

Charles – Bakery owner

Martin Harrow – livery owner

Dollie Harrow – Martin's wife

Edwin Snow - Stable hand at Martin Harrow's Livery

S.R. Snow– Edwin's father

Mary Snow – Edwin's mother

Mr. Beamis– white man guilty of interracial relations

Miles Cornish – Captain – U.S. Army

Melvin Hatcher– Private - U.S. Army

Thaddeus Pratt – Reverend

Jasper Daniels – murdered in Little Rock

Candace Daniels – Jasper's wife (Candy)

Marie - Stephanie's alternate identity

Dr. Luke Smith – Noah's first alternate identity

Isabelle Smith – Ann's first alternate identity

Acquired in Little Rock

<u>Sally's injured mules:</u>

Mule 17 – severely injured side (Beauty)

Mule 4 – injured eye

Mule 7

Mule 8

<u>Noah and Ann's injured mules:</u>

Mule 11 - (Honor)

Mule 20 – (Justice)

<u>Morris's injured mule:</u>

Mule 15 – bought through Martin Harrow

Place of Origin – Fletcher Creek

Katie – Underground Railroad guide

Morris - Katie's husband / Lewis's brother

George - Katie's oldest son

Carmen - Katie's oldest daughter

Ann - Katie's second daughter

Caleb - Katie's 6-year-old son

Rebecca - Katie's sister

William - Rebecca's husband / Matthew's brother (Will)

Matthew- William's brother (Matt)

Sarah - Matt's wife / Andrew's sister

Justin - Matt's oldest son

Freeman - Matt's second son

Elizabeth – Matt's oldest daughter

Agnes – Matt's daughter

Matilda - Matt's youngest daughter

Elijah – Matt's youngest child

Andrew – Sarah's brother

Grace – Andrew's wife

John - Andrew and Grace's newborn baby

Lewis – Morris's brother

Fannie – Lewis's wife

Edna – Lewis's daughter

Pearl – Lewis's daughter

Theodore – Roscoe's alternate identity (Theo)

Abraham – Noah's second alias

Lily – Ann's second alias

Place of Origin – Maumelle

Norman Sweeting – lawman

Lucy – owner of Lucy's Boarding House

Horatio Knapp– Man mugged in alley

Esther Knapp– mugged in alley / Horatio's wife

Murray Strong – Esther Knapp's brother

Henry Parker – Morris's alternate identity

Charles Woolsey – Matthew's alternate identity

One

In Little Rock Arkansas, after two days conducting a public veterinary clinic at Martin Harrow's Livery, what the young doctor and his wife had tried to avoid for months finally happened: Judge Daniel Hall stood in front of them with a drawn gun. Dollie Harrow's desire to elevate her social status had led her to invite the judge, the doctor, and their wives to a mid-day dinner party.

Mrs. Hall walked into the room. The doctor almost choked on his crumpet. Dollie had invited the one man who knew the truth. "My husband sends his regrets. He so wanted to come. Unfortunately, he has been detained."

Dollie felt disappointed but remained gracious. "Tea, Mrs. Hall?"

"Yes, with two lumps of sugar."

Mrs. Hall has no idea. My secret is safe. The doctor took a swallow of tea to calm his coughing.

"My husband told me about your son. How is Ansel?" asked the doctor's wife.

"Still pain-free. Your husband was sent to us by God. You're a lucky woman to have such an intelligent husband."

"Thank you, Mrs. Hall. I agree."

As the Harrows and their guests made small talk,

1

Judge Hall managed to escape the circumstances that had kept him occupied. *I'm so glad I'll be able to personally thank and shake the hand of the doctor who cured my son.*

After serving a scrumptious meal, Dollie went to her kitchen to get dessert. She saw her fourth guest coming up the walkway. Happily, she led Judge Hall into her dining room. "Meet the doctor who helped Ansel."

Judge Hall looked into the eyes of the two he was sure had returned to their vile relationship. "That man is not Dr. Smith!"

Dollie stated emphatically, "I assure you that he is."

"They are Noah Swift Hawk and Ann Williams." He drew a pistol from his pocket. "I told you, if I found you together, that you'd get maximum lashing and a year hard labor. I'm going to whip you both myself, especially you, Ann Williams."

Mrs. Hall stepped in front of her husband. "You will do no such thing. I don't care who they are. This is the man who treated Ansel, and you will not harm him or his wife."

Judge Hall told his wife, "They're breaking the law."

She didn't believe him. "What law could they possibly be breaking?"

Dollie, Martin, Noah, and Ann sat paralyzed. Dollie and Martin didn't understand what was happening. Noah and Ann thought Judge Hall was surely going to shoot them if they moved, probably even if they didn't. Judge Hall explained, "He's an Indian man, and she's a white woman."

"You've got to be out of your mind! That man gave your son a pain-free life. It doesn't matter if he's an Indian or a," she paused, "buffalo!"

The white man, Beamis, who had made a family with a person of color, had escaped because Judge Hall couldn't find them, but he had these two. He wasn't letting them go. "It's the law."

Mrs. Hall asked, "Dollie, do you have the ledger in which you wrote who we were and what we were paying?"

"It's right here." Dollie picked up the ledger.

Mrs. Hall flipped through the pages. "Read this line, Daniel. What does it say?"

Daniel read aloud, "Human, Ansel, stomach pain, one act of mercy from my husband, Mrs. Daniel Hall."

"I had money that day. When Dollie asked how I was going to pay, a feeling swept over me that I should say that you would pay for Ansel's care with an act of mercy. You will honor that payment."

Judge Hall looked at the ledger. He looked at his wife. *Noah is the man who told her how to remove Ansel's pain. She will never forgive me.* He looked at Noah, then Ann. "I'll let him go, but not her." Ann had told him she was going to be with that Indian and be right before God and that he would still be wrong. He strongly desired to whip her.

Judge Hall's wife stepped up to him and held the pistol to her heart. "Then shoot me now because that's exactly what you'll be doing. You'll be putting a hole through my heart if you hurt either one of them."

Mr. Harrow's stable hand, thirteen-year-old Edwin,

sauntered up the Harrow's walkway. Through the window, he saw Judge Hall with a gun pointed at the heart of his own wife, and Mr. and Mrs. Harrow looked as white as the snow that still lay on the ground. Edwin realized there was a worse storm inside the house than the one that had raged across their town a few days before. He crept up to the window and listened.

I'll grant them one act of mercy. I'll allow them to leave this house. As soon as I can get to the arsenal, I'm sending soldiers to track them down and bring them back. I'm going to enjoy ripping the flesh off their bodies. Judge Hall spit the words, "Leave, before I change my mind," from his mouth.

Noah Swift Hawk and Ann Williams shot out of their chairs, grabbed their bags, and flew out the kitchen door.

Edwin already knew all about the Judge. His family had helped Mr. Beamis escape with his slave and their children, and they had helped others before them. He slipped away from the window and ran after them. "Dr. Smith, I can help you!"

Noah recognized Edwin's voice, but he didn't slow. "We have to go! We can't talk with you!"

"I have a place for you to hide."

"We have to get some people!" Ann's long, black hair streamed out behind her as she ran.

"The Bacons said you're traveling with them. I'll tell them to go on without you."

Ann had to spill the beans, "We haven't been honest with you. We're all one family. We have to go together."

"You're a family with Nancy?" Edwin didn't want any of them to tangle with Judge Hall, but especially not the beautiful fifteen-year-old girl who enthralled him.

Ann confessed, "Nancy is my youngest sister."

"Can you hide all of us?" Noah asked.

"Yes. I'll get you to the first stop, then I'll bring them."

Noah was sure Judge Hall wasn't letting them go. Hatred was written all over the man's face. "We're going to trust you to get them and hide us."

"I want your family to understand that I'm on your side. How will they know to come with me?"

"Tell them, Chris and Emma's child says she loves them to the moon and back."

Ann agreed, "Perfect."

Edwin hurried them to his house and opened the door. "Father, railroad procedure, large depot."

The night before, S.R. had met the man he thought was only a veterinarian giving twenty chickens to his son. "Follow me, Dr. Smith." S.R. grabbed his shotgun, just in case.

Edwin left the two people he knew as Dr. and Mrs. Smith in the care of his father and went to get the rest of their family.

At the livery, Nancy asked, "What took you so long?"

"I'll explain on the way. You have to come with me now. Chris and Emma's child said she loves you to the moon and back."

Both of Ann's sisters exclaimed, "What?!"

"Judge Hall found them. We have to go."

5

"Climb up here and tell us where to go." So he could remain with this family Roscoe, the man who had just sold his trading post, flicked the reins across one of his mule's back. "King, forward ho."

Edwin sat beside the girl whose heart-shaped lips he had been thinking about kissing. "It would be easier if you let me drive." Edwin held out his hands. Roscoe handed over the reins. Ann's other sister, currently known as Marie, and her sister's husband, who was still pretending to be Roscoe's nephew James, followed in their second wagon.

They traveled two miles down Old Sweet Home Pike then rode back toward town in the same track. At a wash, they turned off the road, erased the evidence of their departure, and then left no trail by riding in the runoff from the melting snow. They exited onto bedrock that perfectly concealed their route the rest of the way to the only place large enough to hide two Conestoga Wagons, six people, and thirty-one animals.

The opening was only high enough to get in if they took off the wagon bows, so they stopped in front of the entrance to remove them.

James looked into his wife's blue eyes as he helped her out of the driver's box. "Go talk to your sister."

Marie kicked the dirt as she made her way to the leading wagon. *Now, we have this problem again.* She stopped beside her sister. "Do you think you can go inside? If you can't, I'll send James and Roscoe in with the wagons and animals, and we'll stay out here."

"I'm going to try." Breathing short, shallow breaths of fear, the youngest of the three sisters walked to the

6

entrance. She stood beside Marie and looked into the opening. Nancy didn't like it. "Go in and tell me what you see."

"Of course." Marie narrated what she saw as she went, "The entrance isn't high or wide. It doesn't look like we can get a wagon through, but we must be able to, or they wouldn't have brought us here. It's not a long tunnel, and there's plenty of light. I've come to a very large" —she didn't want to say cave— "hollow. There is more than enough room for the wagons and animals. Others have been here before us. I see a fire pit. There are some rails set up as a corral, and it looks like lots of firewood is stacked in here."

"Come get me. I want to make up for the problems I caused the last time a cave came into our lives."

Just then, Ann walked up behind her sister. "Do you want me to walk in with you?"

"You're here!" Nancy threw her arms around her oldest sister. "Marie," she called out as she hugged her brother-in-law, "come out here!"

S.R. told his son, Edwin, "Go back to the livery. Tell Mr. Harrow that you ran away and hid because you saw the Judge holding a gun to Mrs. Hall's heart, and you were afraid."

Edwin hated to leave, but he wanted these people to get away. "May God keep you safe." He hugged each of them. "Goodbye." He hurried away on foot.

Noah's belief was confirmed; *that's what I thought.*

S.R. repeated the same information that he had told other people in the past, "Two days from now, somebody will come and take you to the next stop. That person will ask you, 'Have you made the items?' You say, 'Look in the wooden box.' Keep your fire in the pit around to the right. I'm sure you understand that you can never speak of this place, my family, or any part of this route."

Ann replied, "We understand, and I'm sure you won't tell anybody about us either."

"Do you know how long this trip will take or where we will end up?" asked Noah.

S.R. explained, "I only know this stop. I don't know who is on either side or where you will go. The people I bring here don't know where they are, so they can't tell anybody. That makes it safer because nobody knows anything except their one little part."

That was not the case this time. At every turn, Noah had used his Indian training and had remained oriented to the sun. He had calculated how far they had traveled. Even after the long walk, he believed they were only about half an hour out of town. Edwin's departure had confirmed it. Noah easily could have gotten back, but he didn't think there was any reason to give away that fact. Even though he knew where they were, it didn't help him to know where they were going. Still, he was very grateful. He handed S.R. a coin. "This is to thank you for helping us."

S.R. didn't feel the money was charity. He and Edwin were taking a great risk being their means of escape. He took the Spanish Piece of Eight. In the early spring of 1840, he left Dr. Luke Smith and his family at the beginning of their journey in The Underground Railroad.

Two

Marie asked, "Nancy, do you want to try to go inside while the others get the wagons ready?"

Nancy grasped at excuses to avoid facing her fear. I need more time to figure out how to solve this. "Stephanie, it's only us now, use our real names."

Stephanie didn't drop the subject. "All right, Sally, are you going to try? Ann and I will be right beside you."

Sally sucked down deep breaths and edged toward the opening. Her mind screamed: the cave is going to collapse! She took a few steps into the entry tunnel. I'm suffocating. The walls are closing in. "I can't do it. I'm sorry." She ran out before she was five steps inside. Her sisters walked out behind her. Sally climbed into the wagon with her injured, sedated mule. "I wish I was sleeping like you. I wouldn't know I was even near a cave." Sally rubbed Beauty between the ears. The mule's chestnut colored fur was intact between its ears, but the right side of its body had barely started to heal. Most of its fur had been cut away during a ferocious blizzard that had blown through Little Rock with gale force winds.

Noah walked toward the wagon. He asked the sixty-year-old man they had taken into their family, "Roscoe, come here. What did we bring that can help a person relax and not be anxious?"

9

As intended, Sally heard Noah. "Good idea, brother. I want to be able to go into the cave and not be a problem."

Noah comforted his sister-in-law. "It's all right. Go to the other wagon. Remove as much hay as needed to find the ingredients. We'll take this wagon and some of the animals inside."

Sally left her mule's side and got out of the wagon. She stopped to hug the man she was extremely glad to claim as her brother. "Thank you for understanding." Noah held her and stroked Sally's hair that matched the reddish color of her favorite mule.

Roscoe walked in front of the wagon that carried Beauty and his four sleeping goats. He pulled down on the reins to get the animals pulling the wagon to lower their heads enough to get into the cave. Behind him, Ann held down the heads of the next two. "You didn't have an inch of extra space anywhere. That was good maneuvering."

Ann walked to an artesian spring with a large catch basin. "This place is like Rock House Cave on our farm. Well, what used to be our farm. It's big enough for a large group of families, and it has fresh water inside."

Roscoe followed an aqueduct away from the holding basin. "This goes into the water trough in the corral." Before they went outside again, they examined the fissure where the water went back underground.

Noah and Eli had already released the canvas on one side of the wagon, taken out the bows, and pulled the canvas down tight to compress the hay. Sally held the valerian, fumewort, and St John's Wort in her hands

10

as everybody else, except herself and Roscoe, took in the second wagon and more animals.

"Knock me out, and carry me in after I'm asleep. I'll try the St. John's Wort when I wake up." Sally handed Roscoe the bags.

"I'll go make it." He stuffed the bags into his pocket, grabbed the lead ropes of two animals, and went into the cave as the rest of the family came out.

Eli's told them, "My rule is to replace as much as I use, so if you take in the rest of the animals and the hay, I'll get wood."

Sally followed Eli. "I want to help without going inside. You want to help too, Stephanie?"

Stephanie went with them into the woods as Noah got his horse, Eyanosa, and his two new mules. Mule 11 and Mule 20, like all the numbered mules they had acquired in Little Rock, had their right sides battered by the blizzard then sewn back together by Martin Harrow and Sally Williams when she'd pretended to be Nancy Bacon. Ann followed with Mule 4 that also had a damaged eye, and Sally's other two wounded mules; Mule 7 and Mule 8. Inside, Roscoe asked, "Ann, would you start a fire, so we can make the sedative?"

"Sure." As she looked for kindling, Ann found a wooden box that she carried over and put beside the bags of plants. After Noah and Roscoe had brought in all the rest of the animals and the hay, Ann called them over. "I found this on the woodpile."

Noah opened the box. Inside, they discovered how-to-instructions with a note that said, "Install at least one brake on every wagon."

Roscoe commented, "I guess we'll be going down a steep hill."

Noah studied the schematic. "Maybe we should install two on each of them. One might fail, and then the wagon would roll full speed down the hill." He continued to analyze the document. "This is complicated work. These parts have to be shaped accurately. We won't have enough materials or the time to do this in only two days." He put the papers back into the box. "Let's see what we can find."

Ann searched with Noah. She held the hand of the handsome blue-eyed man she was forbidden to love only because he was part Indian. "These people must know that."

Roscoe called out, "Found them!" Behind the animal food trough, ten brake kits sat neatly stacked under another wooden box. He took out a note. "If you can, please pay three dollars for each brake."

Ann said, "I'll put in the money after I fix Sally's medicine."

Noah and Roscoe each carried a carefully tied bundle of brake parts to the wagons. "Let me buy the brakes." Roscoe Bacon owned more money than all of them because he had just sold Bacon's Trading Post to Arnold Buzzmann, the previous owner of the storm-battered mules.

"By all means." Noah knew the same thing.

Ann looked at the boiling water. "How can we make it right for both Sally and Beauty? Don't we need to make it weaker for Sally?"

Roscoe dug under the hay for their two axes. "We

don't need to make it weaker. We won't let Sally drink a whole bucketful."

When Ann heard the wood gatherers return, she poured a cup of the sedative and then left the cave with Noah. Outside, Ann offered Sally the cup. "You still want to do this? You're going to wake up inside the cave."

"While we were getting wood, I thought maybe I could stay out here until after I eat supper then I'll drink enough of the tea to sleep all night. You can carry me back out here in the morning before I wake up."

"If that's what you want, that's what we'll do." Ann put the cup where it wouldn't get knocked over.

Sally still wanted to atone for being a problem. She and her sisters had an efficient method for turning logs into firewood. "Let us girls chop the wood, please. You men, carry it into the cave. How's Beauty?"

"I haven't looked." Ann took one of the axes Roscoe had brought out.

This concerned Sally. "She might not be all right."

Stephanie tied back her long, blonde hair and reminded her sister, "I'm sure she's fine. She's been this long without anybody looking at her before."

"Knock me out with just a little and take me inside to the animals. If it's big inside, I might be fine once I get in there."

Ann knew Sally wouldn't wake up anytime soon, but she retrieved and handed her sister the sleeping potion.

"Although, I was fine before I lost my lantern in that cave back home." Sally put it down without drinking any. "I want to be able to do it again. Help me."

Ann looked at Stephanie. Stephanie promised, "We'll do whatever we can."

As the girls made firewood and talked about what they could do to care for their injured mules, Ann came up with a plan that might help her sister overcome her fear. "What if Noah or Eli carried you around out here with your eyes closed and then took you into the cave? You won't get scared because you won't know when you'll go in. After you're inside, we'll tell you. If you can't stay inside, you can go back out."

"I'll try."

Ann went into the cave to explain the plan and get one of the men. Eli came out with her. "It's my fault you were in that dark tunnel when you knocked over your lantern. I want to help you. I'll carry you."

"Thank you, Eli. You're a great brother. I love you."

"Jump on." Eli squatted. Sally got on his back, leaned her head against his dark, brown hair, and closed her eyes. He carried her in a large curve, then straight inside. Sally assumed that Eli would carry her around for a long while before he took her in. She didn't go into a panic because she thought she was still outside. "We're here," Eli told her.

"What?" Sally opened her hazel eyes inside a very large space. The animals stood in a large corral, the wagons were parked far to the other side, and a fire burned inside too. It looked like all their camps at night. "I'm fine. Put me down. I'm going to check on our mules." She hurried to the corral. Some of the maggots had already eaten away the infection at their first location and crawled on the mule's fur. I doubt we'd find more maggots out here in the woods. I wonder how many I'll be able to move and how many times I can move them? As well as she could, Sally relocated the insects she was using to treat the injuries, then dripped a few drops of the honey and milk mixture Noah had made the day before to treat Mule 4's abraded eye. After she had done what she could for the mules in the corral, she got into the wagon and moved the maggots around on Beauty.

When Sally went to the fire, Noah told her, "I'm proud of you."

Sally helped Roscoe fix the meal and blessedly, was not at all upset about being inside the cave. All six of them were together, with all their animals, two wagons, money, and plenty of supplies. They felt safe as they got out their bedding and settled in to sleep. Noah whispered to Ann, "God, I thank You for getting us safely away from Judge Hall."

Stephanie interrupted, "Noah, would you pray loud enough for all of us to hear?"

"Maybe everybody doesn't want to hear," he replied.

"I do," Sally encouraged him.

Eli said, "I don't mind."

Roscoe had wondered what Noah prayed about. "Go ahead."

Noah started over, "God, I pray that You are glorified and honored throughout the entire universe, starting in my heart and the hearts of the people here with me. Thank You that You got us safely away from Judge Hall. I thank You for Your providential grace that put us in a livery with Edwin. Thank You for putting Edwin by the window to hear Judge Hall. Thank You for allowing me to help Ansel. Thank You that Mrs. Hall wrote that we would be granted one act of mercy from her husband. Thank You that she is a woman of strong character, able and willing to do what is right with such conviction and beauty. I will never forget how she held the gun in her husband's hand to her heart and told him to shoot her if he was going to hurt me or hurt Ann. Thank You for putting people like her in our path. Continue to help Ansel to be pain-free and to discover everything that causes him pain.

"Heal every animal and every person we treated, our mules, and any others injured by the blizzard, including wild animals. Thank You for every person here with me tonight. Every one of us is a gift to the others. Do not let us ever forget that. Protect us as we travel to wherever You're taking us.

"Comfort our hearts of any sorrows. Give tenfold back to those who sacrificed things they wanted. Thank You for all the abundance You have given me, the first of which is this family here with me tonight. We love You. Protect us, guide us, and use us for Your purposes. In Jesus name, we pray."

Everybody said, "Amen."

"Thank you, brother." Stephanie felt glad that she had asked Noah to share his prayer.

Ann whispered to Noah, "Have I told you how wonderful I think you are?"

"Yes, but you can tell me as much as you want."

"My husband, thank you for your prayer and for having those thoughts. I do think you're wonderful, I love you, and I'm blessed to be your wife." Ann stroked Noah's short, oak-bark colored hair.

Noah looked into his wife's beautiful green eyes. "I'm the one who is blessed to have my Ann as my wife. I love you too."

Even though they whispered very softly, Sally heard them. Because she had chosen to stay with her family, and the soldier she loved had to remain with his unit in Little Rock, she would never lie next to Melvin or hear him say words like that to her. Nor would she ever be able to tell him that she thought he was wonderful. In her heart, she wept.

Three

Morning light sneaked into the cave. Ann worried that Sally would wake, see the walls and ceiling, and be flooded with fear. "Noah." Ann whispered again, "Noah."

Noah opened his eyes. "What wrong?"

"I'm worried about Sally. What's going to happen when she wakes and can actually see that she's in this cave?"

"I don't know, but there's nothing we can do. Go back to sleep."

"You're right." Ann rolled over to her side. Then, she lay on her stomach. She flipped onto her back and continued to worry because she didn't want Sally to suffer.

Noah realized he was not getting any more sleep that morning. "My wife, let's get up and start making breakfast."

"I'm sorry."

"Don't worry about it. I know you're concerned. I am too."

Noah walked to the woodpile to get more logs for the fire and found a basket of eggs. That upset him. It was not because somebody had given them eggs, but because he had felt so safe that he had allowed himself to lose awareness of what was happening around him.

18

He could not protect them if he didn't even know when people were walking around him during the night. The note in the basket said, "From where they came, they return." It had to be Edwin. That also upset Noah. Edwin should not be risking getting himself caught or leading people to us either, but it's nice that Edwin cares. Some people are so good to us. It's too bad that others are so horrible.

Noah walked to the fire with an armful of logs and the basket of eggs. "Edwin left us eggs." He showed Ann the paper.

"I think you should put this note in your medicine bag."

"You're right." He folded the message.

The smell of cooking food woke the rest of the family. Still lying in her blankets, Sally asked, "Where did you get eggs?"

Ann and Noah wondered how Sally was going to react. She got out of the blankets, put on her moccasins, went to the area that had been set up as a latrine, and then joined them by the fire. "Is the coffee ready yet? It sure smells good."

Noah told her, "I think so. Bring your cup, and I'll give you some."

Maybe it just hadn't sunk in yet, but Sally wasn't anxious. They ate eggs, bacon, bread, cheese, honey, and jam, and drank coffee. Noah and Ann also prepared a fresh batch of cedar poultice.

After eating, Sally went to the wagon and discovered Beauty sitting up. When the mule saw Sally, it got up on its front knees and then stood up. "You good girl! Look at Beauty!" Sally got in and rubbed the mule between its ears.

Over in the corral, Noah stopped putting out hay and went to see what was happening. "That's great! I think she'll be fine if we can keep her from getting badly infected."

As if he didn't already know, Sally notified Noah, "She can't stay in here. We have to get her out."

Stephanie walked over. "I don't think we should try to get her to back down the planks."

Ann joined them. "We could take off the side and put the walk boards there. Then, she could go forward, turn to the side, and walk out."

"If we don't knock her over getting the side off, that's probably the best." Roscoe looked at the planks.

Sally offered, "I can stand in here with her and help her not fall over."

Ann rejected the idea sternly, "If she's going to fall, you won't be able to stop her, and you could get hurt."

"Let's see what we can do." Roscoe issued further instructions, "Get our tools."

Stephanie went to the other wagon. "We're going to have to take out this hay to get the tools."

"Then we need to get started." Sally walked over and pulled the canvas back. After they had stacked all the hay by the corral and got the tools they needed, they pried off the boards. Happily, without causing Beauty to lose her footing, Sally led her mule out of the wagon and into the corral.

Roscoe, Noah, and Eli made the side planks permanently removable like they had done with the boards at the rear. After they had accomplished that task, they started installing a brake.

The animals accepted Beauty into the group and didn't bother her at all. The rest of them bit each other and pushed each other away from the hay and oats as if there wasn't enough for everybody or a never-ending supply of fresh water. Putting the two groups together nullified their previously established ranking. Beauty had been the dominant mule in the group that had belonged to the traveling resupply business. Now, she was at the bottom of the whole group. She knew it and didn't assert herself at all. When she recovered, things might change again. For now, all the animals understood that Beauty needed to be left alone.

While Eyanosa, the mules, donkeys, and goats jostled for position, Stephanie, Ann, and Sally brushed them and inspected their injuries. As the women looked at a particular animal, it disengaged from the battle.

Ann took off a wrapping. "It's so unbelievable that Arnold and Russell let these mules get so injured in that blizzard. Sally, you've done a great job taking care of them. They're looking good."

Stephanie disagreed, "They're crawling with maggots."

"I know. Isn't it great?" Sally carefully caught one and looked for another place that looked infected.

"What are you doing? Put that down." Stephanie slapped the creature out of Sally's hand.

Sally reached down and picked it up. "Don't do that again. I need them. These maggots are eating away the dying and infected flesh. They're the doctors."

Ann pointed out, "They do eat rotten stuff."

"Don't they spread germs?" Stephanie asked.

Sally replied, "If they do, they must eat them back up. Every place I've put them is better."

Stephanie wanted to help with the process since she now understood their value. "Here's a place that needs one. Do you see one that can be moved?"

"Not on Mule 20. I'll look on Mule 7," Ann replied.

"We need to give these mules real names." Stephanie joined the search for maggots not already repositioned.

Sally suggested mischievously, "I thought about naming mine: Noah, Eli, and Roscoe."

Ann vetoed the idea, "Even if it is funny, our men wouldn't like it. We better not."

"I want to separate the injured ones for a while, so we can take off and wash the bandages. I don't want to cut up any more blankets," Sally contemplated aloud, "Maybe we should wash the mules too."

Stephanie told her, "It's still too cold."

"You're right," Sally agreed. "I'm worried about the rest of the injured mules. I wished we had been able to get all of them."

Ann picked the wrapping up off the ground. "We've already got all we can manage, and we don't have an unlimited amount of food either. Since we're going to be here for two days, let's wash everything."

The girls looked around to see how they might rig up a rope. Just inside the entrance, they found a series of holes in the cave floor and posts that had been laid on the ground with rope already attached. Ann watched Sally walk right up to the cave's wall to pick one up.

Ann didn't know why Sally was doing so well, but she wasn't going to break the spell by saying anything about it. Stephanie thought the same thing, and so did Sally. As if she had been reading the minds of her sisters, Sally said, "It must be small spaces and not actually being in a cave that bothers me."

"I'm so glad that you're all right being in here." Stephanie was relieved that they could talk about it.

"You think you're glad. How glad do you think I am?" Sally asked.

"You've got a good point there, sister." Ann also wanted to know what had happened when Sally had her secret rendezvous with Melvin Hatcher. "Do you want to talk about Melvin?"

Sally replied with sadness in her voice, "There's nothing to tell. Nothing has changed since last fall. We want to be able to be together, but he belongs to the army, and I belong to this family."

"I'm sorry, Sally, but I'm glad we still have you." Stephanie hugged her sister.

Sally started to cry. "But I know he loves me. He wanted to marry me."

"I always thought he did." Ann joined the hug.

"It makes me feel worse, knowing we can't be together but better, knowing that he does love me."

Stephanie patted Sally's back. "Love has complicated all our lives, hasn't it?"

Ann remarked, "Remember when all we had to worry about was if we were going to starve?"

"Worrying about plain survival was a lot easier," Sally expressed one of the paradoxes of their lives.

As the men fussed with the brakes, Eli saw the women stop putting up the poles, then stand together in a group and hug. He didn't know what was happening across the cave, but he knew the three sisters would be doing the right thing for each other. "We're lucky to have such good women."

"Yes, we are!" Noah agreed emphatically.

Roscoe added, "I think so too, and I'm very glad to be a part of this family." They returned to readying the wagons for the next leg of the trip and talked about where they might be going that would require brakes.

The women washed all the dirty clothes, the animal blankets, and the cut-up pieces of a wool blanket that they had been using as mule bandages. Since they didn't know how often they would be able to have a fire or enough time, they prepared another hot meal for dinner and put bread dough into pans to rise.

Sally went to the wagon where the men worked and looked inside the one that had carried Beauty. "I like what you did with the sideboards. You think I should come back over later and wash out the inside of this wagon?"

Eli answered, "I'd appreciate that. It smells really bad."

"I will. Now, come on over. Dinner is ready."

The men ate their meals, then went back to work on the brakes while the women carried the laundry to the clotheslines. Due to the temperature differences between the inside and the outside, air flowed out of the cave. Stephanie pinned a blanket on the line. "The breeze should dry everything well."

24

Next, Stephanie brushed the mule she had changed from a mean, unusable animal to a tolerant and useful one. She had also changed its name to Redeemed. Ann brushed Eyanosa, the horse given to Noah for saving the life of a man in Ann's hometown of Harmony, Arkansas. The animals stopped jockeying for rank and enjoyed the attention as the girls groomed them.

After Eyanosa gleamed, Ann brushed the uninjured parts of the two mules that Noah had earned for treating the Army's milk cow and the last four of Arnold's injured mules. "I don't want to call these Mule 11 and Mule 20. I know what I want to name them, but I'm going to ask Noah what he thinks." She walked across the cave. "Noah, what do you think about naming your mules, Honor and Justice?"

"My love, they are not my mules. They are our mules, and I think those names are very nice, much better than Mule 11 and Mule 20."

Ann gave Noah a quick kiss. "Good. I'm going to tell Stephanie and Sally." She hurried to her sisters.

"Do you think women are curious creatures?" Noah thought it was strange for those to have been the names that had come into Ann's mind. He decided he would have to ask her about that later.

Roscoe answered, "They're curious for sure. I've never figured out a single one of them, and I've been trying to understand them for sixty years."

"I know. Stephanie asked me for permission to ask for Roscoe's permission to work with Stubborn. I mean, Redeemed. I would have just done it."

Noah contemplated aloud while they worked, "It's

like how they feel about their father. They wanted him to approve of them and of what they did. I think they also want us to let them know that we approve of them. Maybe, if Ann knows that I think who she is and what she does is right and good, she'll stay happy with our marriage."

Eli vowed to do the same, "I'm going to try that too. I want Stephanie to always be happy."

Roscoe said, "As a friend, I'll do the same with all three of them. Let's see what happens."

They went back to talking about whether or not they might, or should, slip out of their escape corridor if it was not taking them in the right direction.

The women brushed clean all the animals, moved maggots, treated Mule 4's eye, put fresh cedar poultice on with the washed bandages, and gave them more hay. After taking care of the animals, Sally hollered, "You men! Come help me get these tubs of water to the wagon." Sally took off the removable boards and scrubbed the wagon with the used soapy water. "Now that I've cleaned the wagon, please help me pour the rest of the water over it to rinse it out."

They dumped out the tubs of water inside the wagon. "Now it's muddy." Eli stood with soapy water on his boots then added, "But I really appreciate the wagon being cleaned of all that manure and blood."

"Then it's a good thing I waited until it was time for you to quit. Come eat supper."

"Good. I'm sick of trying to make this thing attach." Noah felt they had come to a standstill. They could not get the brake to go together the way the instructions said it should work, and they were still working on the first installation. After supper, everybody stayed at the fire and left the rest of the work until the next day. As they lay in their blankets, Eli said, "I'd like to say the prayer tonight."

Noah quickly agreed, "That would be great."

Eli prayed, "God, I also want to say thank You. I am thankful for so many things. For a long time, I didn't know I should be grateful and didn't see what I had. First, I thank You for opening my eyes to see all that I have, for which I'm thankful. God, I'm also thankful that You hunted me down until You caught me. I'm thankful that we have this Bible to read. I'm thankful for this woman who is so wonderful and for the rest of this wonderful family. I'm thankful that even when it seemed like we had lost everything, You were planning to give us something better that we wouldn't have been able to receive if we were still holding on to the things You took away. I'm thankful for all the people You've put around us at exactly the right time. You gave the people in this family to each other by taking Chris, Emma, and Hattie, and by cracking Noah's skull. You also, gave us Roscoe when Judge Hall caused Noah to go to Pine Bluff. You gave us six more mules, more supplies, and more money by sending that blizzard and by letting us help the people in Little Rock. By allowing Arnold to be so stupid with pride, You gave us forty dollars. Thank You for letting me see the blessings in what I would otherwise have thought was a curse. I thank You for Yourself, for being who You are, and for giving us more than we deserve. For dying on Calvary, so that Your Father in Heaven would see Your blood poured out over us, instead of seeing the sinners we are. So tonight, we say thank You, in the name of Jesus."

Everybody said, "Amen."

Ann spoke up, "Eli, thank you for pointing out how we've been blessed by every obstacle. I want to add that we're also blessed to have such intelligent men."

Noah sighed. "If only we were intelligent enough to figure out those brakes."

Roscoe added, "Exactly."

Stephanie assured them, "You'll figure out what's missing tomorrow. Good night, everybody."

Four

Noah lay on his stomach and watched the cave entrance. The faint light of the three-quarters moon filled the opening. Several hours into the night, he saw a slight change at the edge of the opening. Noah got out from under the blankets and slipped to the woodpile as he watched the shadow move along the wall. Noah suspected it was Edwin. He still held his long knife. If it was somebody else, he was ready.

The intruder had come in from the light. Noah had the advantage. He had been in the dark. His eyes were better able to see. In addition, Noah knew somebody was coming in. The person slinking along the cave wall didn't know he had been seen. Noah saw the basket of eggs hanging beside the prowler, and he recognized the gait. He waited in the shadow. After the invader had passed, Noah whispered, "I see you," and touched the middle of the intruder's back with his knife handle.

The sneak jumped and let go of the basket. Noah knew a startle response would cause his hand to open. He was ready and had his hand under the basket handle because he did want the eggs. Noah was surprised but pleased. Even though he had let go of the basket, he had not emitted a sound.

Noah whispered, "I know it's you, Edwin. Come with me." He walked Edwin far enough away from the

29

others to speak. "You could have been killed. You need to learn some things. However, you could have murdered us all last night when you brought the eggs. You are the only person who has ever sneaked past me. I'm very impressed."

"You were sleeping. It wasn't hard."

"Yes, it was. Nobody else has ever sneaked up on me, even when I was sleeping."

"How do you know? If you didn't catch them, you wouldn't know they had been there."

"Good point. However, almost everybody trying to sneak around you means you harm, so I doubt it. I want you to practice. When you go into a dark place from the light, conceal yourself immediately, and wait until your eyes are fully open. Then, check out your surroundings and know what's there before you move.

"In addition, you should not compromise yourself or the people you are helping for something that is not important. You could be found out, and you could lead others to the people you are hiding. Both are bad. Do not do it again! Do you understand?"

"Yes, but you gave us all those chickens and money to buy hay. It's not much, but I can do something nice for you, and it's the middle of the night. Nobody is watching me."

"Edwin, the chickens are yours now, and I gave your father the money for the hay because you're saving me and my family. I owe you much more than a few chickens or bales of hay."

Edwin, being a thirteen-year-old boy who had for the first time been treated as an equal by people he thought were the upper crust, didn't care if he was discovered. These people meant a lot to him. "I didn't mean to make you mad. I'm sorry." Tears started to well-up in Edwin's eyes.

Noah had been stern, so Edwin would never again take a risk that wasn't necessary. He realized that Edwin needed what his own wife needed: somebody to tell him they approved of what he was doing. Noah altered his approach. "I'm not mad. I want you to be careful. You're doing something very important and extremely dangerous: helping people escape from prejudice and injury. We can't afford to lose you; you are much too important."

"I am?"

Noah told him what he knew was true. "Yes, Edwin, you are working directly for God. You're one of the most important people in Little Rock. What would have happened to us if you weren't here? Judge Hall told his wife he was letting us go, but you know he's sending somebody after us. It would be very bad if he finds us."

"I don't believe you did anything wrong."

"I married a woman of a different race. Judge Hall thinks that's wrong."

"That's the same thing the last man said. I don't think he was doing anything wrong either."

"Thank you for being an open-minded person. Now, if you'll still let me have the eggs, I'd love to have them."

"Of course, I'll let you have them."

Noah took all the eggs out of the basket and put

them in the corner of the wagon then retrieved the egg basket he had placed there earlier in the day. "Take both of your egg baskets. Tell me what I told you."

"I'm too important to get caught. I shouldn't take a chance of getting caught or leading other people here for something that's not important. If I go into a dark place from the light, I have to hide immediately and let my eyes get adjusted. I need to be sure to look around real good and know what's there before I move."

"Exactly, and there's one more very important thing for you to remember."

"What?"

"Every one of us loves you, and we will never forget you."

"Even Nancy?" asked Edwin

Noah assured him, "Even Nancy."

Edwin smiled. "Tell her, I love her back."

"I will."

"I love you too." Edwin hugged Noah. "I learned a lot about animals from you, and I learned a lot about people."

"I love you as well. Go home and keep your eyes open for the next people God will bring to you, so you can save them." Noah squeezed his friend tight, then stepped back.

Edwin asked for validation of what he thought he had been told, "God brings them to me, so I can save them?"

"Definitely."

"All right. I'll work for God. You can't work for a better person. Goodbye, doctor." Edwin left the cave with two empty egg baskets but a full heart.

Noah thought, you're right; you can't work for a better person. Noah was very cold from his long talk with Edwin. He got back under the blankets, snuggled next to Ann, and wrapped his cold arms around her.

Ann woke up due to the sudden cold. "Noah, you're freezing. Are you all right?"

"I'm fine. I just had a long talk with Edwin."

"Is something wrong?"

"No. He just wanted to give us more eggs. I told him how important he is and that he cannot risk getting caught over something that's not important. I told him he is working for God saving people."

"You're right, but I think he did come here for something important. I think you are working for God as well. God sent Edwin here, so you could tell him that he's important, that what he's doing is important, that God sees him, and that he is working with God."

"Probably so, and it goes on. You're also working for God. He put you beside me to tell me what you just said, and I think he also put you here for another reason."

"What's that?"

"To warm me up. I'm cold."

Five

Stephanie opened her eyes and saw Sally making french toast. She walked over and sat on the campstool beside Sally. Sally confessed, "I kissed him."

"Is he a good kisser?"

"I've never kissed anybody else to compare, but I liked it very much."

Sally saw Eli coming up behind Stephanie. She didn't say anything. She let Stephanie speak. "I've never kissed anybody but Eli. I don't want to kiss anybody else to compare. Eli is a fantastic kisser."

Eli heard what his wife had said. "If I kiss well, it's only because you do." Eli had also heard Sally's earlier comment and assured her, "I know you feel that you've missed out on something good, and you're sad. Probably it would have been a good life, but there is a man out there who is waiting to kiss you, and he'll be a fantastic kisser because he'll be the man you love."

"I'm not going to stop loving Melvin, so I can't love somebody else."

Stephanie told Sally her opinion, "You don't have to stop loving Melvin to love another person."

"Eli, would you be able to love Stephanie if she loved somebody else in her heart?"

"I love everyone in this family in a different way, but that doesn't mean I love any of you less. Nobody

34

can ever fill the place in your heart that Melvin holds; he's your first love. But you'll be able to completely love the right man and never stop loving Melvin."

Sally hugged her brother-in-law. "I hope so. Thank you, Eli. It's good to hear that from a man." She believed Eli. She had known him her entire life. She knew he was honest and good.

The other three woke up. One by one, they came to the fire. Noah passed on Edwin's message to Sally. "Edwin came again last night and brought more eggs. They're in the wagon. He wanted me to let you know that he loves you."

"Sure, he loves all of us," Sally replied.

"But he's infatuated with you."

Sally didn't know what to say or think about that. "Thanks for giving me his message."

Eli brought up the trouble from the previous day. "I thought about what Stephanie said last night. She said we'd figure out what we're missing. I think we should take that literally. I think we're missing a part. Let's take apart the other brake kit and see if it has another part."

Noah perked up. "Great idea."

After they finished breakfast, they opened the other set of parts inside the wagon, instead of on the ground as they had with the first brake. They discovered there actually was another part. They looked on the ground but didn't find the missing part.

Noah asked, "Should we take this brake off and install a new kit, so the parts fit?"

"I don't know if we'll have enough time to do this one over." Roscoe had found the place and thought they could insert the missing piece.

Eli suggested, "Let's try this part in the brake we've already attached. If it fits, we can use it, and then do the next one with a complete set."

"All right, let's try it." Roscoe agreed then used the part from the other kit and easily fit it right in. They quickly finished installing the first brake.

Meanwhile, Stephanie, Ann, and Sally again put bread dough into every loaf pan they owned, took down the laundry, folded, and packed it, then worked with the animals again. Sally commented, "We sure could use some of Smitty's smelly liniment."

Ann thought back to the previous spring. "Remember how well it healed Dusty after the Butterfield Gang beat him?"

Stephanie looked for maggots. "If we can get these mules there, we'll get some. We should get some even if they're healed. You never know when you might need some."

"How are Honor and Justice?" Sally inquired.

"They're healing well. I doubt they'll have any problems. Did you decide what to name yours?"

"I'm still thinking about naming them after people. These two males, Edwin and Martin and the female, Dollie. What do you think?"

"It's kind of like calling our friends asses. I don't think we should." Ann then informed her sisters, "Edwin brought more eggs last night. Noah talked to him."

Sally replied, "I wondered where the egg basket went until Noah told me about Edwin."

Stephanie delivered her bad news, "All the

maggots must have turned into flies. I can't find any, but the mules seem to be doing well, even Beauty."

The men took the brake kit that was now short a part over to the pile of brake kits, left a note in the money box with a drawing of the part that was missing, put the money box on top of the kit with the missing part, and got a third kit. They made sure all the parts were present before they started.

They got the second brake installed much faster since they knew what they were doing. They had the task done before the end of the day, so they pulled the wagon to the corral and reloaded all the hay and oats into the wagon with the removable side and backboards and the first brake they had installed.

S.R. had told them they would move after two days, so they got everything ready to go. When their escort arrived, all they would have to do would be to pack their bedding and the cooking items. To pass the time, they got out their medicine bags and worked on decorating them while Stephanie read the book of Ezra aloud.

Sally suggested, "Just like Ezra did, we should fast in the morning and ask God to protect us as we travel." They all agreed. After they ate supper, they packed the cooking pots, plates, cups, utensils, and all the loaves of bread they had made. Sally packed her tin cup in the wagon. "I didn't think about the coffee."

They felt bored, so they all went to inspect the animals, brush them, and feed them. The maggots were definitely gone, but none of the mules looked infected, and four of them were well on their way to recovery.

With the willow water, Beauty didn't seem to be in pain. Wearing a clean mule blanket to protect her damaged side from accidental injury, she walked among the other animals. Mule 4's impaired vision didn't seem to cause her a problem navigating around the corral, but she didn't like any person or animal to come at her from the side of her injured eye. Even though Beauty had her own injuries, she always stood just to the right of and slightly in front of Mule 4. All of Roscoe's animals were still fine. The animals had pretty well established who was dominant, had mostly stopped squabbling, and appeared to be content. The sun was not even all the way down when the animals and people were sleeping.

Six

The people hiding in the large depot of the Underground Railroad had to sneak across the gap before daylight, or they'd be seen. The person on the way to guide them, prayed for clouds to cover the moon and walked to the cave. In the dark of the night, he called into the cave. "Have you made the item?"

Noah was up in a flash. "Look in the wooden box."

Everybody already inside the cave put their agreed upon 'danger procedures' into action. If they had to shoot, they didn't want to draw the attention of anybody within hearing range, and they had to get into a good defensive position, so they snatched their bows and arrows, quickly put their backs to the cave wall, and waited several minutes for a response.

"That was the right answer," Ann whispered.

Stephanie shivered with fear. "Something must be wrong."

This time, the voice came from the direction of the corral. "Have you made the item?"

"Look in the wooden box," they all said together.

The man bravely faced six nocked arrows and stepped into the light of the fire. "I already have."

Stephanie didn't believe her eyes. "Thaddeus?" She dashed over and hugged the reverend who had married her and Eli.

"Well, I'll be. I thought you were long gone!"

Eli explained, "Last winter, we didn't visit you when we came through town because we didn't want to put you in a compromised position."

"As you can see, it wouldn't have changed my position. I could have handled it, but you didn't know. We have to leave right now, so get packed."

Noah told him, "All we have to do is hook up."

"Get your biggest and strongest mules into the harnesses."

Sally brought up the topic of her concern, "Some of our mules are injured; two of them badly. One can't see well with her right eye. Another isn't able to walk well. Is that going to be a problem?"

"Show me the mules."

Stephanie and Ann took up the bedding and carried it to the wagon. Roscoe, Eli, and Noah harnessed the biggest of the mules, while Sally took Thaddeus to the four injured mules she thought might be a problem. "These are Honor, Justice, Mule 7, and Mule 8."

Thaddeus looked them over. "What happened to them?"

Sally explained, "The ice and snow ripped into their flesh during the blizzard, but I don't think they'll have any problem because we sewed them up four days ago, and we've been taking very good care of them."

"This was obviously completely avoidable. Your other animals don't have any injuries."

"I know, and that's what makes me so mad." Sally took him to Mule 4. "She has a lot of damage to her eye and doesn't like anything to approach from that side."

Sally had the eye covered with a cloth strip full of shredded potato. "I can take it off."

"Leave it on. Let me see the other one."

"Be prepared to be furious and shocked." Sally took him to Beauty and removed the blanket.

Thaddeus looked at the mule with so much of its fur and skin removed. "Why didn't you shoot her?"

"Why does everybody say shoot her? Doesn't she deserve mercy? She didn't do anything wrong."

Thaddeus tried to defend his comment, "Sometimes, shooting an animal is mercy, Sally."

"I'm not going to let you shoot her."

"We'll give them both a chance."

The men had the mules harnessed to the wagon and had driven the wagons to the cave opening. "Do we have enough time to move the hay to the other wagon and put Beauty in the wagon?"

"No. If they can make it past the gap, we can stop, but not before. Are the brakes installed on both wagons?" Thaddeus inquired because it was going to matter very soon.

"Yes," Noah assured him.

Thaddeus inspected the brakes to be sure they had been properly constructed and installed.

"Did you see the note about the missing piece?" Eli wanted to be sure that the part got replaced.

"I saw it. I'll take care of it. Let's go."

Everybody, except Thaddeus, looked at Sally. Eli asked, "Are you going to be able to walk through the tunnel?"

"Eli, will you help me like you did when we first

41

got here? This time, don't take me right through. Let me get adjusted first."

"I'll carry you. Get on my back again and close your eyes." When his sister-in-law was on his back, he did the exact same thing he had done when he'd brought her into the cave. Thaddeus wanted them to leave as quickly as possible. Eli was not going to carry Sally around inside while the others waited outside. To help Sally feel safe and cared for, like she really was, he carried her a long way after they were out. He stayed far enough behind the wagons so that Sally could not hear them well, but he could still see them.

Thaddeus sat beside Noah in the lead wagon. "I see you decided to do what you promised God."

Noah had to correct Reverend Pratt's erroneous assumption. "No, I didn't. I went to Pine Bluff because I was too afraid to trust God, but God did something wonderful. He put it into the hearts of my family to find me. They trusted God, not me."

"God's grace is wonderful for sure."

Eli finally said, "We're out."

Sally did not have any reference point to know how far they had walked. When Eli let her down, Sally believed he had carried her around inside the cave long before taking her out. "You're the best brother ever. You've kept me safe three times by carrying me in caves, and twice you kept me safe from men who had the wrong intentions. I can't thank you enough. I love you very much." Sally hugged Eli and then suggested, "We need to catch up. Let's run."

They ran until they were by the mules. Sally

stopped beside Beauty and Mule 4. Eli continued forward to join Roscoe in the second wagon. Ann and Stephanie had been watching to see when Eli would let Sally know they were out of the cave. When they saw her get off Eli's back, they dropped back to walk with her. Sally checked on Beauty and Mule 4 because she hadn't given them any willow water that morning and was afraid they were in pain.

"Beauty doesn't seem to be in pain." Sally notified her sisters, "We still need to keep a blanket over her. I don't want brush or anything else to touch her side."

"How's Mule 4?" Stephanie asked.

"She's walking with the others but in the middle of the herd."

Beauty walked on the left so that her injured side faced toward the center. As they traveled through the close brush, the wagon pushed forward a branch that snapped back after the wagon had passed. It whipped Beauty on her left side. She was startled and took off. The rope tied to her halter jerked her back. That threw her injured side into Blanco. Blessedly, the blanket cushioned the impact.

The mules behind veered around the collision, which got the lead ropes tangled. They jerked each other with their tangled ropes and soon fell into a panic. Ann, Stephanie, and Sally unhooked the lead ropes attached to the wagon, which stopped most of the problem. Soon, they had all of the mules untangled and decided they didn't need to fasten the ropes to the wagon.

The men ahead were oblivious to the chaos at the

rear, but it didn't matter because the women were completely capable and handled the confusion. However, to avert any more mishaps, they took up positions on both sides of the wagon, to control the branches that snapped back.

They arrived at the reason for the brakes. Everybody looked at what was ahead. Thaddeus pointed, "We need to get down this incline and across that gap before daylight."

Roscoe exaggerated, but not by much. "That's almost as steep as the trail into Pine Bluff."

Eli added, "But wider."

Stephanie gave her opinion, "I don't think we should try it."

Thaddeus reminded them, "You're not the first. Everybody else has gotten down. We can do it."

Ann peered down. "I guess this is the reason that nobody looks this way for escapees."

"Exactly. Nobody believes it can be done, but it can." Thaddeus had led several wagons down the slope in the past.

Stephanie demanded, "Why didn't you tell us about this before we set out?"

Thaddeus told her the obvious answer. "Because you wouldn't have come and tried."

Noah had carefully studied the slope. "We can do it. We're strong, like the eagles at Pine Bluff, and we're protected and guided by God."

Thaddeus explained how to proceed. "Attach four strong mules to the back of each wagon. I'll drive the first wagon. Noah or Eli, you drive the other. Keep the brakes on hard. The rest of you, walk beside the mules at the rear. Direct them to pull back on the wagons from the rear."

Noah answered, "Eli has the most strength. He can apply the greatest pressure to the brakes."

"I'll do it. Let's figure out how to hitch the mules to the back." Eli walked to the rear of the lead wagon.

Thaddeus had discovered that most people did not want somebody to tell them how to handle their animals. He offered advice but did not insist. "I'll show you my suggestion."

To previous travelers, Thaddeus had just been the man showing them the way. The Williams family had the advantage of already knowing Thaddeus. They trusted him. "Show us," Eli replied.

Thaddeus put a mule blanket over Diamond and then rigged a heavy survival pack around its rump. It was held low and was prevented from slipping up by looping the straps around the mule's rear legs where they joined the body. Then he tied a rope to it, looped it around Diamond's front legs, and tied knots that wouldn't allow the rope to constrict. He tied a quick release knot in the rope going to the wagon. "If the wagon goes out of control, pull this release. It's better to lose some of the mules than all of them. Eli, if that happens, jump off the wagon, and let it go." Thaddeus had given the same instructions to everyone he had taken over this hill. Nobody had lost a wagon yet, but he always wanted people to know what to do if that happened.

After they roped seven other mules the same way,

Thaddeus called them together. "God, get us safely down this hill. Calm all our fears and the fear of the animals. Guide the animals, our thoughts, and our actions to respond correctly to everything as we traverse the hill that You've placed here to provide the means of escape from this town. In Jesus' name, I pray. Amen. Get into position. We need to move on."

Everybody got to his or her place. Thaddeus flicked the whip and started the wagon toward the incline that looked more like a sheer drop. Ace and King were the first to put their feet to the slope. Before the weight of the wagon was even behind them, the mules skidded and tried to hold themselves back. Chief and Blue were the next over the edge. As they leaned back against the incline, the tendons in the fronts of their legs stretched to the limit to keep from going rear-over-head down the precipice. As soon as the front wheels went over the edge, Thaddeus leaned hard on the brake. He had to keep the wagon from rolling over the mules.

When the rear wheels went over and joined the downwards push, the falling tongue jammed forward into the harness, pushed the front mules, and pulled Rose and Honey, roped at the rear. Between their own aversion to the pull and Noah pulling back on their halters, they held back and helped stop the forward thrust. Behind him, Ann pulled back on the halters of Chocolate and Blanco. The whole rig went over the edge. Animals and humans strained to keep from flying full-speed into a heap of boards and mule flesh at the bottom.

Eli sat in the seat of the other wagon. He watched

the wagon roll over the edge at an angle he thought was impossible. I shouldn't follow to what has to be sure destruction. Especially with nobody at the rear, in case Stephanie and Sally need help. He called back, "If we lose control, promise you'll let go."

"We'll be fine. Go on." Stephanie had set her mind to the task. Waiting was getting on her nerves.

Eli urged Quick Silver and Diamond, followed by Shaggy and Hector, to follow the first wagon and start the fight against the weight of the wagon and gravity. Eli pushed as hard as he could on the brake. It moved forward with less resistance than he thought it should. "Pull back!"

Sally directed Smiley and Big Jenny to slow the downward roll. The rope's slack disappeared and jerked Redeemed. It reminded the mule of the past. The mule switched back to its stubborn way of thinking and resisted the forward pull. Jumper pulled back beside it. Stephanie realized they would soon be rolling too fast for her and Sally to keep up. Stephanie swung up onto Redeemed, pulled back hard, and hollered, "Jump on!" Even as a very intelligent mule, the go forward command of the lead rope combined with the hold back orders coming from its halter confused it. It seemed that the mule thought about the situation and gained a greater respect for Stephanie. She was the one telling the mule to do what it wanted to do; resist being pulled forward against its will. The mule became permanently redeemed in her relationship with Stephanie.

Sally jumped onto Smiley and pulled back to tell Smiley to resist. Even with the mules pulling back, the rear wagon gained on the wagon in front of them. Since the hay wagon was lighter, they had harnessed the strongest mules to the other wagon. Even so, they should have been able to slow the wagon more. Stephanie and Sally pulled back on the mules as hard as they could. The mules tried to slow down, but the brakes barely engaged the axle. Eli got on the floorboard, propped his back against the seat and pushed the brake lever with both feet. The wagon slowed, but nowhere close to enough. The wagon ahead of them, with stronger mules and brakes depressed firmly against the axle, held back the front wagon better. They were going much slower than the wagon closing in from the rear.

Eli yelled, "We're going to ram you!"

Noah and Ann looked back and saw the other wagon barreling down on them. Noah called forward, urgently, "Let the wagon roll faster!" He and Ann didn't know how much farther it was to the bottom or how much to ease up on the backward pull, but they released some tension off the halters.

Thaddeus ordered Roscoe, "Get in the back of the wagon. Keep your eye on Eli's wagon. Tell me how much faster we need to go." He stopped pushing so hard on the brake and rolled faster.

"They're still gaining on us!" Roscoe called out. Thaddeus let up on the brake only a little more. He feared that they would flip over if they went much faster.

Pushing back against the forward thrust might work better than pulling back from the rear. I'll use

Redeemed to help stop the momentum from the front. Stephanie pulled the release and untied Redeemed from the wagon.

The wagon rolled even faster. Sally screamed, "Are you out of your mind?!"

Stephanie called out, "Just keep trying to pull back!" and then directed Redeemed to the front.

Roscoe informed Thaddeus, "They're coming even faster now." Even though Thaddeus thought they were already beyond the limit, he eased up the pressure on the brake.

As Stephanie rode past him to the front, Eli yelled, "What are you doing? We need Redeemed to pull back!" The seat dug into Eli's back as he pushed against the brake lever and pulled back on the reins.

Stephanie positioned Redeemed between Diamond and Quick Silver. She barely slowed until the mule's hind end touched the front of the harness then she pulled back hard. The wagon slowed significantly. They stopped gaining on the wagon in front. Both wagons still moved down the slope much too rapidly.

They weren't far from the bottom. Thaddeus thought, if we don't flip or veer out of control, we may still make it. For several harrowing minutes, they rolled at the slowest speed they could accomplish, which was much too fast. They barely kept the wheels on the ground as they tried to preserve the delicate balance between not rolling over the mules harnessed at their front, not flipping, not going too slow for the wagon at the rear, or going too fast for the wagon in front.

The front wagon was almost to the most dangerous

part of the descent; the bottom, where the steep slope made a sharp transition to level ground. Thaddeus would have to move faster to gain enough space between the wagons, so he could slow enough to make the trajectory change.

Thaddeus called back to Roscoe, "We need to slow way down to change to level ground, and so does Eli."

Roscoe passed the information to Noah. Noah took hold of Honey's short mane, leaned forward, and pulled the release knot, so he could change position. The wagon surged forward.

Ann's ride, Blanco, stumbled. Ann hit the ground. She knew she couldn't run fast enough to keep up. Still, it was try or be trampled or crushed by the wagon. She jumped up between the ropes and ran.

Noah realized his mistake, but it wasn't possible to fix it. The ropes that trapped Ann inside kept Noah out. He couldn't ride over and pull her on with him. Ann ran for the rear of the wagon and for her life.

"Slow down!" Noah screamed.

Thaddeus pressed the brake. Ann and the rear wagon barreled toward him. Roscoe reached out and grabbed Ann. As soon as he had Ann in the wagon, he called out, "Go!"

Thaddeus thanked God and let the wagon roll.

Noah thanked God and slowed Honey. To join Stephanie's backward shove against the rear wagon, he maneuvered Honey into the space between the wagon's falling tree and front wheel.

Thaddeus called back to Roscoe, "Tell me when they're ten yards back."

Ann questioned him, "What're you going to do?"

"We need to slow down significantly, without being rammed from the rear, or we won't be able to transition from this angle when we get to the bottom."

Ann moved to the edge of the wagon and called for Blanco. Noah saw her. "Don't try!" Ann ignored him, made the jump, and landed on the back of Blanco. She urged Blanco to keep speed with the wagon and not pull back. The space increased between the wagons.

Roscoe notified Thaddeus, "Now!"

Thaddeus put all his weight on the brakes and pulled back hard on the reins. Ann reined in Blanco at the same time and resumed the backward pull from the rear.

The wagon slowed. Everybody prayed her or his version of, "God, slow us down and keep us from wrecking." They begged and willed the animals and the wagon to slow enough to make the trajectory change safely. They slowed drastically. The rear wagon gained on them quickly.

Wham! The wagon slammed against the sudden change of angle. It bounced and skidded but stayed upright. In the clearing at the bottom, Thaddeus steered out of the path of the next wagon.

Ann released Blanco and dropped back. She put Blanco against the front of the wagon opposite Noah and pulled back on the halter to once again tell Blanco to slow as best as it could. The wagon slowed, but not enough. Stephanie, Noah, and Ann needed to push back as long as possible then move out of the way at the last second.

At the rear, Sally still pulled back on Smiley's reins. Smiley resisted going forward. The other three mules, with nobody to direct them, did not pull back at all. They ran along behind. Sally steered Smiley to Big Jenny. She leaned out to get her halter then pulled Big Jenny into the fight against their speed and further arrested the wagon's submission to gravity. It rolled much slower than at any other time during the descent. With enough time, they could bring it to the slow pace they needed. Nobody believed they had the time.

Noah hollered to Ann and Stephanie, "Ride away when I tell you. Keep pushing back until I tell you." The wagon approached acceptable velocity, but they were at the bottom. "Now!" Noah, Ann, and Stephanie urged the mules forward and out of the way. Quick Silver and Diamond navigated the change in slope. Eli pushed on the brake with both feet. Sally commanded Smiley and Big Jenny to stop. Their legs stopped running, but their feet slid over the ground. Shaggy and Hector stopped trying to resist the push of the wagon and changed to running forward. They crossed the transition to level ground. The front of the wagon momentarily stopped as its forward momentum tried to drive the wagon straight down into the ground.

Sally jerked Smiley's halter as violently as she could. In that split second, with no forward pull, Big Jenny and Smiley stopped. The rear of the wagon rose. Sally wrapped her arms around Smiley's neck. Ann, Noah, and Stephanie watched in horror as the wagon pulled the two closest mules off their front feet and into the air while Sally dangled from Smiley.

52

"It's going to flip!" Ann screamed.

Stephanie cried out, "No! God, no!" The wagon was sure to land upside down, crush Eli into the ground, and sling Sally, Smiley, and Big Jenny over the top, only for the ropes that tethered them to jerk them to the ground. All captured in an endless second of terror, the mules hung suspended on their hind hooves. They snapped back into time when the weight of the three dangling at the rear countered the upward movement before it reached the tipping point. The mules still ran forward at the front and pulled the wagon off the hill and forward. The back of the wagon that had reared above crashed back to Earth with the sound of cracking wood. They rolled onto level ground and then slowed to a stop.

Seven

Stephanie jumped off Redeemed. "Eli, are you all right?"

Wedged between the seat and the brake lever, the final maneuver of the wagon had slammed Eli hard into the brake lever and then against the edge of the seat. He lay crumpled in the floorboard.

"Sally!" Ann grabbed her sister into her arms as Sally slid off Smiley.

"I need you!" Stephanie screamed, "He's dead! He's dead! Oh, my God! He's dead!"

Everybody ran to the front of the wagon. Stephanie reached toward Eli. Noah ordered, "Don't touch him!" He told her more softly, "You can damage him more." Noah gently felt Eli's wrist. "He's not dead."

Stephanie replied, "Thank You, God." Eli regained consciousness. Stephanie probed for assurance, "Darling, are you all right?"

"I can't move. I think my back is broken."

With tears streaming down her face, Stephanie resumed repeatedly screaming, "No, God! No!"

Ann ordered her sister, "Stephanie, stop screaming! Somebody may hear you!"

Inches from Ann's face, Stephanie accused her, "I told you we shouldn't go down. This is your fault!"

Ann turned away. She went to check on the wagon

and look at the animals. Noah got on the wagon and carefully flexed Eli's foot. "Can you feel that?"

Eli grunted in pain. "Hurts like the devil."

"Good." He flexed the other. "How about this?"

"I feel it too but not so much pain."

"Good." He touched the tip of each finger and waited for Eli to respond.

Each time, Eli said, "It hurts."

And Noah said, "Good."

Stephanie scolded loudly and angrily, "It's not good! It hurts, and this is your fault too!" She turned to Thaddeus. "And you. How dare you take people down this hill! "

Eli ordered his wife, "Stephanie, stop."

Noah explained, "Stephanie, it is good if it hurts. If he can feel, then the nerves are working, and his back isn't broken." He felt Eli's sides and his back. There was plenty of blood. "Can you move your head?"

Eli rolled his head slightly. "Yes, that hurts something fierce."

"Move each finger." Eli curled them, one after the other. "Now, your feet." He could only flex one.

"You're back is battered, but it's not broken. This ankle is either broken or badly strained." He turned to Roscoe. "May we use some of those mattresses?" They brought three and positioned them on the floorboard beside Eli. "I want to help you lay flat. I'll try not to move you too much." Noah helped Eli onto the mattresses as Roscoe and Thaddeus pulled them across the footboards in front of the driver's seat.

"Can he ride?" Thaddeus asked.

"It will hurt, but shouldn't cause further damage."

"Then, we need to move on. We have to get across the gap before daylight." While Noah examined Eli, the animals not attached to a wagon had made their way down. They had joined their herd of animals and people at the bottom.

Eight

At the top of the mountain in Little Rock, Captain Miles Cornish and Judge Hall had spent their third night looking into the gap with spyglasses. Captain Cornish asked, "Why do we keep coming here?"

"Every time people have gotten out of Little Rock, this is the only place we've never looked."

"That's because there isn't any way to leave going this way."

"Just keep looking. If they're going this way, they'll try to get across during the night."

Nine

Stephanie tried to sit beside Eli on the floor. "Stephanie, I'm going to be all right. Sit in the seat and drive the wagon."

Ann rejoined the people. "All the animals are here. The rear axle of the hay wagon is cracked, but it's still together. Big Jenny seems fine, but Smiley is in pain from being jerked into the air with Sally hanging from her neck. Strangely, Beauty looks like she's walking better. All the other animals, including Mule 4, are none the worse from the descent."

Thaddeus urged them on, "Let's go. Be as quiet as possible." He didn't understand what had gone wrong. It should not have been so hard to slow down. Now Eli was badly hurt, and that upset Thaddeus very much. He was mad that he hadn't inspected the brakes well enough to protect his charges. They had spent quite a bit of time checking on Eli and getting him ready to travel farther. The sun was barely below the horizon when they made the short ride to the gap. When they arrived, the sun popped the very top of its head into their part of the world. Through the cloudless sky, it bathed the gap with light. Blessedly, neither God nor nature had produced the clouds for which Thaddeus had prayed. Above in the town, the Judge called an end to his watch when the morning light painted the valley below blood red. He and Captain Cornish turned and walked away from their vantage point, just as Thaddeus took a spyglass from his pocket and looked up toward the town to see if there was anybody looking into the gap. The escapees crossed unobserved. They had gotten through the most dangerous stretch of the journey.

Thaddeus imparted their next set of instructions. "Right here you can't be seen by anyone, so do what you need to do for Eli. I don't know how long it will take to get to the rendezvous, but your next escort won't pick you up until tomorrow morning at the earliest. Keep heading west through the forest, stay between these ridges until you come to an uncrossable waterway. Your contact will say, 'It's a foolish person who waits here.' You should say, 'Fools find fools that find the foolish way.'"

"Aren't you going to take us all the way?" Sally asked.

Stephanie confronted him, "After your horrible plan to take us down that hill, which practically killed Eli, you should at least make sure we get safely to the end of this section."

"This is the end of this section. The next section you will travel unescorted. Stephanie, I'm very sorry about what happened. I've taken others this way and never had any problems. It's not that I don't care. I care more about this family than I have any of the others I've helped, but there will be others I'll have to take out of town, and I can't be discovered. I'm supposed to be back in my house before daylight. I don't even know how I'll get back now that the sun is up. Please forgive me for allowing any of you to be injured."

"No, I won't," Stephanie refused to forgive any of them. In her mind, they all had caused Eli to be hurt because they hadn't cared about anybody but themselves.

Thaddeus felt the arrow of Satan's influence pierce his heart. He asked to pray for them, "May I pray with you before we part?"

Stephanie turned and walked away, but Eli spoke up, "Thaddeus, there's nothing to forgive. It's just something that happened. Noah says I don't have a broken back, and I'll get better. Stephanie will forgive you in time. Please, pray."

"Protector of the widows, orphans, the downtrodden, and the weak, watch over this family. They mean so much to me. I married Stephanie and Eli. I would never, ever want any harm to come to them or the rest of this family. I told Noah to do what he promised You he would do and that was to live with and love Ann until death. You brought them back together, proving that You joined them and that nothing should pull them asunder. I also know taking people this way is what You want me to do. When I found it, You showed me a vision of leading streams of people over that slope. I don't know why You let this happen to Eli. Of all the people that have come this way, why did You let this man who I care about so much be injured? I know You have a reason, and we may never know what it is. Now, I ask that You heal him completely. Let nothing remain less good than it was before; no impairment or weakness. Instead, make all of them stronger in body, mind, and spirit, and me as well.

Protect them, not just on this journey away from Little Rock, but also for the rest of their lives. I ask in the name of our Savior, Jesus."

Everybody except Stephanie said, "Amen." Stephanie had heard what Thaddeus had prayed, and she wanted everything to be true, so she silently said, amen, but she was furious that the man she loved had almost been killed. She believed it could have been avoided if other people had made different decisions.

Eli thought he could help his wife, as well as Thaddeus. "I would like to say a prayer for you. God, thank You for Thaddeus who has helped us get safely out of Little Rock. We know taking people over that cliff is a good thing because it is the only way to get away undiscovered. I thank You for preventing Noah and Ann from having the flesh lashed off their bodies and from serving more hard labor and for keeping Noah in this family. Forgive every one of us who has made any choice out of wrong motives or has done the wrong thing out of good motives. Heal our spirits, minds, hearts, and bodies. I ask that You get Thaddeus safely back home. Comfort him, and don't let this discourage him from continuing to help others. Let him know how much You love him, and we love him. In the name of Jesus."

The whole group that was circled around Eli completed the prayer with an, "Amen."

Stephanie knew Eli was telling her that she was wrong, and it made her madder. *How can he think I'm wrong and not them?*

Thaddeus hugged Noah, Ann, and Sally. He

reached over and shook Eli's hand as he lay in the floorboard of the wagon, then turned and shook Roscoe's hand. Thaddeus walked toward Stephanie to hug her. Fiery darts flew into all their hearts as Stephanie turned her back and walked away.

Thaddeus went east into the woods and headed back to Little Rock, as the other six people, sixteen mules, ten donkeys, four goats, one horse, and two wagons moved due west. All of them had very heavy hearts and believed one way or another that God, family, and friends had let them down.

They were all unaware of the miracle that God had provided for their safe getaway when He had set into motion the string of events that had prevented them from arriving at the gap too soon. They didn't know that God had protected the escapees and all those living at Little Rock who had helped them.

Ten

Roscoe looked up the valley. On the south-facing side of the northern range of mountains, a pine forest had grown that would make it hard for a wagon to pass. On his left, on the north-facing slope of the southern mountain range, was a hardwood forest of large oaks and hickories with much more space between the trees and not much undergrowth.

"Follow me." Roscoe drove toward the hardwood forest.

In the other wagon, Eli groaned with every bump. Stephanie tried very hard not to jar him, completely unsuccessfully. "Darling, we need to stop. We're hurting you."

"I know how much you care about me, but stopping isn't the answer. You can't make me more comfortable, and we can't just sit in the woods until I heal. Get us to camp then make me willow tea."

"We should stop and make some now."

"We need to get to the river." Eli lay on his back. As he passed below in the wagon, he looked up into a leafless hundred-year-old oak that had provided a perch for a scarlet tanager. The brightly colored splash of red flitted from bare branch to bare branch as it followed them through the forest. Eli concentrated on enjoying the bird, so he would not emit groans of pain.

63

Every breath was extremely painful, so he gave up trying to enjoy the bird and went back to moaning.

Walking behind the wagon, Ann heard what Stephanie had suggested. Ann believed her sister when Stephanie had said it was her fault. If she had not wanted to take revenge because she and Noah had been told they did something wrong when they got married, this would not have happened. If she had not wanted somebody in Little Rock to treat her and Noah respectfully and then stupidly stayed at the Harrows, they could have left peacefully, and Eli wouldn't have been hurt. Instead, Eli was injured and in pain. I can make the sedative, and he wouldn't feel the pain.

Since they walked at the rear to make sure all the animals stayed with them, Ann whispered, "Noah."

Noah moved closer to speak softly, "What?"

"It's my fault that we're in this situation because I wanted to pretend that we're somebody important. I want to do something to help fix this. I need ingredients out of the wagon to make the sedative for Eli. I'll stop to make it while the others keep going. I can keep Eyanosa with me and then use him to ride back when I have it ready. I know you can find what I need."

"It's not your fault any more than mine. I felt the same way, and I made the same choice. I wish God had slammed me around and not Eli. God is teaching me that I have a problem with pride."

"I do too, but Eli being injured and Stephanie being mad at me hurts me worse."

"You're not making it alone. How can we get what we need out of the wagon?"

"You get in the wagon. When Roscoe turns and Stephanie can't see, throw what we need out the side from under the canvas. I'll pick it up, then you come back, and we'll make it."

"I'll get it all into a pack, and then I'll throw it out. I saw a dead branch hanging from a tree a short way back. I'll bring the hatchet. It should be enough dry wood to boil water." Noah ran to the front wagon and climbed it. He thought the closed pucker strings would prevent Roscoe and Sally from seeing what he was doing, but Sally felt the wagon bounce when Noah climbed in. She peeked in through the small opening of the front canvas and watched Noah put items into a pack, strap it on, and then wait. When Roscoe steered around a boulder, he jumped out. She looked back and saw him run into the woods and hide behind a boulder.

Sally informed Roscoe, "I'm going to walk a while." She jumped down on the opposite side of the wagon from Noah. When Stephanie passed her, Sally said, "I'm going to see how Beauty and Mule 4 are doing." Sally stayed hidden as she peeked around the back. Ann sat on Eyanosa. After both wagons had navigated around the bolder, Noah ran over to the horse and jumped on with Ann. They rode away and left the animals to follow or not.

Sally thought, if they want to be alone, now is not the time. She decided she would stay at the rear and do what she had told her other sister. Beauty followed along with the others, but kept to the right, slightly in front of and close to the side of Mule 4. Neither appeared to be suffering, but they stayed in the middle of the group. Sally walked beside Beauty and looked under the blanket. Scabs covered most of her side, but she couldn't see any infection.

She walked behind Beauty and tried to move up between her and Mule 4 to look at its eye. Beauty moved over and closed the space between the two animals. Sally tried to push between them, but Beauty continued to block her. Sally backed out and walked up beside Mule 4 on the left side. The mule saw her and didn't flinch. Both animals let her stop them and look into Mule 4's eye. It still looked cloudy, but she couldn't see any visible abrasions. She decided to experiment because she thought Beauty was purposefully protecting Mule 4. She tried to bring Mule 4 behind and then up beside Beauty on Beauty's right. Immediately, Beauty made the same maneuver and positioned herself to the right and slightly in front of Mule 4.

Sally realized just how good of a mule she had acquired. She rubbed Beauty between the ears. "You're such a good girl. Even though you're injured, you're protecting your herd." Sally didn't like it that Arnold and Russell's mules had suffered, but she was glad that the snowstorm had given them Beauty, and Mules 4, 7, 8, 11, and 20. She hurried Mule 4 and Beauty to the front of the herd then left them to care for each other. Sally stood in place and counted as the animals walked past her. They were all there. However, Snowflake was back a little, pawing the ground. Sally checked her feet and legs. She felt her stomach and discovered the source of her slowness. She checked Bella and Fancy.

Sally told the male goat, "Billy, I see you've been

busy." She hurried back to the rear wagon. She said to Stephanie and Eli, "Guess what?"

Having no idea what, and not in the mood for Sally's guessing game, Stephanie snapped, "For Heaven's sake, just tell us if it's important."

Sally knew Stephanie was upset at Noah, Ann, and Thaddeus, but she hadn't done anything wrong. "It's not important. I'll go tell Roscoe." She walked away and then sat beside Roscoe. "Guess what?"

"Give me a hint," he replied.

"It has something to do with the goats."

Knowing what happened with his animals every year, he guessed. "The girls are pregnant."

Sally was surprised. "How did you know?"

"It happens every spring."

"Then why do you have only four goats?"

"I sell all the kids and the excess milk that I don't use myself."

Sally passed on the more critical detail, "Anyway, we need to go slower. Snowflake is falling behind."

Roscoe pulled on the reins to slow them down.

In the other wagon, Eli had told his wife, "Stephanie, stop attacking everybody."

"Don't tell me what to do. They're all wrong, and they don't care that you're hurt."

"They do care, and you're making it worse."

"How can you take their side?"

"There aren't sides. We're all on the same side."

"They're all selfish, and all they care about is what happens to them."

"That's not true. They care about what happens to

all of us, and you're the one being selfish. Noah and Ann had to rebuild Cadron Ferry, and they have to hide to be married. What do you want them to do? Let Judge Hall whip them, or put them in a real prison, so we could ride safely out of Little Rock? That is being selfish!"

"Of course, I don't want them to be whipped, but they didn't have to have their little dinner, so they could be the la-de-da doctor and his wife."

"They were asked by their host to stay and have a meal with a friend. They were being polite."

"They were putting on airs, and you know it!"

"Don't talk to me, Stephanie." Eli thought it was ridiculous for her to be mean to everybody.

"Don't worry; I won't!" Stephanie clamped her mouth shut and clenched the reins. Her fingernails cut into the palms of her hands. Blood dripped onto the mattress beside Eli and landed on his face. He looked up and saw blood dripping from his wife's hands. "You're bleeding. Let me see your hands."

She unclenched and showed Eli her palms.

"I'm sorry, honey. I shouldn't have said that. I love you. I want you to talk to me. I just don't want you to be mad at everybody."

"I'm sorry too. I just can't stop feeling mad."

"I'm going to get a bandage." Eli tried to rise up and then fell back in pain. "Ahhh!"

"Don't try to move, darling." She called out, "Sally, I need you!"

Sally heard Stephanie call for her. "Stephanie needs me." She ran to the rear wagon.

"What's wrong?"

Eli told her, "Stephanie needs bandages on her hands, and I can't get off the floorboard."

Stephanie showed Sally her hands. Sally looked at four half circles cut into the palm of each hand. "How did that happen?"

"I was holding the reins too tightly."

"I think you should have realized sooner. I'll get what we need." Sally went to the front wagon, got the first aid kit, and then returned to the rear wagon. She placed the first aid kit on the seat and climbed up.

Stephanie apologized, "I'm sorry that I snapped at you. What did you want to tell us?"

"Snowflake was falling behind, so I checked her and discovered that she's pregnant. Then I checked Fancy and Bella. They are too. I can feel a lot of feet." Sally put iodine on Stephanie's hands and wrapped them with bandages.

"How many do you think are there?" Eli asked.

"I think they're all going to have at least two kids."

Stephanie said, "I want to see if I can count how many. Will you drive, so I can go feel them?"

Sally didn't want Stephanie to know that Ann and Noah were gone. Stephanie would really be mad if she knew they were gone. "You won't be able to feel with these bandages on your hands."

"I guess you're right." Stephanie slowed.

"I'll call out if you need to go slower or stop."

Stephanie hugged Sally. "I'll be listening. I'm sorry I acted mean, Sally. It's just that I'm so upset that Eli is hurt. Will you forgive me?"

"Of course, you're forgiven." Sally held onto Stephanie for the longest time.

As Sally climbed off the wagon, Stephanie told her sister, "Thank you for forgiving me." It didn't occur to her that she should do the same and forgive Ann, Noah, and Thaddeus.

Eleven

Sally stood on the ground and let the animals pass. Beauty and Mule 4 passed in their new formation, along with the others. Making up the rear guard was Billy with Bella and Fancy. Snowflake had stopped. The head of one kid was already arriving into the world. Now, everybody would know that Noah and Ann were gone. It was too bad, but nature had called her hand. Sally called out, "Stop! Snowflake is having her babies now!" Roscoe and Stephanie reined in the mules. They stopped, and both walked to the rear.

"Where are Ann and Noah?" Stephanie asked.

"I don't know," Sally replied.

Stephanie snapped at Sally again, "So, you choose to tell us that the goats are pregnant, but you didn't think you should mention that Noah and Ann are gone?"

"I didn't want you to know because you're so mad at them. Noah packed something, and then they rode away on Eyanosa."

Stephanie was furious. "You let them run away and leave Eli injured?!"

Sally tried to refocus everybody's attention. "How long will it be before the baby goats can walk?"

Roscoe explained why they were not going further. "She's going to have them both today. Every other year, all three of them had their babies within days of each other. Kids can walk after a short period of time, but not long distances. Also, the doe and kid have to stay at the place where it's born for at least an hour to bond. Since she's going to have the other kid too, and we have to stay so she can bond with it. We won't be moving from this spot today."

As Roscoe finished explaining, the first baby plopped onto the ground. Snowflake immediately licked her baby's face to remove the birth membrane and fluids. The baby drew its first breath. Snowflake nibbled away all the birth goo and licked until her baby was clean then nudged it to her udder to take nourishment.

Sally tried to think about what they could do to keep going. "We could get them in the wagon and carry them, but there's not enough space for them to give birth."

Fancy started pawing the ground and pacing. Roscoe told them, "Fancy's getting ready to give birth."

"I'm going to go tell Eli." Stephanie walked back to the wagon. "We're stopping here. Snowflake is giving birth, Fancy's about to give birth, and Noah and Ann are gone."

"They're gone? Where did they go?"

"How should I know? Sally saw Noah pack some things in a pack and ride away with Ann on Eyanosa."

"You were so mean. They think we don't want them, and now they've left us. I've never had any brothers or sisters until Ann, Sally, and Noah. They mean a lot to me. We need to find them."

Sally walked over. "Eli, since we're going to wait here, would you like willow or a sedative?"

"I'm upset, I hurt, and I don't want to deal with all this. Put me to sleep."

While Snowflake gave birth to kid two, Roscoe made a fire. Sally climbed into the wagon to get the willow, fumewort, and valerian. "It's all gone."

"What's gone?" Roscoe asked.

"Noah and Ann took what we need to make a sedative."

Stephanie had her mind completely set on thinking the worst of her sister and brother-in-law. "If I ever see them again, it will be too soon." She threw a log onto the fire and sent sparks flying in every direction.

Roscoe and Sally put snow into the washtubs to melt it for the animals to drink. She also put snow into their pots to prepare the mid-day meal. Stephanie walked over to Eli, sat beside him, and silently fumed. He didn't want to hear her talk about how horrible Ann and Noah were, and she didn't have anything good to say about anything. She listened to Eli's labored breathing and wanted to clobber Ann.

Noah and Ann rode up on Eyanosa. "What happened? Why are you stopped?" Noah feared that something bad had happened to Eli.

Stephanie heard Noah talking. She jumped down to give him a verbal thrashing.

"Snowflake and Fancy are having babies," Sally informed him.

Noah lowered Ann to the ground as Stephanie stalked over and accused her, "If you had to run off to be alone, fine. But to take the valerian and fumewort is horrible and unforgivable!"

Ann defended Noah and herself, "Stephanie, stop thinking the absolute worst about us. We did not go anywhere to be alone. I know we created all these problems, and we feel horrible that Eli is injured. We wanted to do something to help, so yes, we did take the fumewort, valerian, and willow because we made some medicine for Eli. We didn't tell you because we didn't want you to stop and miss the next rendezvous." She took the canteen to Eli. "We made you the sedative. Do you want it?" Ann asked.

"Yes, please." Eli drank a large draught of the sedative straight from the canteen because he really wanted to be free from the pain and turmoil. Eli was soon asleep and breathed much easier.

Noah and Ann gave hay to all the animals. Snowflake's two kids nursed. Fancy's first-born of the year had its two front feet and head out and was about to take its dive into the world. Since they had to wait, Stephanie sat on the wagon seat beside Eli. She also wanted to stay far away from the others, who all sat around the fire on campstools not far from the goats.

Roscoe commented, "I don't think we can ride through this forest in the dark, but I don't know what will happen if we aren't at the river in the morning. This whole thing may fall apart."

"Should we just take our chances, head toward Harmony, and forget about this route?" Ann asked.

Noah pointed out the problem with that plan, "Judge Hall will be watching the roads to Harmony.

These people have a secret route. I think we need to stay on this path."

Ann imparted her concern, "I don't know how to make this right for the rest of the family."

Noah suggested, "Maybe I should go and lead them away. The rest of you can go home. They don't even know about anybody but me and Ann."

Sally stood up and put her hands on her hips. "Absolutely not. If you go, I go with you."

Ann agreed with Noah. "It would be safer for the rest of the family if Noah and I aren't with you. I think we should part."

Sally absolutely did not want to separate. "You can't do that. We need to stay together."

Stephanie walked over from the wagon. "We don't need to stay together. They should go. We aren't safe when they're around."

"We'll leave." Ann got up and went to pack.

Sally ordered, "Stephanie, apologize right now."

"No," Stephanie refused.

Sally confronted Stephanie, "You want our sister to leave? What is the matter with you? Don't you love her?"

"No, I don't. I want to get Eli to a real doctor, and I can't do that if we have to hide in the woods."

"Then take the wagon and Eli, and go to a doctor. I'm going with Ann and Noah. Roscoe, what are you going to do?"

"We should stay together and take Eli to a doctor. We can ask the person at the river where we can find a doctor. Will that be acceptable to you, Stephanie?"

"We can go to the river, but if we can't get to a doctor, then I'm taking Eli back to Little Rock."

"Thank you, Stephanie." Sally was relieved that the family wasn't breaking apart. She went to tell Ann and Noah that they didn't have to leave. Ann sat in the wagon with Noah, but they weren't packing. Noah held Ann as she cried. It broke Ann's heart that Stephanie had said she didn't love her and wanted her to leave. "We're going to stay together and go to the river. We're going to ask whoever is there how to get to a doctor."

Twelve

Stephanie turned toward the woods. "What was that?"

A low growling came from several places around their camp. Everybody tensed. "Coyotes or wolves. They must have smelled the goat babies. This time of year, they have pups. They'll be very aggressive." Noah held out a rifle.

Sally refused to take one. "Somebody may hear the shots."

"It won't matter if we're dead, and these animals won't stop attacking." Noah handed one rifle and two pistols to each of them and then their bows and arrows. Each of them would have only three shots, plus several arrows. Stephanie laid her arrows on the floor then stood guard over Eli. The others surrounded the goats with the larger animals then spaced themselves around the group.

"How many do you think there are?" Ann asked.

Noah answered, "Maybe a dozen; it's hard to tell when they're slinking around."

Roscoe cocked his rifle. "If you have a clean shot, shoot."

After several minutes of waiting for whatever predator was out there to make a move, everybody was fraught with anxiety. Sally screamed, "Do something!"

"They're studying us to find the best way to attack." Noah hoped the vicious animals would go away, but he knew that wasn't going to happen. He had fought wolves in Indian Territory. Seven Indian warriors had barely survived, but all the wolves had ended up as skins in Indian lodges. Noah saw the familiar yellow orbs and sank an arrow between them.

Suddenly, the whole pack dashed from the woods. An enormous animal bounded toward Sally. Terror filled her. Please let us be far enough away from Little Rock. She fired her rifle then ran into the herd. Several of the wild dogs ran past the mules and donkeys toward the highly appetizing aroma of newborn goats.

The hungry, vicious predators encountered an onslaught of sharp hooves. King sent a canine body flying. With an open gash on the bridge of its reddish gray nose, it again dashed between Shaggy's legs.

A snarling ball of teeth and claws charged Ann. She pulled the trigger of her rifle. Only a puff of smoke rose from the flash in the pan. They were widely spaced around the animals, so nobody could see her. A few more strides and the coyote would have her. She threw down the rifle and pulled her pistol. With its lips curled back and its teeth exposed in a bloodthirsty snarl, the coyote sprang toward Ann's neck. She fired the pistol. The bringer-of-death slammed Ann to the ground. Blood poured over Ann's body. She wiped it away from her eyes and reached for her other pistol.

Eli's sedated brain registered the gunshots as two coyotes raced toward the wagon. Stephanie shot one through the heart. She didn't know if she could bring down the other in time. Eli saw what was headed his way. He grabbed an arrow, jammed it into the mattress with the arrowhead up, and rolled to his side. The coyote sprang onto the wagon and skewered itself. Stephanie yelled, "Two are dead!"

The coyotes again attacked as a pair. Sure of their meal, they came at Roscoe. He stepped back into the mass of mules behind him. Wedged between Big Jenny and Little Jack, he fired his rifle and dropped one. Its partner continued its dash for dinner.

Little Jack kicked sideways and hurled the invader toward Big Jenny. Big Jenny thrust her rear feet and lobbed the limp body into the snow.

The coyote shook it off and rejoined the assault on the donkeys between Sally and Ann. Sally returned to the edge and fired her pistol, but the coyotes had altered their strategy. She again missed as they veered into the herd.

Trying to stomp and kick the three assailants under their feet, the mules blocked Ann's line of fire. "Three made it into the herd!"

I have to protect the goats. Noah pushed into the cluster of animals.

Coyotes, angling to give others in their pack a chance to get to the kids and drag them out, darted at and drew the attention of Ann and Sally.

Ann sunk her last bullet into a coyote that streaked into her line of fire. It yelped, turned, and came for her. She dropped the empty pistol and nocked an arrow.

Through the chaos, Sally fired at Ann's attacker. This time, she didn't miss.

Just then a ravenous animal bit Mule 4's nose. Afraid, in pain, and unable to make sense of all the movement, the partially blind mule dashed out of the group and into the trees. Two coyotes ran after it. Ann released her arrow. Her target continued its pursuit of the mule with an arrow in its rump.

"I'm not letting them kill my mule!" Sally ran after them.

Stephanie screamed, "Sally, stop! Get back to the animals!"

Sally continued into the woods. Ann ran after her with only her bow and arrows.

A canine attacker again tried to get at Stephanie and Eli. With a nocked arrow, Eli stood beside Stephanie, already aiming her gun. In the blink of an eye, with both an arrow and a bullet in its lungs, the coyote breathed its last.

Stephanie scanned the trees. "I don't see any more."

Roscoe didn't see any either, but he knew three were in the group of animals, and he still had two loaded pistols. He ducked down and spotted a coyote trying to bite Redeemed on its belly. Redeemed reared and kicked, but couldn't get at it. The mule also couldn't move away because all the other mules and donkeys surrounded it. Roscoe dropped the coyote. With only one bullet, he scanned for the others.

Noah drew his knife as Fancy charged and ran the coyote away from her baby toward Billy. Billy attempted to impale the attacker with his horns. His hard skull sent the animal reeling. Even with a ripped open side, it got up and tried again. The other wild dog lunged for Snowflake's baby. She kicked it away, but the coyote leaped back into the fight and drew Fancy away from her baby. The injured coyote ripped long gashes into the soft flesh of the kid's neck. Noah grabbed the coyote by the tail. He yanked it over and plunged his knife into its chest.

The remaining vicious attacker clamped its fangs into the kid and then dragged the helpless baby while dodging stomping and kicking hooves.

In their attempt to destroy their attackers, the mules kicked wildly. Instead of making contact with a canine body, a hoof took Quick Silver's leg out from under it. The mule crashed to the ground on top of the coyote pulling the kid past.

Stephanie screamed, "Sally and Ann ran into the woods behind two coyotes!"

Noah forced his way out of the animal mob. "Which way?" Stephanie pointed.

The wild dog bit at the body that had it pinned. Quick Silver got back to his feet. Before the instrument of destruction got off the ground, the mule had stomped it into mangled blood-soaked fur.

Roscoe picked up the crushed kid with its throat ripped open. *Blasted coyotes killed it.* "Do you see any more?"

"No, but two ran after Mule 4 into the trees. Sally ran after her mule, so Ann went after Sally, and then Noah followed to save them all."

Roscoe hurried to Stephanie and Eli. "We should stay here, in case more come or those two circle back."

Eli was clearly in excruciating pain. Stephanie told him, "Lie down."

"Not until I know we're all safe." Eli struggled to breathe with his smashed-up ribcage.

Stephanie ordered him, "Then, sit!"

Since he could barely stand, Eli sat on the wagon seat. Roscoe went to look over their animals.

In the woods, Sally realized what she had done. She stopped her pursuit and raced back along her trail through the snow. She saw Ann running her way covered with blood. Panic filled her mind. Sally frantically asked, "Are you hurt?"

"It's coyote blood." Ann hugged her so tightly that Sally could barely breathe. "What did you think you were doing? What if those coyotes had turned back on you? Don't ever leave the group like that!"

"You're suffocating me. Let me go. They're going to kill Mule 4!"

"Maybe, but her life isn't worth yours."

Noah caught up with the girls. Neither looked injured. He asked anyway, "Is everybody all right?"

"Yes." Ann let Sally out of her arms and turned toward Noah.

Noah went into high concern. "You're bleeding! You are not all right!"

"I'm fine. I shot a coyote. It bled on me. "

Noah looked at his wife. Like war paint, she wore the blood of her vanquished enemy smeared across her forehead and cheekbones, down her neck, and over her chest. She looked more savage and powerful than any woman he had ever seen. Noah still wanted them out of the woods. "We need to get back to camp. Come on."

Sally objected. "We haven't rescued Mule 4!"

Noah told her, "I'm sorry, but she'll have to make it on her own." Two of the coyotes had gotten away. Noah assumed they would come back. As they hurried back to the camp, he kept a constant, intense scan on the woods.

The family and their animals had killed several coyotes. The coyotes had probably killed two: Mule 4 and the newborn goat. The coyotes would have been better off remaining hungry.

Thirteen

When they got back to the wagons, Ann washed the blood from as much of her skin as she could. Noah hoped Stephanie would talk with him and walked to the wagon. Eli was sitting on the wagon seat. "Eli, we should get you into the wagon. You'll have more space, and we can protect you better in there. Can you walk?"

"Maybe, but I don't think I can get down, and I don't want to try."

"How can we move him without hurting him?" Stephanie wanted Eli in the safest place they could get him.

Noah explained his plan, "We can take the side boards off the hay wagon and nail the backboards to them to make a firm platform. We'll hold it beside the wagon and pull the mattresses and Eli on. We'll carry him around then prop one end up on the back. Two of us will get inside and pull the mattresses and Eli into the wagon. Then, we can take the boards apart and put them back on the wagon."

Roscoe added, "If we put Eli in the other wagon, we can put all the hay into a tarp and hang it from the top, then the goats will have the whole wagon bed. We need to get Bella into the wagon before she starts to have her kids. She and Fancy can bond with their babies in the wagon, and we can keep moving."

Stephanie agreed, "I think that'll work." They reloaded all their guns, in case the fight resumed. Next, they got Eli into the wagon. Stephanie lay beside Eli for a moment. Even injured, Eli thought about his favorite hobby. "I sure would like to have some of the coyote skins."

"I'll ask Noah to help me skin at least one." Stephanie stroked Eli's hair until the adrenaline wore off and the sedative put him back to sleep. Then she went to help get the hay wagon set.

"Eli wants to have some coyote skins. Is there any way one of you would help me skin one?"

Noah was glad to be able to do something that Eli and Stephanie wanted. Maybe it would help to mend their fractured relationship. "I'd be glad to help you. I don't think we should stay here to skin them, but we can gut them here and skin them later."

"I'll help too," Ann offered.

Sally led Fancy into the wagon. "She still looks fat. I think she has another baby inside."

Fancy's kid that had been born was now dead. Roscoe hoped she did have another. "If she does, she'll have it in the wagon."

Snowflake's two babies were nursing and well bonded with her. Roscoe put the babies into the wagon while Noah led the mother in. They wanted to create the most room possible for the birthing, so they kept Billy out of the wagon.

They gathered coyote bodies, slit open their bellies, and cut out their innards. They made short work of the task and quickly had coyote bodies hung on the sides of the hay wagon. They ate the meal Roscoe had started before the attack, cleaned up, and then buried the fire with snow.

When Roscoe said, "It's time to leave," they had been there three hours.

"What about Mule 4?" Sally wanted to give it a chance to get back.

"It's been over an hour. She's not coming back."

So very sad that Mule 4 was gone, Sally climbed onto the seat of the front wagon. She had tried to save her from the injuries she had acquired during the blizzard but had ended up losing her to coyotes. She didn't want to think about the coyotes killing her mule. Instead, she tried to occupy her mind by looking for a way around the obstacles with Eli's hospital wagon. Roscoe followed with the goat nursery. Ann and Noah walked behind to make sure all the animals stayed with them and to guard the rear in case the coyotes came back.

Expecting an attack at any moment, they wove through the trees fully armed. The only thing they saw were doves. Ann decided target practice with her bow was in order. "I want to shoot a dove."

Noah thought it was a good idea. "We might as well try to get enough to eat. Dove spirit, we ask for permission to take lives."

Ann and Noah shot at the cooing doves that sat on the branches above. Two fell from their perches. The rest of the flock took flight through a barrage of arrows.

"Tonight, we eat roasted doves." Noah smacked his lips for emphasis as they gathered the fallen doves and the arrows that had failed to hit their marks. Noah watched Ann, with her clothes still red with coyote blood. She expertly cut open the doves and removed their innards. She was his spirit woman. He pulled her over to kiss her. "I could ravish you if it wouldn't be totally inappropriate in the eyes of Stephanie."

"She's wrong, but I've hurt her too much, and she's hurt me too much, and we shouldn't add to the problem. But I want you to know, if you loved me in this forest right now, we would melt the snow out of the entire valley."

"Well, we wouldn't want to cause a flood." Noah kissed her long and lovingly, but they waited to share their love. Instead, they caught up with the others and hung the birds at the back of the wagon.

"My wife, look at the wagon. Death circles the wagon as dead coyotes and doves. However, inside new life is blooming as baby goats."

"We've been given a vision of the circle of life." They felt completely in tune with nature and each other.

In the last rays of light, they arrived at the bank of Fletcher Creek, running swollen, fast, and deep. Close to the water, hundreds of bright yellow narcissus flowers pushed through the snow. They tried to lead the animals to the creek to get a drink without crushing the flowers. It wasn't possible. The twenty-seven animals trampled many of the beautiful flowers. They brought the animals back to the camp and fed them in a communal pile.

Roscoe brought food and water to the goats in the wagon. He discovered Fancy nursing two kids. Fancy must have stolen one of Snowflake's kids to replace the kid she lost. He looked over at Snowflake. Snowflake's two kids slept beside her. "Fancy was pregnant with triplets! She has two in here." Except for Eli, who was still asleep, they all came over to look.

They roasted the doves, baked sweet potatoes, and boiled corn. Meanwhile, to give them protection from coyotes, they moved everything inside the supply wagon and stacked it all at the ends. They completely blocked the front of both wagons with one-and-a-half by two-foot containers stacked on top of each other, all the way to the top of the canvas opening. At the backs, by separating the two stacks of boxes, they created a small slit that they had to press through sideways. Inside one of the eighteen-foot long wagons, they had a fifteen-foot-long space to sleep. In the other, was fifteen feet of space for three goats and, they hoped, eventually six kids.

When they settled into the wagon for the night, Eli and Stephanie went all the way in. That protected Eli more, and neither would be getting out for a guard shift. Ann and Sally were next. They lay with their feet overlapping Eli's and Stephanie's feet. Noah was closest to the back and overlapped head-to-head with Ann and Sally. Roscoe took the first three-hour shift. Noah was scheduled to take the second shift. Ann planned to take the last shift.

Roscoe climbed into the wagon at the end of his shift. He handed Noah Eli's pocket watch and then slid into the blankets. When Noah's three hours were up, he stayed on watch and let Ann sleep. She was capable, but he didn't want to take a chance with her life if coyotes sprang on her out of the dark. It was almost morning when Noah heard something approaching. He sounded the alarm.

Ready to blast coyotes to smithereens, everybody grabbed their loaded rifles. Except for Eli and Stephanie, they got out of the wagon. With her rifle in her hands, Stephanie looked out the narrow opening into the receding darkness.

The nighttime visitor came into the light of the fire. They all let out a cheer. With hooves and fur stained red, Mule 4 rejoined her herd. Beauty immediately took up her position to the right front of her friend that was covered with fang and claw injuries, as well as dried mule and coyote blood.

Fourteen

While they examined Mule 4, Ann told Noah, "You didn't wake me up."

"I know," he replied, "I lay awake and worried the whole time Roscoe was on duty, and I knew I wouldn't be able to sleep with you out there, so I just stayed on guard. Now that the last two coyotes are stomped into pulp, I should be able to sleep. I'm going to get into the wagon and do that after we take care of the animals."

An hour later, Mule 4 had received her eye treatment. All the injuries from the coyote fight had been treated with cedar poultice, held on with red ribbons and the bandages they had made during the spring blizzard. They also had given the animals a dose of willow water for pain, taken them to the creek for more water, and back to camp for food.

Eli ate before he drank more sedative. He lay in the wagon and tried to breathe. Noah checked on him. "You have cracked ribs. Is it all right if I put cedar and garlic paste on you? I also want to bind your foot and ankle with a splint."

Eli gave his permission. "Do what needs to be done. Did you get any of the coyote skins?"

"We gutted them all. We haven't skinned them yet. Should we just salt the skins when we do?"

"That would be good. I wish I could help, but I hurt too much, and I'd rather be asleep."

"Don't worry about helping. We can do it. It's going to hurt but try ten deep breaths. I don't want you to get pneumonia."

Eli inhaled. His lungs expanded and pushed on his ribs. In pain, he groaned loudly. Stephanie flew to the wagon. "What's wrong?"

"Nothing's wrong, honey. I'm trying to breathe deep to keep my lungs clear. It hurts."

Stephanie commanded, "Don't hurt him, Noah."

"It's going to be worse, and he could die if he gets pneumonia." Noah wrapped Eli's chest loosely with a layer of cedar across his back and garlic paste on his chest.

Eli painfully raised a foot. "Will you salt the coyote skins until I can work with them?"

"I was up all night. I'll work on the coyote skins after I wake up." Noah wrapped the foot and ankle tightly, applied cedar and more layers of clean wool blanket pieces, then bound a short splint diagonally across his ankle to hold his foot immobile but in a flexed position. He wrapped that with more wool blanket pieces to try to make it more comfortable. Noah asked as he finished, "Is that all right?"

"Sure. Much obliged, Noah. I'm glad you're here to take care of me."

After Eli was as well treated as Noah could get him, Noah told Stephanie, "I'm done."

She moved next to Eli. "I'll get started on the coyotes, my darling." Stephanie gently kissed Eli and then once again stroked his hair to comfort and relax him until he slept. Noah also lay asleep in the wagon when Stephanie slipped out.

Roscoe, Sally, Ann, and Stephanie sat silently at the fire and drank coffee. Ann was still hurt that Stephanie had said that she didn't love her and that she wanted Ann to leave. Even though she was glad that the coyotes had hurt neither of her sisters, Stephanie was still mad that Eli was injured. When their coffee cups were empty, they started skinning coyotes. Ann could feel the tension hanging over them like a wet, suffocating blanket. It was clear that Stephanie didn't want to be around her, and it made for a long morning.

Roscoe skinned and then butchered a coyote. He started a pot with water, a leg of coyote, a pound of apricots, a diced onion, two cloves of garlic, salt, ground black pepper, apple cider vinegar, molasses, dry mustard, ground chili pepper, and sugar. As his coyote barbeque simmered, he skinned more coyotes.

After she had skinned three of the coyotes, Ann escaped. She walked a short way up the creek past the animal watering area and out of view then lay among the narcissus on her folded tarp. She lay quietly and faded into the background.

A river otter family came out to play. They jumped on each other, wrestled in the snow, and dove into the water on top of each other. The littlest one tried to escape to land, but its older sibling pulled it back into the fun, just in time for another otter to jump on them both. They all scrambled out of the water onto the steep bank on the far side of the creek, scurried to the top, then slid down the snow and plopped into the river at the bottom. They reminded Ann of the fun Sally, Stephanie, Roscoe, and she had in the mudslide at Pine

Bluff. She wished they could be happy again. The snow melted beneath Ann. She felt several hard, round objects pressing into her stomach then sat up and pulled the tarp back. All the otters dove into the water and fled away, safely hidden beneath the surface.

She felt around in the snow until she had one of the rotten black globes then worked on removing the thick husk. When the husk popped off, she cracked open the shell and then ate the walnut. She felt around in the snow until she had all the walnuts from under the tarp beside her. Ann decided to spend her time doing something constructive, so she gathered walnuts. She found the large tree with the deeply furrowed bark that was the maker of the walnuts and concentrated her search under its branches. In a few hours, the tarp had a large, heavy cache of still-in-the-husk walnuts, which she dragged back to camp.

"I found walnuts." Ann opened the tarp.

Sally asked, "What happened to your hands?"

Ann looked at her black fingers. "I guess it's from touching the walnuts. I'll wash." She got soap and warm water and then scrubbed and scrubbed. The shade of her skin remained the same.

"That's some good dye." Sally climbed into the wagon, "I'll get gloves, so we can shell these."

With gloves to protect their hands, they beat the husks off the walnuts. "I think we should keep these and make dye." Ann crushed the husks then dumped them back onto the tarp. In a separate pile, they put the inner shells and the nutmeat into a third pile. The pounding woke Noah. He joined them, "This is great.

Not only is this great food, but the husks are excellent for getting rid of intestinal parasites. We should all take the treatment, just in case."

Ann agreed, "I'll try it." So did Sally and Roscoe.

Stephanie told Noah, "You're not a doctor."

"Even though he wasn't supposed to train me, the medicine man of our tribe taught me a lot, but you don't have to drink any."

"Really? Will you teach me?" Sally asked.

Noah agreed, "It's a 'learn-as-you-go' process, but I'll tell you what I know when we come across things like these black walnuts."

"Thank you." Sally gave Noah a big hug and then continued to process the nuts.

By the end of the day, they had all the nuts shelled. Ann folded all the nutmeat inside a large square of duck cloth and tied it up. She guessed they had five pounds, and that didn't include all the nuts they had eaten as they had shelled them. In a separate square of duck cloth, Noah wrapped the shells he had pounded into a powder, along with several unbroken halves to use as measuring tools. They pounded the hulls into pea-sized pieces and poured them into ten-gallon washtubs. They had salted, folded up, tied, and stacked all the coyote skins in duck cloth.

The coyote bodies lay buried in the snow until they decided if Roscoe's recipe was any good. Roscoe ladled the coyote barbeque onto mashed white potatoes. From downstream, the sound of a person whistling floated by. They put down their plates of food and picked up their rifles.

A very thin woman approached the wagons. "It's a foolish person who waits here."

Since they had agreed it would be better for one person to reply, Roscoe replied, "Fools find fools who find the foolish way."

"Then we'll be the fools. What do you have there?"

Sally looked at cheeks like caves sunken into the woman's face and clothes that swallowed her body. She and her sisters had been close to that state the previous spring. "Coyote barbeque on mashed potatoes."

Ann warned her, "But we haven't tried it yet."

Roscoe offered for her to join them. "Would you like to try some? I think I'm a good cook. I'd love to have you try it with us."

"I don't mind if I do."

Roscoe handed her his untouched food then went and got a small pot. When he returned, the woman said, "This is excellent. Maybe you'll tell me how you made it and let me have some of those coyotes."

Roscoe told her, "Help yourself to as many as you want. I'll write out the recipe after we eat."

The woman pointed to the wagon where Stephanie had gone with two plates of food. "That one doesn't like people?"

Since she really wanted to fix things between herself and Stephanie, Ann explained, "That brings up a request we have. She went to take food to her husband. He's injured and needs a doctor. We don't know where you're going to take or send us, but if there's any way we can go to a doctor, we need to get him there."

"There's a man who's sort of a doctor not far away,

but he's asked regularly about his patients. There must be people looking for you, so it wouldn't be a good idea."

Ann looked at her stained fingers. "I think I can solve that problem."

"Will it compromise our travel or safety if we don't move on immediately?" Roscoe asked.

"It doesn't matter how long it takes you to move on." The woman held out her plate for more coyote.

"Can we get him there tonight?" Noah asked.

"It wouldn't be safe to go at night. We should load up all those coyotes and go to a different place tonight, then you can take your man to see the doctor in the morning."

Noah picked up the pot of cooked food. "We'll get packed up."

Ann said, "Throw that out, so I can clean the pot."

"I have some children who are hungry," the woman commented.

Ann spoke up immediately, "We'll take this food to your children."

Ten minutes later, as the large waxing moon rose, their new guide sat beside Roscoe in the first wagon. Eli and Stephanie rode in the back with the remaining coyote bodies packed into washtubs filled with snow. Sally drove the second wagon. The animals remained tied at the rear by their lead ropes.

Fifteen

Ann walked beside Noah at the rear. "I think I can dye my skin with the walnut husks and take Eli to the doctor. When Judge Hall comes asking the doctor who's been there, he can honestly say a brown-skinned woman brought a man. I don't know how you feel about my skin being almost black for a while."

"If it helps Eli and Stephanie, it's good."

The gaunt woman led them downstream and then stopped. "We don't have much farther to go, but there are too many animals, so water them here."

When all the animals had drunk as much as they wanted, and the travelers had filled their canteens, they traveled to a group of five cabins. A very slender man came out of one of the cabins, followed by four children with skin stretched over their skeletons. The man was clearly angry. "What are you doing? How could you bring people here?"

"They have food. How many more of our children do you want to die?"

Roscoe saw emaciated faces peeking out of the other cabin windows. They waited for the angry man to speak. "Do they have enough for everybody?"

They had tubs of coyote bodies. She assured her husband, "Yes."

"I'll accept them into our community, at least for the night. Have them set up camp and bring the food."

Roscoe looked at the starving faces in the windows. "How many people are here?"

"Twenty-two, including the children."

Ann carried the pots of cooked food they had brought from the camp to the woman's children. They stuck their hands into the pot and greedily, hungrily, shoved food into their mouths. They gulped the life-giving sustenance down so fast that they soon had hiccups. The newcomers parked the wagons beside their guide's house. Roscoe instructed the man and woman who appeared to be the leaders of the group. "Come to the back of the wagon."

"Give these to each family." Roscoe handed out skinned coyote bodies. "Bring the wash tubs back. Ma'am, how many days to the next place we can safely buy food?"

The woman's husband replied, "Two days."

Roscoe motioned to Sally. "Make five copies of the recipe for coyote barbeque." Roscoe owned all the food. I'll give out everything, except two days supplies for the six of us. He looked at Noah and Ann. "Help me divide this food into five stacks."

Roscoe handed Stephanie a bolt of cloth. "Unroll the duck cloth as far as from one hand stretched out to your other, then cut it straight across. Cut me five pieces." Eli woke up as Stephanie cut the cloth and passed them out. Ann and Noah laid them on the ground behind the wagon.

"What's happening?" Eli asked.

Stephanie let him know what was going on. Eli watched Roscoe pass out smoked hams, roasts of beef, dried fruit, potatoes, carrots, rice, beans, salt, sugar, coffee, tea, pepper, flour, split peas, corn, saleratus, oatmeal, vinegar, pickles, bran, salt pork, lard, and many other items. Noah and Ann divided it into the five stacks. Every person came out of their cabin and hungrily watched the food stack up.

The husband of their escort said, "I'd say this is too much, but we're starving. We gathered just before my wife left to look for travelers. I asked God to spare us and send us food. I hoped God would send us a few meals. Suddenly, you are here with all this food."

Roscoe had already piled into the duck cloth sheets everything he had bought to feed six people for six months. "I can get more as we go, and one more thing." He brought out a medium-sized box and handed it to their escort.

The woman opened it. Her husband looked over her shoulder into the box. "What is it?"

She picked up the packets of folded papers and read, "Tomatoes, beets, carrots, peas, corn, okra." She stopped reading the packets. "Vegetable seeds."

Roscoe received so much pleasure and felt so blessed by helping that he thought of something else he wanted to give them. "I want to give you something else." He climbed out of the much emptier wagon and walked to the other wagon. He took down the rear boards, put up the walk planks, and went into the wagon. He came out with Snowflake, followed by her two kids. "Don't eat these. Wait a week, so the kids drink all her first milk then you can milk her once a day. Let the kids nurse the rest of the day. She has a male and a female kid. You can breed them in about eight months. It's best if you take the two females and breed them with somebody else's goat, but you can use this male."

"This gift means life to our community. I'll give life back to you and take your injured man to a doctor. Of course, I'll also lead you safely to your next transfer. Right now, I want to protect these goats from predators." Their escort took Snowflake and its babies into her cabin.

Sally had the coyote barbeque recipes ready. When she handed a young woman one of the sheets of paper, the woman, who could barely carry her tiny baby asked, "Will you tell me what this says?" Sally picked up two corners of the cloth. "I will, and I'll get this end if your husband gets the other."

The young man knew how weak his wife was from nursing the baby. "Thank you."

"It's a recipe for coyote barbeque. I'll help you start a pot tonight. It will be ready in the morning." Sally carried the food into their cabin and helped put it into their empty cabinets.

Other families tried to pick up the duck cloth sheets of food. All of the women and some of the men were too weak. Ann helped a couple with two young children.

Noah called out, "We need some help."

Stephanie peeked out the back of the wagon. "What do you need?"

"We need to help these people move this food."

Stephanie looked at Eli. "I should stay with my husband."

"I can't help, but I can send you. Please go help." Eli waved her out of the wagon.

"I'll be back." Stephanie helped the last couple while their escort and her husband carried their own stack of food.

Sally and the young man took the cloth and washtub back to the wagon. Roscoe took the washtub. "In the future, we'll need this to water the animals, but you can have the cloth if you want it."

"Thank you. I'll keep it."

Sally told Roscoe, "I promised to show this family how to make the coyote barbeque. I'll be back later." She walked with the young man back to the cabin then put together a meal they could eat immediately.

"It's a simple meal, but it tastes so good. After weeks of starvation, it's the best food I've ever eaten." The exhausted mother ate the last bite. "Would you mind if I lie down?"

Sally assured the woman, "That's perfectly fine. I don't mind at all. You need to be rested to care for your little one." The woman went to the small room with their one bed.

Sally turned to the woman's husband. "Do you want me to tell you what to do with the coyote?"

"I would."

"First, I'll cut off a leg, and then I'll show you one way to cook a coyote."

"I hate that I don't know the names of the people who are being so good to us. I should pray for you, but since you're in the Underground Railroad, none of us should know each other's names."

"God knows us all, and we can pray right now."

The man began, "God, heal the injured man in the wagon. Heal and strengthen all the people in our community who are starving, and get these travelers safely to the place You want to take them." The man offered, "You're welcome to stay in our home tonight."

"There isn't enough space in the wagon. I'll get my blankets and sleep on the floor." Sally told the man, "Break the bones and cook the marrow out then use the broth to cook everything you eat until it's all gone. Your wife needs that nutrition to feed the baby." While he cracked the bones with a hammer, Sally went to get her blankets and pack.

In the cabin where Ann had helped carry the food, she explained to the family how to cook the coyote. The father cut pieces of smoked beef and handed them to his children and wife while popping pieces into his own mouth.

"I don't think I have ever eaten anything that tasted better." The women ate the beef and started stewing apples.

"How long have you been without food?" Ann asked.

"Two weeks with almost no food and longer rationing food. One of the daughters of the woman who brought you here died four days ago."

"I'm so sorry." Ann thought about eating fancy food at the Harrow's because she had wanted people to respect her and Noah while a child died of starvation. As God heated up the furnace to purify her heart of pride, Ann felt even more horrible than she already felt about that meal. The woman of the house started a batch of cornbread in the oven while Ann and the man of the house cut up the coyotes then packed the meat with snow into a wooden box.

In a different and very cold cabin, Noah asked, "What can I do to help?"

The woman with six children stated their major need, other than food. "We need firewood. Matt has been so ill that he can't chop wood, and the rest of us are also too weak."

"Where's your axe? Do you have a lantern?" The woman got the axe and lantern. "Where's the wood?"

She led Noah to the stack of wood. "Everybody here is too weak to chop now. They barely have enough wood for their own families."

Noah started to chop logs. "What's wrong with your husband?"

"I think he has worms. I saw something that looks like insect eggs in his stool."

Noah instructed her, "Take your children back inside." He chopped until he had enough to fill the stove then brought it in and got the fire going before he went back out to chop more firewood. The woman served cold food to her family and started bread dough, so it would rise when the house warmed up. So they could keep the fire stoked during the night, Noah made firewood, carried it into the house, and filled the wood box.

He went out to chop the rest of the stack and thought about how he had chosen to stay with the Harrows, so he could be warm and not have to hide in a shed or hotel room. He had been prideful. He had wanted to be Dr. Luke Smith. Without a shred of heat, the people of this community had gone through a blizzard while starving. He looked at himself and squirmed as God focused the lens.

Stephanie didn't escape God's discipline either. She helped newlyweds butcher two coyotes while they talked and ate cold food.

"Do you want to give one of these to your sister?" the young man asked his wife.

"Of course, her children need food."

He didn't want to upset his wife, but he wanted to help her family. "I didn't know what you were feeling."

"I was mad, but she is my sister, and those are my nieces and nephews. I'm so regretful that I didn't share with them," she apologized to her husband.

Stephanie was curious. "You don't have to tell me what happened, but I'm very mad at my sister and her husband."

The man looked at his wife. Maybe they could help another family before it got to the point it had with them. The woman burst into tears and let all her hurt spill out. "Katie didn't want me to marry William. She told our father I was going to marry him, and he forbade me. He said William was beneath us. So, we ran away and got married."

Stephanie remembered that Tom had gone against his parents' wishes when he had married Hattie. If he had not, she wouldn't have Eli.

"My sister told our father we went to Arkansas. He tracked us down and found us. Show her." The man took off his shirt and showed Stephanie the bright red scars that covered his back.

"Your father did this?" Stephanie asked.

Her face grew red. "With his own hands. He made me watch. My sister and her husband watched too."

William explained, "His heart was so full of rage that he was frothing at the mouth as he flogged me. I told him, 'You can whip every bit of flesh from me. I'll still love your daughter and want her as my wife.' Her father fell to his knees, clutching his chest. He looked at my wife and saw her face. I guess he didn't want whipping her husband to be the last thing he ever did. He said, 'Forgive me, love him, and be happy,' and then he fell over dead."

"After we buried father, Katie told me our mother hadn't really died, but had left with another man. When I left our father as well, it was too much. If Katie had told me, I could have done things differently. Father would be alive, and my husband wouldn't have been whipped.

"Trying to make things right between us, Katie moved here this fall. I didn't want to forgive her. When she asked me for food this winter I wouldn't share, even though we still had food and they didn't. I thought she was going off to help people escape, so she could feel better and was getting food for herself. So, I didn't give her any of our food."

The woman sobbed until she could talk again. "Four days ago, Katie carried Ann's lifeless body to our house. She said, 'She's dead. I forgive you.' She forgives me, but I'll never forgive myself."

William held his wife as tears streamed down their faces.

Stephanie cried too. "Her name was Ann?"

The young woman nodded her head up and down. "I killed my niece." Waves of sorrow and self-loathing wracked her body.

Stephanie told her, "You didn't know she was going to starve. Forgive yourself."

"I can never make amends for taking the life of Ann. She was innocent. She didn't deserve to die."

Stephanie realized that she knew something that might help. "No, Ann didn't deserve to die, but we've discovered something these last two years. God takes away, but He also gives back. Both my parents died three winters ago. Our farm was burned to the ground, including all our animals and all the crops we had planted. If I stay with my sister, I can't ever go home to the place where we were born. My husband may have to leave his father, or I may lose one sister and maybe both. How can a person make sense of life or make a decision between horrible choices? It just isn't possible. We don't know the future, we barely understand the present, and the past is a horrible mess. All we can do is trust that God knows what's happening and is working everything out."

"God did bring you here." The woman hugged the stranger she barely knew but knew completely.

Stephanie hugged her back. "And He brought me to you, so I could understand that I need to forgive my sister." When the three of them finished chopping up the coyotes, they carried half to Katie's cabin.

Katie opened the door and was surprised to see her sister. "Come in." William, his wife, and Stephanie stepped into Katie's cabin. They had all suffered over the death of the child and didn't know what to say.

Katie's husband finally said the only thing he could think about, "You killed my child."

"I'm so sorry. I didn't know that would happen. I never wanted anybody to die. I would give up my own life to bring her back. You don't have to ever forgive me, but I want you to know how horrible I feel and how very sorry I am."

"You should feel horrible," Ann's oldest brother stated firmly.

Katie took her sister in her arms. "I will forever miss my wonderful daughter, but I don't want to lose my wonderful sister. I've missed you. I forgive you. I've done so many things wrong to you and to all of us. Will you forgive me?"

The two women held each other and cried. The younger woman told her sister, Katie, "I forgive you."

Sixteen

Roscoe gave away almost all the food. Even though it was nothing more than just enough to keep the animals from wandering away, he used the empty crates to close in the fourth side of the corral they had made with the two wagons and the cabin. He closed the boxes with contents and stacked them at the front end of the wagons. He had seven thousand, seven hundred, and fifty dollars and the ring hidden in his bag. In his strong box, he had the money from the sale of the trading post, the store's final operating money, and the money he had earned caring for ill animals in Little Rock. Therefore, he stayed in the wagon with Eli.

Stephanie had slipped out Katie's door to find Ann, but first, she looked in the dark wagon. "Eli, how are you, darling?"

"Eli's asleep. He ate some food and drank a lot of water. I helped him use the bedpan, then he drank more of the sedative."

"Thank you, Roscoe. You're a good man." Stephanie walked to the cabin where Ann had gone and knocked on the door. A man opened the door.

Stephanie stood outside. "I've come to talk with my sister."

"She left. I don't know where she went."

"Thank you." Stephanie assumed Ann would be

with Noah. She walked to the cabin were Noah had gone and saw him outside chopping wood. "Is Ann here?" she asked.

"No. I'm sure she's around here somewhere. Do you want me to help you look?"

Stephanie declined. She wanted to talk with her sister alone. "I'll find her." She went searching. Stephanie finally found Ann staring into the dark as she sat on empty boxes she had pulled around to the backside of the goat wagon.

"May I pull over a box and join you?" Stephanie asked.

Ann was happy that Stephanie wanted to be within twenty feet of her. "Please do."

Stephanie got a box and returned. Trying to decide how to proceed, Stephanie sat beside Ann for several minutes and looked into the darkness.

Ann spoke first, "Stephanie, I want you to know that I was totally wrong. I was filled with pride. I wanted revenge for being told that Noah and I weren't good enough, for being forced to rebuild the Cadron Ferry and also for being forbidden to love Noah, so I decided to stay and have lunch as Mrs. Doctor Luke Smith. I was stupid, selfish, and prideful, and I caused Eli to get hurt. I would rather have my own back smashed than to have hurt any of you. I'm very sorry for what I did. I know I can never make things right, but I want to do what I can."

"I know you didn't mean for Eli to get hurt. I do understand that you were treated horribly, and I would have wanted to get revenge too, but it was stupid to think it was wise to have dinner with some uppity people."

"I know it was stupid, and God has been whipping me for it. The worst part is that you don't love me, and you don't want me around you."

"I was upset and worried about Eli, and I blamed you. I treated you very badly. I love you very much. I'm sorry I said that I didn't. I don't want to be going through all this, but I don't want you or Noah to be whipped either, so if this is what I have to do to protect you, then I'll do it."

"I promise that I'm going to think very hard about the consequences of what I do and not take any chances ever again, and I'm going to dye my skin and hair with the walnut husks. I'll be disguised, so I can take Eli to the doctor tomorrow. Nobody else will be in danger, and I won't draw attention because I won't look like anybody Judge Hall is looking for."

"That's a very good idea, but I'm going too. I think we should all dye ourselves and then go directly to Harmony. We can dye all the animals and the wagons, and we should dye Snowflake before we go. If they do come here looking for us, she won't look like any of our animals."

"I don't want to make you dye yourself. It may take a long time to wear off."

"It's my choice. In the morning, after Eli's awake and I tell him, I'll dye him too."

"We don't know what it may do if it gets in his injuries. Let's ask Noah."

"He's not a doctor, Ann."

110

"He's trained in Indian medicine."

"You just said you weren't going to pretend to be a doctor's wife."

"There's a difference between pretending to be a doctor's wife like I did in Little Rock and getting advice from somebody who knows about medicine."

"You're hopelessly deceived."

"I'm not the one who's not seeing reality, Stephanie; you are."

"So, it's all right that my husband is injured as long as yours isn't?"

"No, it's not all right that Eli is injured. I would never want any of us to be injured. I didn't know that he would get hurt. I want him to get better. I want to take him to the doctor in a way that won't draw anybody's attention to us, so no further injuries will happen to any of us."

"I'm going to my husband, and don't bother dying yourself because you aren't getting anywhere close to Eli, and neither is Noah." Stephanie stormed away.

Ann emitted a huge sigh of frustration, hurt, and regret. She got off her box and went to talk with Noah. As he chopped and she stacked the wood in the shed, Ann told Noah, "I just don't know what to do. I thought we were resolving the problem. When I told her not to put the walnut dye on Eli until we asked you if it would be safe, she got all upset again. She said you're not a doctor, that I'm hopelessly deceived, and she doesn't want us to get close to Eli. She's being completely irrational."

"The walnut dye is safe. Leave her alone. Arguing with her is only going to make it worse."

Ann didn't ask God for guidance before she suggested, "Maybe we are selfishly endangering everybody by making them sneak around with us. We should go back to our plan to go on our own."

"I agree. Let's dye ourselves and leave tonight. It will be a huge turmoil again. We need to sneak away. First, I want to check on this man. Come with me." Noah and Ann carried a load of wood and went into the house.

Noah asked Matt, "Can you give me a stool sample? I want to see what your wife told me she saw."

"Maybe." Matt took a piece of bark and went to the outhouse. Fifteen minutes later, he came back with the sample on the bark carrier. They could clearly see small white dots.

"These are parasite eggs; probably tapeworms. We have what you need. Since you are infected, others may be as well or may become infected. You need to boil all your water for fifteen minutes before using it and cook everything very well before eating it. Twice a year, for three months, everybody needs to drink the walnut hull and clove mixture I make. Bury your outhouse and start a new one farther away. At the end of the year, bury that one and start another. Then, start a new one every year."

Matt's wife told them, "I'll tell the others, and I'll watch how you make the medicine."

Noah went to the wagon, rolled up their bedding, tied them to their packs, and then passed them to Ann.

"Are you two staying in a cabin?" Roscoe asked.

"It's too small in here, and I'm making some

parasite medicine." He handed Ann the washtub of walnut husks, the packages of ground shells, and the nuts. Earlier, Roscoe had heard Stephanie and Ann fighting outside the wagon. He feared Noah and Ann would leave, so he watched them go back into the cabin. Noah, Ann, Matt, and his wife made a large batch of the parasite killer in the couple's giant cast iron pot. Noah filled the pot with walnut husks then packed some of the raw husks in with his crushed shells and put the package in his pack. He put a third of the packages of nuts in Ann's pack. Ann ground a dozen cloves and then added it to the pot of walnut skins. An hour later, the dark brown potion was cooked. Noah poured the hot liquid into smaller tin pots. When Roscoe saw Noah and Ann put the pots outside in the snow to cool, he stopped watching and went back to sleep. Eventually, the parasite killer was ready. Noah took the first dose. He gave some to Ann, not only so that everybody would know it wasn't poison, but also because Noah wanted some just in case he or Ann had any unwanted creatures inside. Noah filled his India rubber canteen with the medicine and then left all the rest for the people of Fletcher Creek.

One of the young children tried a swallow. "This is horrible. I don't want to drink it."

Her father commanded, "Drink it anyway."

Noah wanted to take the hot, soft, cooked hulls with them. "We'll throw these away and leave your pot outside. Everybody, go to sleep. Have a good night."

Outside, Noah moved empty boxes and quietly filled them with the raw walnut husks. He put the

113

package with the other two-thirds of the nuts on top then silently led Eyanosa, Honor, and Justice out of the corral. On their way to the creek, they put the empty pot by Matthew's door.

Noah and Ann poured creek water into the washtub holding the cooked walnut husks. When the husks had made a tub full of dark brown water, they stripped in the cold night under the bright moon. Ann looked at her husband. He was power, provisions, security, and love. "Let's flood the valley."

The white skin of her bare breasts reflected the moonlight. Noah always wanted her, but it was different this time. Ever since he had seen Ann drenched in coyote blood, he had felt more than his physical attraction, and his emotional attachment. His spirit wanted to join the power of the masculine with the power of the feminine and become one spirit with Ann, like the Calumet. He laid their blankets on the ground. They lost themselves in the love they shared.

When they used their blanket coats to stain themselves, the water was colder than the night air. After blackening their own skin, Ann and Noah dyed Eyanosa completely, and then the legs, tails, manes, and blazes on the noses of Honor and Justice.

They dumped the used husks into the creek, which quickly swept them away, then dressed and put on their short winter coats, so they could use their long, now dark brown, blanket coats as mule blankets. With their survival pack rope, they tied one pack on Honor with the washtub on top then ran the rope to Justice and tied on the other pack.

Noah jumped onto Eyanosa and pulled Ann up in front of him. She held the lead rope attached to their mules. Dark skinned people on a brown horse, instead of a gray, dappled appaloosa, rode away beside the creek, leading mules with dark brown legs, faces, manes, and tails. Nobody would describe them in a way that Judge Hall or even their family would recognize them.

Seventeen

After traveling a few hours, Noah and Ann decided to stop and sleep. When Noah prayed, as he did every night before they slept, the spirit led them to the realization that they should have asked for guidance before making such an important decision and it was wrong to abandon their family. They should protect them, not desert them. They decided to sleep for a few hours, wake with the sun, and then go back to the cabins.

When Sally went to the wagons in the morning, she found the family had two more goats and two fewer people. She feared that Stephanie had finally driven Ann and Noah away. "Where are Ann and Noah?"

Roscoe told her what he thought, "They stayed with that family." He pointed to the house he had seen them enter the night before then walked over with Sally and knocked on the door.

"Are any of the people with us here with you?"

The man in the house said exactly what they did not want to hear, "They left last night."

Stephanie took hay to the animals in the corral. "Eyanosa, Honor, and Justice are gone."

Sally glared at Stephanie. "This is your fault."

Stephanie replied, "They're just being their same selfish selves, running away when we need them."

Stephanie redirected the focus. "Right now we can't worry about them. We need to get Eli to the doctor." She walked over and knocked on Katie's door. "When can you take us to the doctor?"

"We've already had breakfast. I can take you now."

Stephanie asked, "How long before we're back?"

"I'm not telling you where we're going, but it will take all day."

Sally and Roscoe had already gotten King and Ace into the harness of the wagon that contained Eli asleep in the back. Stephanie climbed onto the front seat. Katie didn't want to compromise the location of the man she thought could help, so she planned to go the long way. Katie handed Stephanie a blindfold. "For everybody's protection."

Stephanie tied it on as she and Katie rode away. Since she couldn't see, nothing distracted her. She had to deal with her own mind, which told her all the reasons they'd be better off if her sister and brother-in-law were still with them.

Ann and Noah had not slept well and had gotten up very early. They lay in the woods on the hill behind the cabins and looked through their spyglasses. They saw the wagon ride away from the community. "They must be taking Eli to the doctor."

Noah offered some alternatives. "We could follow then sneak close enough to hear, or we can stay here and watch what happens."

Ann expressed her choice, "Let's stay here, and watch. I want to know if they're glad we're gone."

Shortly after Stephanie and Katie left, Katie's

husband went to the two who had remained and told them some news, "We found a clue by the creek."

"Take us there," Roscoe told him.

When Sally and Roscoe left with their escort's husband, Noah figured he knew where they were going. Not needing to follow, he and Ann made their own way to the place where they had used the dye. They didn't know how long they had before the others would be there, so they quickly found a hiding place and were barely out of view when Roscoe and Sally arrived. Sally rubbed the wet dirt on her arm, washed it in the creek, and then showed her arm to Roscoe.

Noah thought, smart girl.

Sally looked for, found, and then followed the hoof prints for a short distance. She contemplated the evidence. "Let's get ready to move on, Roscoe. There isn't any reason to wait. They aren't coming back."

"How do you know?" Roscoe wondered aloud.

"They left a completely obvious trail, so we can find them."

Sally got Jumper and went to find out what she could. She rode as fast as she could while still being able to follow the trail. When she found the place where they had slept, Sally saw that they had circled back toward the cabins. She didn't follow the trail. She went straight back and started making a batch of cedar and sedative.

The man who had told her that Ann and Noah were not in their cabin came over to watch. "What're you making?"

Sally explained, "I'm making something to put my brother-in-law to sleep, and this is something to help stop infections and pain."

"Did you use this on those mules that are all sewn up?"

"Yes, and we've used it on all of us."

"Can you show me where you get these things and the walnuts?"

"I don't know where you can find all of these around here, but I can tell you what they look like. The lady taking my brother-in-law to the doctor can show you where the walnuts are."

"I don't want to have to depend on her for the walnuts. I need them."

"Won't she tell you?"

The people who lived at Fletcher Creek did not trust each other much, and they didn't work together. Matthew explained, "Maybe she will, but I don't want to depend on anybody. This is too important to take a chance. The man you were looking for said I have tapeworms, they're sucking the life out of me, and they may be in my family. I need walnut husks."

"You can have all these."

"Please!" he begged.

Roscoe offered, "I'll take you."

"Do you know anything about trees?" Sally asked.

"Not really."

Sally got paper from the wagon. She drew as she described what she hoped to find. "Willow trees have long flowing branches like a woman weeping with her hair thrown over her head. Cedars look like Christmas Trees with blue cones that look like berries. Valerian has fern-like leaves and tall, hollow flower stems with clusters of small, pale blue flowers. Fumewort's mauve flowers grow on spikes on a ten-inch tall plant with deeply divided greenish-gray leaves. Have you seen any of these?"

Matthew picked up the cedar picture. "This is everywhere," then the fumewort drawing, "I saw something like this, but the flowers are yellow. There's a big bunch of these by the small spring." He pointed to the willow tree picture.

Sally negotiated, "If you take us to these, we'll take you to the walnuts."

Matthew was highly disappointed. "I can't walk that far."

Roscoe knew their supply was low, so he offered the obvious solution. "We can ride mules. Can you ride with only a blanket and halter?"

"I've always used a saddle and bridle. I have some. I think mine will fit your mules."

Roscoe instructed him, "Bring them, along with gloves, some kind of pouches, and that duck cloth."

"I'll get them and tell my wife, then we can go." A few minutes later, they were on the hunt for willows, fumewort, and walnuts. Maybe they would happen to find some valerian too. Matthew and Roscoe rode Blue and Big Jenny since the saddles fit them. Sally rode Jumper with only a blanket and halter.

Eighteen

Katie, Stephanie, and Eli arrived at the home of the doctor. Katie said, "You can take the blindfold off now." She jumped off the wagon and knocked on the door. "We have an injured man in the wagon. Please come see him."

The man went out to the wagon and examined Eli. "He's obviously already been to a doctor. Why do you want me to look at him?"

Stephanie explained, "The person who did this isn't a doctor. We want you to examine him and do anything that needs to be done."

"You could have fooled me." As the doctor removed all the wrappings on Eli's foot and around his body, Eli woke. The man looked him over. He gingerly felt his back, stomach, chest, and sides. When the doctor prodded Eli's ribs on his badly bruised side, Eli cried out in pain. The doctor listened to Eli's breathing, especially his lung on the side that had so much pain from his touch.

"Breathe deeply."

Eli tried. It was very painful. "I can't."

The doctor listened to his stomach then gently moved his arms, hands, legs, and feet.

"What do you think?" Eli asked.

His examiner told him the diagnosis. "The skin on

121

your back is ripped up and bruised. You have a sprained ankle and broken ribs. You shouldn't travel if you want those ribs to heal right. You need to lie on a flat bed and not bounce. There isn't anything I can do better than what was already done, except wrap your chest tighter and give you a painkiller."

Eli declined, "We have a sedative that puts me to sleep, and we have a painkiller."

Stephanie asked, "How much do I owe you for examining him?"

"Do you want me to put everything back on or are you going to do it?"

Stephanie knew the question meant he would charge more, but she wanted Eli cared for properly. "Please, do what's best for him."

Stephanie and Eli both noticed that the man put everything back on exactly the same way as Noah had, but this man wrapped the cloth around Eli's chest much tighter.

This smells like cedar and garlic. The doctor put a small amount of the green material from the man's back into one pocket and some of the paste from his chest in the other. I'll examine these later. The doctor finished the work, "One dollar."

Stephanie gave the man his dollar. "Thank you for looking at him."

On the way home, Stephanie sat blindfolded. "When do we need to go across the creek?"

Katie heard what the doctor had said about the man not traveling, but they would eat up food. "We can leave tomorrow morning if you're ready."

Eli tried to stay awake to listen to the conversation He lay in the back, feeling every bump. Being wrapped up so tightly, it didn't hurt as horribly, but he could barely inhale.

Katie heard what the doctor had said about the man not traveling, but they would eat up food. "We can leave tomorrow morning if you're ready."

Stephanie sat silently and thought. She knew Katie had heard what the doctor had said, but she hadn't offered for them to stay in their community. Stephanie decided to force the issue. "Eli shouldn't travel, and we should wait for the others to come back."

Katie couldn't just refuse. "None of us has space for you to bring him inside."

"We'll stay in the wagons or set up our tent." She remembered what Eli had offered when they had first arrived at Roscoe's trading post. "We already gave you all our food, so we'll hunt for more. We'll do all the work, and I'll go to Little Rock and buy more food."

Katie thought it over. They were all city folks who were hiding in the woods for various reasons. None of them knew how to survive in the wild, which was why they were in the situation that had taken the life of her daughter.

"Will you teach us how to live out here?"

Stephanie answered, "Of course, Katie."

"You live in your wagons and do all the work. If we don't still have plenty, you buy more food before you leave. Teach us how to live out here, and I'll let you stay until your husband can travel. And Rebecca shouldn't have told you my name."

You shouldn't have just told me hers either. Since she wanted the woman to let them stay, Stephanie said, "Call me Marie. My husband is James."

Eli thought that shouldn't be any trouble. Noah can teach them. He didn't know that Noah was gone, so he relaxed and stopped trying to stay awake. Soon the sedative put him back to sleep, and he wasn't aware of anything.

Stephanie didn't know what to do. She kicked herself mentally. Now, Noah and Ann would have to be Dr. and Mrs. Luke Smith again. That was if they even came back. If they didn't, then she, Sally, and Roscoe would have to do the work of a whole community. They might not agree to the plan, and even if they did agree, they might not be able to do it, but Eli needed time to heal.

Stephanie wished Ann and Noah were there. This was not what she had wanted, and she couldn't believe that Ann had actually left. They would not have survived the coyote attack without Noah and Ann. Noah had taken care of Eli as well as a real doctor had, and Noah had helped Eli immediately. They wouldn't have eaten doves, mussels, sturgeon, or walnuts. They wouldn't know how to make the cedar poultice, the willow tea, the sedative, butterfly weed tea, or garlic paste.

None of which would have mattered because they would have been burned into ashes from the fire when the Butterfield Gang had burned down their farm. Now, they would be a lot less safe without Noah while Eli was injured.

Stephanie knew Ann and Noah cared about Eli and didn't want him to be hurt. While she rode blindfolded back to the cabins, she wondered why she had been thinking the way she had. Looking back on the last two days, she felt as if she didn't know who the woman was who had acted so horribly. She had done exactly what Katie and Rebecca had done; let anger destroy their family. She hoped it would not cost a life like little Ann who had starved because her mother and aunt were fighting.

Nineteen

First, Matthew took Sally and Roscoe to the willow trees. Branches painted a pale green by the sunlight shining through the translucent springtime leaves made the trees glorious. Sally showed them how to gather what they needed. They chopped away six-inch square sections of the outer bark from multiple places on all five of the trees. Each of them slipped the pouch strap for their portion over his or her head, and then harvested the pink inner bark. All happy that they had gotten so much, they got back on their rides and continued the excursion.

Sally called for an emergency halt. "Stop! Those are sassafras trees!" She jumped down beside slender, green-skinned, white-spotted trees with five-petaled yellow flowers at the ends of the branches that had leaves shaped like a glove, or were three-lobed or an oval. The same flowers adorned the large mother trees. However, instead of green skin, they had deeply furrowed bark. Sally scratched the skin of a young sucker and inhaled the cinnamony aroma. She pulled it up, along with the six-inch long root that ran to the mother tree. "I love sassafras tea. Help me pull up all the little suckers around the mother trees. We can harvest all of them and still leave a thriving grove." Sally tied all the young trees behind Roscoe's saddle.

After they had gathered the sassafras, Matthew took them to an outcropping of loose rocks. Bright green plants with yellow flowers pushed up from the small spaces where life was able to take hold and grow. Sally dug up several whole fumewort plants with the small amount of soil that had been their homes. She added more soil to the root balls, wrapped them with a piece of duck cloth, and slipped them carefully into a bag to keep them safe.

Matthew gathered a couple for himself. "I showed you where to find your plants. Take me to the walnuts."

When they arrived at the walnut tree, Roscoe told them, "Put on your gloves, and we'll gather as many as we can tie up in that piece of duck cloth." The temperature had risen drastically all morning, melted most of the snow, and revealed the huge multitude of narcissus that covered the creek side. As they gathered the walnuts among the bright yellow flowers on the beautiful spring day, they felt that winter was finally over. They searched in the melting snow until they had filled Matthew's cloth with walnuts. They tied the corners of the duck cloth into a sack. The three of them tried to raise the heavy load onto Big Jenny's back, but they couldn't accomplish the task. Sally was only fifteen, Matthew was very weak, and Roscoe couldn't do it alone.

"We can shell these here and take only the husks and nuts."

"Let me try one. I may not have the energy." Matthew worked on beating the husk off.

He said, "I won't be able to do enough of these." He put the walnut meat into his mouth. "Not bad."

127

Roscoe suggested, "Leave half of them here. You can come back when you have more strength."

Sally contemplated. "If we had something else to hold them, we could divide them into smaller sacks, and then all of us could carry some." An idea came to her. "It's warm enough that we could just wear our coats and use our shirts as pouches."

"Good idea, except not you." Roscoe wasn't letting Sally go without her shirt, even wrapped in a coat. They tied the bottom of Roscoe's and Matthew's shirts closed, filled them through the neck hole, and then used the arms to tie the shirt bags closed.

"Mount up," Roscoe instructed Matthew.

After Matt was on Blue, Roscoe put a shirt full of nuts in front of him. Matt only had to hold it in place. Sally sat on Jumper. She took Roscoe's shirt bag and one corner of the duck cloth bag still on the ground. After Roscoe mounted Big Jenny, he and Sally pulled up the bag they could now handle. They got it situated in front of Roscoe.

Roscoe tapped Big Jenny. "Let's go home. We can find cedars any time."

"I'm very tired. That suits me fine." Matthew had what he needed: more husks and the location of the tree. When they got home, Matthew rode Blue to his cabin's door. Completely exhausted, he dropped his shirt of nuts to the ground. "Thank you. I have to go lie down." Matthew tried, but he couldn't drag the nuts into the house.

Roscoe lowered his large cloth bag of nuts. "I'll get it for you." He got down and took the last sack of nuts from Sally.

Sally said, "I'll put up the mules."

Roscoe followed Matthew into his home with a shirt full of nuts. Matthew called out, "I'm back, honey." He handed his wife the pouches of willow bark and fumewort plants.

Roscoe put down the shirt and then got the other two bags. "Where do you want me to put these?"

Matthew looked around as he tried to think of a place to put loose nuts.

"I'll be back." Roscoe left. He returned with two of the empty wooden crates that had been part of the corral.

Matthew was already in bed. His wife had brought her husband the food she had prepared while they were gone. Matthew thought it felt good to be in a warm cabin with a hot meal waiting for him. He also had the medicine he needed to kill the worms inside of him. He believed he would escape the death he had felt stalking him.

Since he had just found all the other husks in the corral boxes, along with the package of nuts, Roscoe informed Matthew's wife, "I'll bring more boxes of walnut husks over later." He didn't need empty boxes and was glad to leave them for Matthew.

Twenty

Roscoe saw Sally at the corral and walked over. Sally informed him, "I'm going to take all the animals to the creek for a drink. Can the baby goats walk that far?"

"I think so."

A young man, who looked to be Sally's age, asked for the five oldest children of the community, "Can we help you get your mules to the water?"

Sally didn't see any reason why they shouldn't help. "That would be lovely."

As they herded the animals toward the creek, Roscoe instructed them, "The proper procedure is to keep the animals together, avoid Mule 4's right side, and don't startle any of them. They're all skittish after the coyote attack."

"You fought all those coyotes?" the youngest looking girl asked. Sally and Roscoe told them all the details. The children were all very impressed.

The oldest boy walked beside Sally. "Thank you for giving us all the food and for taking my father to find the walnuts."

Sally pointed to Roscoe. "Thank him. The food was his. He gave it to you, and your father helped me find some plants I needed, so it was a good trade to show him the walnuts."

"Thank you all the same. I wish there was something more we could do for you."

"You are doing something for us. You're being friends and helping us get to safety."

"Still, I wish there was something I could do."

Sally told him, "Maybe something will come up." Sally wondered how they had ended up in their situation of desperation. "Why didn't you have any food?"

"I don't know why we didn't have enough. We ate what we had but then didn't have money to get more, so we ate our horses. We had always lived in town. My father was a carpenter. We just bought what we needed. We don't know how to live out here."

Katie's oldest daughter had brought Snowflake and her kids, along with the other animals. "My sister died. We never should have come here, but we're here now, so we need to learn." She watched Sally talk to Matthew's oldest son and was glad they would leave soon. Even though she was thankful for the food, she didn't want any competition for the heart of the young man who was ignoring her and paying way too much attention to the very beautiful new arrival.

They arrived at the watering area that was a large bend in the creek with a very wide, shallow platform on the inner side. When the water was low, the area was dry land. Now in the early spring, the water was a few feet deep across the platform, with deep fast water in the channel on the outer side of the bend.

The goat babies got in water for the first time. They jumped, played, and bumped into the other animals until Billy was thoroughly annoyed and charged at them. That caused their mothers to put Billy in his place.

They would not allow anything to attack their babies, not even Billy. Roscoe led Billy away from the other goats, but Billy went back and put up with the irritation, even though his kids splashed and bumped him.

Upstream, Roscoe and Sally filled their canteens while the animals drank downstream. When they could see that all of the animals had lost interest in drinking, they moved them out of the water to go back to the cabins. They had just started away when they heard the sound of an approaching wagon.

"Hello at the creek!" Katie called out.

"Welcome back. What did the doctor say?" Sally asked.

Stephanie heard Sally, so she took off her blindfold and got out of the wagon. "He said James has cracked ribs, his ankle is sprained, he's scraped and bruised, and our brother-in-law cared for him as well as any doctor would have. Also, that James should not be traveling."

"So, he's going to be all right?"

"Yes. Thank God!"

"Perhaps you should thank God, and thank our brother-in-law," Sally replied.

Stephanie looked at Roscoe, who was staring her down, along with Sally. "I know. Thank You, God, and our brother-in-law."

"We better water these mules." Roscoe took King and Ace out of the harness and over to the creek. Sally put Big Jenny and Redeemed into the harness. After the last twomules got their fill of water, they went to the cabins together.

That night, they made their fourth meal since God

and Roscoe had brought them food. The whole community and their guests ate together outside around a fire. Even though they still looked like skeletons, the people were gaining strength.

Sally felt Noah and Ann were still around, but she wanted to be sure. It looked like they could approach unseen from the woods on the far side of the corral, so she slipped into the wagon and wrote a message. "We have to stay here for James to heal. Wait to come back. I want Marie to realize exactly how important you are, and how much she loves you." Along with the note, she hid pots of food and hot coffee.

Noah and Ann saw Sally put the pots on the backside of the corral. When everybody was asleep, they slipped into the camp, ate the food, and read Sally's note. After they got back to their fireless camp, Noah took the package of powdered walnut shell, went back to the corral, and left a walnut dust heart beside the empty pots.

Noah returned to Ann. "What do you think about staying away or going back?"

Ann explained her point of view, "If Stephanie thinks we make decisions for selfish reasons, staying out here to teach her a lesson will prove it. I don't think we should do that."

"I agree. If we need to stay, then we should help, even if Stephanie doesn't want us around. That's the truly unselfish thing to do. Since we already dyed ourselves, we can go back into camp as different people. That way, the people here can say the two white people left. Later, dark-skinned people came."

"Everybody will know us because of our eyes. What advantage will that give us?"

"It covers our trail better if the people here choose to do so. Let's go camp at the creek as if we came in through the Railroad. We know the code phrase."

"This time, she won't have a reason to take us to her home."

"If we haven't figured out a solution, we'll tell her who we are."

"All right. We'll go back to the creek in the morning."

Sally made sure she was the first one up to check on the pots. The food, coffee, and note were gone. Beside the empty pots, she saw a tiny heart made of walnut shell dust. She brushed the heart onto the ground, put the pots with the other dirty dishes they hadn't cleaned the night before, and then gave food to the animals.

Twenty One

At the request of Katie, the people of Fletcher Creek congregated and ate the previous night's leftovers with the people who had provided food and still had the medical treatment they needed. Katie told them, "The injured man shouldn't travel. I told them they could stay if they did all our work. Tell them what you want them to do." Katie turned and requested the help she had been promised. "Are you ready to start doing the work of the community?"

Rebecca took William by the hand. "You don't have to do anything for us."

Stephanie looked at Katie. "What would you like us to do?"

"I'll show one of you the next step to help people move through the Underground Railroad, and then you can start making the trip every day or so to pick up anybody who knows the code."

Roscoe motioned for Stephanie and Sally to go with him into the wagon. They got into the wagon. Roscoe told them his concern. "I think I should be the one to take over. I don't want either of you girls to be out there alone. We won't know anything about the people coming through or anybody else who might be out there."

Eli was awake and heard Katie's request. He knew

135

they were supposed to help, but he agreed with Roscoe completely. They would move on before he would allow the women to be in danger, and he wasn't going to change his mind. He spoke up, "People won't try to take advantage of Roscoe like they would a beautiful woman alone in the woods. I don't want either of you to do it. Promise me you won't."

"I promise, darling. There will be plenty we can do here, and I want to stay close to you."

"Then, we agree." Roscoe got out of the wagon. "I'll do it."

Katie requested, "May we ride? I'll ask to borrow my sister's saddle."

"Yes." Roscoe went to get Shaggy and Rose out of the corral. Rose was the gentlest of all his animals, and he thought she would be the best for Katie. Noah and Ann watched them leave the small community, then followed carefully to avoid detection. A few hours later, they came to a sharp bend in the creek and stopped.

"Whoever is moving on, should wait here until a person comes from the other side." Katie pulled a rope from her pocket. "This is the signal. Tie this thin rope like this." She made the proper configuration. "Tie it exactly here with a long loop that you attach here and here. It will make a triangle within a triangle. Nobody will know this configuration and the exact branches to use unless they're in the Railroad." Katie again demonstrated how to tie the complex pattern.

"If they see this signal, whoever is on the other side, will shoot across an arrow tied to a thin line. Draw it over until you have the heavy rope with a harness

136

attached. The people crossing secure the harness to their wagon and use their own animals to pull it across. Keep the lead rope on this side and use it to pull everything back. Also, you should use the harness on all the animals to swim them across.

"This is how you tie the knot so it won't come loose. The rope will already be secured on the other side of the creek." Katie took down the piece of rope and showed him how to tie the knot then handed him the rope and had him tie the knot several times before she pointed to a branch and said, "You leave this rope, so the people crossing can practice before they set the signal. They leave the rope here when they go."

"I got it. I'll take this rope and keep practicing. I'll get you to verify that I've done it right. Are we ready to go back the other way?"

"Yes. Now, we go upstream. I'll show you how far I go looking for travelers."

Noah and Ann watched, but they weren't close enough to hear. They assumed they knew what was happening and didn't follow. Instead, so they could get situated and be found, they rode away from the creek and then moved along at a steady canter upstream. Along the way, they rode through a grove of sugar maples. Ann felt happy. "Since we're not leaving, we should come back and tap these maples."

"I'll bring you back."

"Thank you, my husband. How can we make a fire pit?"

"We'll look for clay and bake it into bricks."

They believed it would be highly unlikely for two

137

different groups to get to the creek at the exact same place. They also wanted to know what was farther upstream. Not far beyond the walnut tree, they found a deep pool created by a beaver dam and decided it was a good place to stop. They didn't see any of the beavers that had built the dam, but they knew they were still around because of the recently felled trees.

Noah told Ann what was on his mind. "It will probably be a long time before they get here. Ever since I drew those pictures for Martin, I've been thinking about making a collection of plant pictures with descriptions that explain the kind of place they usually live and specific places I've actually found them. I was wondering if you have one of those binders of paper."

"I do, and I think that's a wonderful idea. I saw the drawings you made for Martin. They were very good. I'll get it and a pencil." Ann lay on the blanket beside Noah. She watched Noah draw the first picture for his book before scurrying chipmunks caught her attention.

Noah was working on his second drawing when a man riding a mule with long shaggy hair and a woman on a medium-sized, short-haired mule approached. The man said, "It's a foolish person who waits here."

"Fools find fools that find the foolish way," the person drawing replied.

"Then, we'll be fools." The woman then asked, "What do you have there?"

"It's going to be a book of medicinal and edible wild plants." The man with blue eyes and extremely dark skin looked up.

When the other person looked at her, the woman

looking for travelers in the Underground Railroad knew who they were. The chance of two people with dark skin having blue and green eyes was about zero. She hadn't looked much at the folks who had left two nights before, but she knew they had blue and green eyes. It was obvious they were pretending to be other people.

The woman knew the people traveling in the Underground Railroad had reasons to hide. She decided these two wanted to be with the others but needed to be somebody else for their family's safety and for the safety of her own community. She figured they were the people actually being tracked. Katie decided the man drawing had to be the one who had given medication to her brother-in-law.

The doctor in her area had said that the care given to the injured man had been the work of a doctor. Marie had agreed to do all the work so they could stay while her husband healed. It would be a good thing for them to feel obligated and get the help of a man with that kind of knowledge. The man had just said he was making a book about medicinal and edible plants. Clearly, she had only one viable option. She went along with the deception.

Because of the animals, Roscoe had known who they were before they were even close. Even though they were a different color than the last time he had seen them, he saw the 11 and 20 seared into their flesh. He was so glad they hadn't left that he wanted to hug them. However, doing so would defeat the obvious plan of Noah and Ann to be new people.

Roscoe told the folks they had come to help, "Pack

up, so we can move on." His mind churned. How am I going to get Katie to take them to her home?

"What do you know about medicine and finding food in a place like this?" asked the woman who had come to help them on their secret journey.

The black-skinned woman promoted the man who stood up with his book. "He knows a lot." She rolled up the blankets they had been laying on and strapped them to their packs.

"Could you help people who are starving?"

The newly arrived man suddenly had an idea and answered, "No, we have very little food. We've had to find what we eat as we travel. So far, we've done very well for ourselves, but we don't have any food to share."

"I mean somebody who is sick because they were starving but now has food."

The two dark-skinned people mounted their animals. The woman mounted a mule with black legs, nose, tail, and mane. The man got on a horse almost as black as himself. "I'd have to look at them to know if there's anything I could do to help, but we shouldn't stay in one place very long." He didn't want to agree too easily. Even though he was sure she knew who they were, he thought they should all retain deniability.

Katie didn't want any more of her children or anybody else in the community to die. Even though they had food, she knew they were all in bad condition. "They're my family. What can I do to convince you to look at them?"

The woman with green eyes accepted. "He'll look at them. Then we can decide what you can do for us."

140

So they would come and help her family, Katie accepted the open-ended agreement. In addition, she looked forward to having these people around for a while. She had barely talked to anybody but the woman with the injured husband and the man beside her at the moment, but she knew they were well educated and intelligent. This man was obviously also on the same level. She missed the people from the top rungs of society with whom she and her husband had socialized before they had gone looking for her sister. As much as she loved the extended family that was now around her, it wasn't the same.

"Let the mules have a drink before we go, but be careful. The creek is deep and fast, except right at the edge." Katie rode into the creek. Noah and Ann allowed their mules and Eyanosa to wade into the creek beside her. Roscoe also joined them. They sat quietly on their mounts and allowed all the animals to drink.

Suddenly, a different family of the community came out of the woods and trapped them. The dark woman whispered, "Don't move."

Everybody turned his or her head in the direction the woman was looking. That caused the mother of the newly arrived family to startle and go into defensive mode. She raised her black and white striped tail and fired. Much to the relief of those sitting on their animals in the creek, they were far enough from shore that the thick, viscous substance fell into the water short of them.

Unfortunately, the overwhelming smell still filled the air. Tears flowed from their eyes, and mucus ran

141

from their noses. The mules threw their riders, then darted toward land and sent the skunk family scurrying away. Most of the people landed in the shallow water close to the bank. When Rose had reared up, she had sent her rider into the deep, fast-moving water.

The current instantly swept Katie to the beaver dam and pinned her under a log. The force of the water made it impossible to push away and prevented Katie from moving to the surface. A healthy person with normal strength could have escaped, but she was an almost starved woman. Katie knew she would soon be with her dead daughter. Unable to hold her breath any longer, she thought, I'll see you soon, Ann. Water filled her lungs, as four hands pulled her free and then out of the water. Noah slung the woman over his shoulder. Gravity started to pull the water from Katie's lungs. He carried her quickly to the shore using Roscoe's shoulder to help navigate the logs of the beaver dam. As soon as they were on solid land, Noah put the woman on the ground.

"What do people do?" he asked.

Roscoe told Noah the only method he had ever heard about. "My cousin almost drowned. They blew smoke into his bottom."

"We don't have any way to do that," Ann stated.

Noah said, "I could try blowing into her mouth."

Roscoe believed he should attempt it. "You might as well try. Otherwise, she's dead anyway."

Noah put his mouth over the woman's mouth and tried to force in air. He felt resistance. He tilted her head back and tried again. Water dripped out of her mouth,

142

but Noah unsuccessfully tried to force air into her lungs. He felt inside her mouth, pulled out a leaf, and tried again. This time the air did move into her lungs, but nothing seemed to happen.

Ann encouraged Noah, "Don't give up. Keep trying." He blew into her mouth again.

Roscoe made a suggestion. "Maybe we have to push the water out of her." He pushed on her chest a few times. More water dripped from her mouth. Ann stood in suspense, watched, and prayed that the woman wouldn't die. Noah blew air into her lungs again.

Suddenly, Katie coughed. Water spewed from her mouth. Noah sat her up, so the water she coughed out wouldn't run back into her mouth. Katie sat on the ground, supported by Noah and Roscoe, and drew in a large breath of air that forced more water out of her lungs and into her lap. The woman tried to breathe air in and coughed water out. Roscoe massaged her back to comfort her and encourage her lungs to expel the water.

The woman finally said, "I'm all right."

Ann replied, "Thank you, God."

"You stay here and recover. I'm going to go find the animals." Noah followed the trail the mules and Eyanosa had left when they had crashed through the woods to escape the overpowering fumes of the skunk's defense. It looked like the animals had stayed together. Noah thought, maybe I'll be lucky, and they'll all come to me if Eyanosa does.

Noah had been teaching Eyanosa the same way he had taught the horse he had ridden out of Indian Territory. A few times, when he had whistled for

143

Eyanosa, the horse had come to him, but not consistently. Noah didn't want to search the woods for hours. He whistled and hoped his horse would hear and go to him.

Eyanosa had just had a terrifying experience with the skunk smell. It knew the whistle was Noah, safety, food, and comfort. When Eyanosa heard the whistle again, he whinnied back and trotted toward the whistle. Noah moved toward his horse, and his horse moved toward him in a duet of need, respect, and love that flowed into the forest as a human's whistle and a horse's whinny.

When Eyanosa saw Noah, the horse broke into a full gallop and charged. Noah thought he was going to be run over, but Eyanosa screeched to a halt and rubbed his head against his friend. Noah hugged his horse's neck, rubbed its nose, and scratched between its ears. He did the same to the four mules that had followed the leader of their herd on their dash away from the noxious fumes. Thankfully, they had also followed Eyanosa to Noah.

Noah was very pleased that none of them had a strong lingering smell of the skunk. Blessedly, none of the repulsive substance had made actual contact. He mounted Eyanosa and then rode toward the setting sun and the creek. When he got to the creek, he didn't recognize the area. We must be upstream. They rode downstream. Noah observed the surrounding forest and made a mental note of everything, especially anything that he could add to his book about plants. An hour after he had left his family and their almost drowned escort, Noah rejoined them.

Ann ran to Noah and looked into his darkened face. It was still the most handsome face she had ever seen. "You found them all. I knew you would."

"How's our escort?" Noah got off Eyanosa then hugged and briefly kissed his lovely, very dark-skinned wife.

"I'm fine. Thank you for saving my life. You and…" Katie stopped. She didn't know the names of any of them, "this man."

Roscoe knew Stephanie and Eli were going by James and Marie again. He decided he would use an alternative name as well. A name popped into his head. "Theodore."

Katie did not believe that was the man's real name, but she said, "Do you go by Theo?"

"Either is fine."

Noah wanted to get home before night fell. He held out his dark hand to help Katie up. Katie thought the water of the creek would have washed off fake color. Maybe they aren't the two who left. The others already knew her real name, so there wasn't any reason to say anything else. "I'm Katie."

As soon as Roscoe had given his name, Ann started thinking. "I'm not going to destroy any chance I have of reconciling with Stephanie. We can't be Luke and Isabelle." She decided to speak before Noah said anything. "I'm Lily. This is my husband, Abraham."

"Well, Theo, Lily, and Abraham, let's go."

Noah thought they would follow the creek. Instead, Katie took them into the woods. If they followed the creek, it would be dark long before they got back to the cabins. Katie knew the area well and took the faster way home. That made Abraham happy because he was able to observe even more of the forest. He saw bear tracks. A fat bear would be wonderful. Fish and fowl will be healthy and good to eat. He also noticed oaks, sumac, chickweed, white mustard, and hickories.

When Katie arrived at the cabins with two slaves, her husband was livid. "If slaves want to be free and go west, that's fine, but you've lost your mind bringing Exodusters here. I told you the last time; don't ever bring anybody here again."

Stephanie and Sally heard Katie's husband and peeked out. Katie and Theo had two black-skinned people with them. They also thought it strange that Katie had brought more people to their community.

"They saved my life. I almost drowned, and do not treat me as if I'm stupid. I wouldn't bring them here if we didn't need them."

"And just why do we need these two?"

"He's a doctor, and he knows about plants and how we can live out here."

"I thought these others were supposed to do that for us."

"He can do it better."

Sally jumped out of the wagon. Ann looked into the eyes of her sister then got off the mule branded in its rump with the number 11. Sally had hoped Ann and Noah would stay away long enough for Stephanie to realize she needed them, but she was glad to have them back. Sally heard Katie say the man was a doctor. "That man is a doctor? Could he look at James?"

Eli had been upset beyond reason because Noah had not been to see him in two days. He would not take the sedative, and he had demanded that Noah come see him. Stephanie had not told Eli that she had caused Noah and Ann to leave. Sally hadn't either. When she saw Noah's face, Stephanie begged, "Please, look over my husband." She desperately wanted Noah to go to Eli. The man she loved was very upset, and it was her fault. She was tremendously grateful that Noah was back.

Abraham looked at Katie's husband for permission. Katie looked her husband in the eyes as she answered. "Go ahead, Abraham. Settle in out here somewhere. We'll talk more tomorrow." She went into her cabin with her family.

The doctor climbed into the wagon. He held his finger in front of his lips as he moved over to Eli. Eli looked at the man's face and blue eyes. His skin was different, but Eli knew Noah when he saw him. He would have said, "Where have you been?" but he saw the signal not to say anything.

Noah looked Eli over. "These are way too tight." He removed the bandages.

Eli informed Noah, "That doctor wrapped them tight. I hurt less."

"Your lungs have to expand. With an injury like this, they are even more likely to fill with fluids. I know it hurts more, but you have to expel the fluid. Sit up, breathe in deep, and exhale hard."

Noah helped Eli sit up. Eli took a deep breath, then held his side as he coughed repeatedly.

147

"I'm sorry it hurts. Since you coughed so much, you don't have to exhale hard right now."

Sally got into the wagon with a pot of cedar poultice and a cup of sedative. Noah wanted to find out if anything had gone wrong inside. He carefully listened to Eli's lungs and stomach. His lungs sounded worse. Next, Noah checked Eli's ankle, foot, and back. There wasn't any sign of an infection, and Eli could flex slightly at the ankle. "I'm sorry I didn't get to see you sooner. You'll be as good as ever when you heal."

Eli didn't know why Noah had skin as black as night. He knew Noah wouldn't have been gone without a good reason. He was just glad that Noah was back.

"James, will you take this sedative now?" Nancy held out the cup.

In order for Noah and Ann to know that they were using their Little Rock names, Eli said, "I will. Nancy, tell Marie to come see me."

"Theodore brought us here. I'm Abraham, and my wife is Lily. She's talking with Marie right now, but I'll tell Marie to come see you first."

"No, let them talk. Thank you for checking on me. I'm glad you're here."

"You're welcome. I'm very glad to be able to check on you." Abraham could already hear James breathing easier as the tension left his body.

Abraham and Nancy got out of the wagon and walked over to Lily and Marie. "Marie, he wants to see you when you're done talking."

Marie told Lily, "I'll talk with you again later." She hurried to James.

148

"Is everything all right with you and Lily?" James asked.

"It will be." Stephanie lay beside James on the mattress and stroked his hair. "You should know that they left and that it was my fault."

"I've been waiting for you to tell me something. It's been upsetting me that you haven't been telling me what's happening."

"I'm sorry. I've done so many things wrong lately. Will you forgive me?"

"Of course I forgive you. I love you. Nothing will ever change that. Let's forgive and love everybody."

"Thank you for forgiving me, darling. I'll forgive everybody too. I promise."

After James was sleeping again, Marie went to talk with the others. "Abraham, do you think James should travel?" Marie wanted to compare his opinion to what Katie's doctor had told her. Somewhere inside, she trusted him, but she also still wanted to validate his medical ability. It was one thing to make a cedar poultice. It was another to deal with a major injury, and James was too important for her to take a chance.

"If somebody would die if we didn't, he could. The best thing for him would be to not travel."

"These people said we can stay here until he heals if we teach them how to live out here. What can we do for them?"

"They all said that, or Katie said that?" Lily asked.

"Actually, it was only Katie."

Abraham questioned the woman's ability to decide for all of them. "Does she speak for the whole

149

community? Because her husband seems to believe he has authority over her."

"They do seem to have some contention over who decides." Nancy had noticed the same thing.

Marie also told them, "Rebecca said she didn't want us to do anything for them. The others haven't said anything one way or the other."

Abraham pointed out that it didn't matter. "Regardless of what's happening between the people here, they do need to learn how to live out here, and James should heal while not bouncing around in a wagon."

Those were the same words spoken by the doctor. Marie felt reassured. "Right, so what can we do?"

They spent some time talking about what they could do. Lily suggested, "We could teach them how to tap the maples and make maple syrup and sugar, but we'd have to build a fire pit."

Theo added, "And we could show them where to find plants they can use as food or sell as a cash crop."

"If the people here want us to do it, we could teach them math, reading, and writing," Nancy thought that would help the people of Fletcher Creek the most.

Marie decided they had plenty of things they could do to help. "Tomorrow, we'll talk to the people living here at Fletcher Creek and see what they want."

Even though the most meaningful, loving endearment they shared was the affirmation of their marriage, Abraham decided he didn't want to allow anybody to track them because he always used the endearment 'my wife.' "I'm ready to go to sleep. See you when you come to bed, my beautiful one." He left Lily to speak with her sister. Theo and Nancy also said they were going to the tent for the night. They all wanted to give Marie and Lily space to talk.

Marie expressed her feelings to Lily, "I don't want to fight. I love you. I know you love us and want to do what's best for all of us. I'm sorry for being difficult and mean. Will you forgive me?"

"Of course, I forgive you. I love you and James very much, and I do want the very best for you both. I'm sorry for being prideful and pushing my beliefs on you. I hope you'll forgive me as well."

Marie embraced her sister. "I do."

Twenty Two

There was something Matthew wanted Nancy and Theodore to do for him. When he saw Nancy come out of her tent, he went to speak with her. He was the first one to ask for something.

"I don't want you to think that you can only stay here if you do something for me."

"Thank you," Nancy replied.

"But there is something I would like to ask. If you'd be willing to do it, I would really appreciate it."

"What would you like, Matthew?"

"I want to learn what you know about plants. Anything we can eat or use for medicine. I know you won't be here very long, but I'd like to learn as much as I can while you're here."

"Actually, I want to search the forest and see what's here, so that would suit me fine. In addition, we are very fortunate to have Abraham here. We can both learn a lot from him and Theodore."

"Who's Abraham?"

"Katie brought him here last night."

Matthew had the same thought as Katie's husband. "She sure is bringing a lot of people here."

Nancy asked, "Are you going to be able to go riding today?"

"Maybe not as much as yesterday."

Inside the tent, Abraham heard Nancy talking about going into the woods alone with a grown man. He got up and went out of the tent. "I heard the two of you talking. I'd like to go with you."

Matthew said, "Let's go before Katie gets up and wants us to do something different."

"Matthew, we're going to eat first." Nancy was willing to help, but she wasn't going to be bullied.

"Go on and eat. I'll go get more pouches and the duck cloth again." He started away and then turned. "Call me Matt."

Abraham said, "Bring some paper to make notes."

Matt replied, "I can't read or write."

That gave Nancy an opening to make her offer. "While we're out in the forest, I could teach you. Nobody would see you learning, except Abraham and me. We could even teach all your children then maybe Katie could continue after we leave."

"I'll think about it." If I tell Sarah and then I'm not able to learn, what will she think? Then he thought what would she think if I had a chance to learn and didn't even try. Matt knew they didn't have any paper or anything with which to write. Rebecca knows how to write. She probably has some. He went to his brother's cabin.

William opened the door. "Good morning, Matt. Come on in. What can I do for you?"

"Will, I was wondering if you have any paper and something I can use to write."

"Why do you want it?"

"Don't worry about why. Do you have any?"

153

"I think so. How much do you want?"

"Ten sheets of paper and a pencil."

Will walked over to the table and opened a box. He counted out ten sheets and then handed them to his older brother, along with a pencil. "Good luck. Maybe you can help me with the same thing some time."

Matt hugged his brother. "Maybe. Thank you, Will." He went home to get the other things he needed.

"Honey, where are those sacks?" he asked.

"I'll get them. Are they going to do it?" Sarah knew that her husband wanted to learn how to find food.

"Yes." He took the sacks, kissed her, and went back out the door. He picked up the paper and pencil he had left outside and walked over to the wagons.

When Lily woke, Abraham wasn't beside her. She heard him talking to James. "How much does it hurt to be awake? I don't want you to get pneumonia."

"I surely don't feel good."

"Could you stay awake for a few hours and try to breathe like Theodore did when he had pneumonia?" Abraham helped James sit up and drink butterfly weed tea.

"If that's what I should do, I'll do it."

"Good. I'm going to take Nancy and Matt into the forest to look for food. I'll put this sedative here. Try to stay awake for a few hours before you drink it."

"That's what he asked for you to do, so we can stay here?"

"Yes. Isn't it great?"

"What does the rest of the family have to do?"

"I think Lily and Marie are going to take them to

some maple trees, show them how to get the sap, and how to make maple syrup."

"I wish I could help. That's what we did last spring when I first went to the farm. My life changed forever the day I rode with Marie and Nancy out to the farm to ask Lily if I could work for them."

"I'm glad she said 'yes' because now we're brothers."

"Me, too. I wonder if there is anything I can do. I want to help."

"It depends on if you can take the pain to sit. I heard Nancy say something about teaching how to read and write. They would need to learn math as well."

"I could do that for sure. I'll see how long I can sit. As you said, that would help me keep fluid out of my lungs."

Marie called from outside, "Breakfast is ready."

Abraham said, "Be right there." Marie was already getting into the wagon with food and water for James.

"Good morning. Thank you for tending to James." Marie hugged Abraham. Unlike Nancy, who hugged him all the time, it was one of the few times that Marie had hugged him.

Abraham told her, "You're welcome. I'm sorry for everything I did wrong. Thank you for the hug."

"I did plenty of things wrong myself. I love you, brother."

"I'm glad. I love you too."

Abraham got out of the wagon and went over to the fire where the other three members of his family sat on campstools eating boiled oats.

"I see we're eating my favorite breakfast food." Abraham ladled oat porridge into his tin pot. Katie knocked on all the cabin doors and told everybody to wait until their guests had finished eating then go over to their fire. When everybody had gathered, Katie said, "These people are going to help you, so they can stay."

Rebecca told her sister, "Katie, they gave us all their food. They shouldn't have to work for us."

Katie ignored her and asked the others, "What do you want?"

Marie poked her head out at the rear of the wagon. "You can tell us your requests, but we do have some suggestions."

"What do you want to do?" the man with the new baby asked.

Marie offered their first recommendation. "There are some maple trees not far away. We can teach you how to tap them and make maple sugar. You should be able to make enough for everybody here and possibly have some to sell. Would any of you like to learn how to do that?"

William and the man with the new baby stepped forward. However, William wanted his thoughts about the helping requirement to be known. "I'd like to learn, but I don't want you to feel obligated to do it."

"I'm happy to do this. I've made maple sugar every spring for many years."

Matt spoke up, "I've already made plans with Nancy and Abraham."

Katie objected, "But we need Abraham to look at all of us and see if there's anything wrong."

156

Theo said, "I can go with Matt and Nancy."

Matt's oldest son piped up, "I want to go with my father." He admired his father and wanted to do whatever his father did. On top of that, his father was going with Nancy.

Matt started to object because he didn't want his son to see him struggle to learn to read and write. He held his tongue because it suddenly occurred to him that his son should learn the same thing, and the best way to get him to try was for them to do it together. Matt looked at Will. He asked quietly, "Ten more sheets and another pencil."

Will knew for sure what was going on. He left the group and came back with the whole box of paper and pencils. "I want to go with Nancy and Theodore."

"What are you going to do?" Rebecca asked.

Will looked at his brother. Matt spoke up, "We're going to learn how to find plants we can eat and use for medicine." He didn't mention learning to read or write.

"Do you need so many?" Katie asked.

Nancy saw Will come back with a box marked, '500 sheets'. She had the idea that grown men might not want to learn in front of their wives or children. "It will take a lot of people to forage, but I think this is enough for now. Later, we might need more."

"Theo, I'm going to get my pack and the things we'll need." Nancy went into the wagon.

"Lily, will you help me?" Marie asked.

"I would love to help," Lily replied.

Theo asked, "May we skip a day or two of looking for people along the creek?"

Katie affirmed. "I think so."

Theo asked the men planning to go with him, "Can any of you ride without saddles?"

"I have two saddles," Will told him.

"May we use them?"

Will left with his nephew to get the saddles.

"For the first lesson in maple gathering, please come over by the wagon." Marie had already spoken with James. He knew what he was supposed to do and was propped up at the back of the wagon. Marie proudly said, "Meet my husband, James."

Twenty Three

None of the people of Fletcher Creek had met or even seen the injured man except Katie. Katie's husband said, "Pleased to meet you."

Rebecca and the young man Nancy had helped the first night shook the hand of the man leaning against a mattress and a stack of crates. Not wanting to be the only man not participating, the last man stepped away from his wife and two children. He also greeted the man in the wagon.

Katie's oldest son asked, "May I learn?"

"Of course," Marie told him.

Katie's daughter requested, "If children can help, I'll go with Nancy and Theodore."

Nancy saw Matt wince. "Not today. I can only work with a few at a time."

Carmen thought you want to have Justin to yourself and then walked over to the wagon.

James started the lesson. "The question is, how do you get what's inside a tree out of it without hurting the tree."

Everybody stood silent. James repeated, "How would you get out what's inside a tree?"

Carmen spoke up, "You'd have to make a small hole if you didn't want to hurt the tree."

"Excellent answer and exactly correct." James

159

smiled at the girl. Carmen perked up. Maybe she was in the right place after all. "Where do you think the sap we need is located?"

"What's the sap?" Carmen asked.

Marie spoke up, "The sap is the plant's food. Trees make their own food then send it all around inside to feed itself."

Katie's oldest son suggested, "They must have some tubes or something inside." Katie watched her children. She thought her husband probably knew the answer.

"Very good. It would require a tube or tunnel in some area that moves the sap around." James affirmed the boy at the edge of becoming a man. "Just under the bark is the part of the tree that moves the sap."

The man with the baby spoke up. "So, we have to make a small hole to get just under the bark and drain the sap out."

"I see this will be very easy because you are all so smart. That is exactly what we have to do."

The man looked at his wife holding his baby. She was smiling and proud that her husband had known the answer.

"So, what we need to find is something you have here that we can use to make a small hole that will go through the bark, and something that will let the sap drain out."

"How small of a hole do we need to make?" Katie's husband asked.

"About an inch," James replied.

The man with the two children asked, "Do we have

to use the same thing to make the hole and drain the sap?"

"No," James answered.

Carmen was also following the reasoning. "I think we're going to need buckets to catch the sap when it comes out, and the tube draining the sap has to be long enough to reach the bucket."

"You are thinking exactly right. Do you have those things?" Marie asked.

Katie's husband instructed the group, "Let's go look for what we might be able to use and bring it back here." They all went to look as Matt, his son, his brother Will, Theo, and Nancy rode away.

Katie's husband came back with a hand drill. He held out his hand to James. "I'm Morris. This should make holes."

Next person back came with a hollow metal tube, three feet long. He had heard Morris introduce himself, so he did the same, "I'm Andrew. This came out of a trunk we used when we came here. If we had some way to cut it, we could make tubes to drain out the sap."

Carmen arrived with two buckets on a shoulder pole. "We all have some of these, but we use them to get water."

Her brother arrived with a spike and hammer. "We can make holes with these."

Standing behind her son with nails and rope, Katie said, "We'll need to hang the buckets."

As the last man returned, Morris said, "Couldn't you find anything, Lewis?"

"No, but I thought maybe we could make sacks out

of duck cloth covered in beeswax, and I know where there's a beehive. Any of you know how to get the wax out of a beehive?"

Everybody shook his or her head from side to side. Nobody wanted to try to figure out how when they would most likely end up with bee stings.

Abraham spoke up, "Let me look everybody over then we can go to the beehive and see if we can get some wax. Maybe we can also get some honey."

Abraham examined each of them. As far as he could tell, they should all be fine with continued food, but he told them, "I'm not a doctor. I don't know everything, and I can very easily be missing something, but I think other than not having enough food you are all fine, except this young fellow has a club foot."

A teenage boy spoke up, "The last man who was here said my father has a tapeworm. Now I have to drink this horrible stuff every day. Can I stop?"

Abraham pretended he had no idea about the tapeworm, but he was glad the boy had brought it up. "No, you can't stop. Do you know what's in what you're drinking?"

"Walnut skins and cloves."

"If that's true, you should all have what this boy's father is drinking. He ate tapeworm eggs somewhere. Others probably have as well. Do you have that drink, more walnut husks, or cloves?"

"We have a pot of the medicine already made up and more walnut husks. Father wouldn't want me to give any of it away. I don't know about cloves."

Abraham informed the people, "We need to get a lot more, so we can have enough for everybody."

Morris said, "Freeman, bring the medicine. I'll talk to your father."

"It's too heavy to carry." Freeman made up an excuse to protect his father's medicine.

Morris walked over to Matt's cabin and knocked on the door. "Sarah, give me the tapeworm medicine."

"No, Matt needs it."

"Let us all share it, and Abraham will make more."

"There aren't any more cloves."

Morris pushed past her into the cabin. He saw the pot on the stove, strode over, and picked it up. So he couldn't take it, Sarah tried to grab the handle. The pot overturned. All the liquid poured out onto the floor. "Now look what you've done! You have no right to take Matt's medicine. That man made it for Matthew."

Sarah's little daughter Agnes reminded her mother, "He told us to share it with everybody, Maw."

The rest of the people stood outside the door. Abraham told them quickly, "I know how to make something." He had thought and hoped that they would share. "It would be best to have cloves and some mugwort as well, but just walnut husks are good. I'll make that for everybody."

Lily suggested, "Maybe one of these people could go to Little Rock to buy cloves and mugwort."

Morris conveyed the flaw in the request. "We don't have money. If we did, we would've bought food."

"How long does it take to ride from here directly to Little Rock?" Lily asked.

"It's two days," Morris told her.

Abraham stated firmly, "We need to use these walnut husks. I'll go out and look for prairie sage."

Now that the first batch of medicine was gone and she needed something, Sarah decided she would let them use the walnut husks. "Take them."

Katie spoke up, "Marie, Nancy, and Theo can show you where to get more."

"Bring a box." Abraham walked toward his campfire.

Lily told Abraham, "If I only have to boil the husks, I can make it for you. You go look for sage and the beehive."

"That's all you have to do. Thank you, Lily. Anybody who wants to come with me and Lewis, let's go."

Marie declined the beehive hunt, "We'll work on cutting this tube into sections."

Andrew, along with Morris's son and daughter, stayed to help work on making the sap drains, but Morris decided to go with his brother.

Twenty Four

As they walked, Morris whispered to Lewis, "That's the same man who was here the first night. Their mules are sewed up the same, and he doesn't speak like a Negro."

Lewis pointed out, "His skin is black."

Morris told his brother, "I'm going to spill water on him."

"Don't do it. They're in the Railroad. They have their reasons to hide." Lewis pointed to a tree. "It's just up ahead on that tree."

"The dead one laying down?" Abraham asked.

Lewis told him, "No, the living tree behind it. I'll wait here. You go look."

Abraham scanned the entire area as he quietly walked to the tree with inch wide layers of hanging wax formed by thousands of six-sided cells. It was crawling with bees. Each layer was a drawn down half circle only about four inches at the longest sheet in the center. It seemed too small for the number of bees swarming around the structure.

There was also a dead tree lying on the ground a few yards from the active nest. It looked like it had been down for a while since the broken end had weathered. Abraham knocked on the trunk as he climbed over and around the branches along the length of the tree until he

165

heard the dull thud he suspected. "Bring the axes over here."

Lewis and Morris walked to Abraham. Morris handed him an axe. "Here you go."

In a few minutes, Abraham had chopped a wedge out of the top of the tree and looked inside. "We have really been blessed. Come look."

The brothers both looked in the opening. "How far do you think it goes?" Lewis asked.

Abraham knocked on the truck as he continued down the tree. "I don't know if the comb goes this far, but I think the tree is hollow for six feet. The honeycomb could fill the whole thing."

"Let's chop out a wedge on this end too?" Morris took a swing and barely notched the log.

Abraham told him, "You're too weak. I'll do it." He cut out another wedge. They looked in the hole.

Lewis excitedly exclaimed, "We better get everybody and figure out how to collect all of this."

Morris didn't want any interference. "Maybe we should cover these holes, so the bees don't go back in while we're gone."

"Good idea." They stuffed pieces of duck cloth into the holes before they hurried home.

In the forest south of the cabins, Theo explained how he explored, "If we want to know what's here, we have to create a search grid. We start at a fixed point and lay out a square. We walk the section and document everything of value in the square, or that we didn't find anything in that section."

Matthew informed Theo of his past procedures, "I

did that! I started at the creek where you watered your animals, then rode up to where I could just see my starting point, and then rode back toward the cabins. I've looked at a lot of these woods, but I don't know what to look for."

"Let's do it again. First, we'll let the animals drink at the creek."

In the first section, they found chickweed. Nancy took out a sheet of her own paper. "Get a sheet of paper and a pencil."

"I'm sure you know there are such things as letters and numbers. We'll use them to identify each section. We'll start with the first letter and the first number. At the top of your page, make a mark like this." Nancy wrote a capital A. "The same letter can be written two ways. This one is upper-case A." She showed the letter to their students. It didn't seem to mean much to them.

Theo asked, "Have you heard of an A-frame?"

Matt answered, "I have." He exclaimed, "So that's why they call it an A-frame!"

"Since this is the first section, and an upper-case A is the first letter, we'll use the first number as well." She wrote a zero. "This is the symbol for nothing."

Will asked, "If it's not the symbol of anything, why use it?"

"I don't mean it doesn't stand for anything." She picked up a handful of the chickweed. "How much of this do I have in my hand?"

Justin replied, "A handful."

She dropped it. "How much do I have now?"

Will answered, "None."

Nancy explained, "That is what this symbol stands for; none, nothing, zero."

Matt didn't want to use zero. "I understand, but this section isn't nothing. It's the first something. What is the symbol for one?"

Nancy wrote the number one. "It looks like this." Everybody wrote the number 1. "This section we're going to call A1, and this paper is the symbol for everything in section A1 because we marked it that way. This plant is chickweed. You can eat it." She picked the roots off, put the rest in her mouth, chewed it up, and swallowed. "Try some."

Theo had already eaten several handfuls, so the others tried it. Will chewed some. "I like it. It's tart."

"We can write the word chickweed on the A1 paper. You have to put letters together to do that. You can copy it from my paper."

They all copied the markings, not knowing what they were.

"Now, get another paper." When they all had another sheet, Nancy explained what was next. "To remember what chickweed is we make a page for chickweed. Write the same word on the top of the paper."

They all wrote chickweed again. "On the chickweed page, draw a picture of what it looks like." Nancy started her own drawing. "Try drawing it."

"I'm drawing it right?" Justin asked.

"That's good. Also, do a close up of one leaf and one flower."

Justin made a very accurate drawing. When all of

them had the pictures done, Nancy explained the next step. "Since we don't have colors, we have to write it. You don't have to do that now. I will, and later, you can copy what I wrote." She read as she wrote, "Light green leaves and tiny white flowers." Nancy offered, "I can tell you what the other letters and numbers are if you want to learn."

Matthew was the first to say, "I want to learn."

"Me too," Will told her.

Justin added a condition, "I do, but only if you don't tell anybody what we're doing."

"I won't," Nancy agreed.

Will started copying the markings on Nancy's paper. "Good. Nobody tells anybody that any of us are learning anything."

Matt suggested, "Perhaps we should say we're learning which forest plants we can use."

Will changed his mind. "You're right. That's better."

Justin, Nancy, and Theo also agreed. Nancy went on with the lesson and showed them how to make each upper-case letter in order. They practiced writing the letters and saying their names.

Twenty Five

When Abraham, Morris, and Lewis got back to the cabins, Marie had packs on six donkeys.

"What's happening?" Morris asked.

Marie explained, "We made all the drain tubes. We filled your storage barrels with water, so we can use the buckets. We have a drill, nails, ropes, and cloth covers. We're going to ride to the maples and get started."

Lewis informed them, "But I found the biggest honey hive ever to exist, and we're going to go back and get it. It's so big; we need everybody to help."

Abraham added, "Also, we need all the buckets and canteens to bring back the honey."

Even though Morris hadn't said a word, Katie told those already packed to gather maple, "Marie, we can wait until tomorrow to start the maples. We're going to do what my husband wants."

They loaded up every axe in the community, their six survival pack tarps, every shovel, and all the rope anybody had. Andrew's wife Grace went back into her cabin with their baby boy. None of the small children could walk or ride all the way to the beehive and back, so Sarah offered, "I'll stay with Grace. If you want to go to the beehive, I'll also watch Caleb."

"Thank you, Sarah." Katie knelt beside her youngest son and hugged him. "You go with Aunt Sarah, Caleb. Ma and Pa will be home later."

"Elijah, let's play." Caleb took his cousin's hand and helped him get to the sandy place where they liked to play. Morris watched his youngest child. Nobody had asked the six-year-old to do it. Of his own will, Caleb had made himself the helper of Elijah, who had feet that didn't work well. Morris felt proud of Caleb. He didn't know that his daughter, Ann, had given much of her share of food to her younger brother. Caleb knew why his sister was gone. Even in his young mind, he knew he should do something to make his life worth the loss of Ann.

Grace sat in the rocker on her porch. "Fannie, bring the girls over." So she could visit while the others were gone, Fannie herded her young daughters onto the porch to play dolls with Agnes and Matilda.

Morris notified those staying behind, "We'll be up at the north ridge just east of the lower springs."

Everybody rode a mule. In addition, they led five donkeys behind them. When they arrived at the beehive, Morris offered his advice, "I suggest we chop through each side here and here and take the top off. That way, we won't lose any of it."

Abraham took up an axe. "All right, Marie, Lily, and I will work on the log if you'll drag the branches over there. We can come back later and get them for firewood." Abraham hacked off the dead branches in the way then chopped through the shell of the hollow trunk opposite Lily.

The people of Fletcher Creek dragged the lopped off branches to the pile for Marie to chop. Before long, they had cut from one to the other of the wedges that Abraham had chopped out on the first trip.

Twenty Six

In the southern part of the forest, after their mid-day meal, Nancy decided they'd had enough practice writing letters. "Let's go see what other plants we can find in section A1." They folded their papers and tucked them carefully into a pocket before mounting up and riding on to discover what else lived in the forest.

Theo advised them, "Look for colors."

Shortly after they resumed their search, Will called out, "I see yellow." They rode toward the yellow and discovered dandelions.

Theo jumped down and picked a handful. "We can eat these, and we can make wine from them."

Justin asked, "Do you know how to make them into wine?"

"I sure do."

Matt informed his son, "That doesn't mean we'll be making, or you'll be drinking, any wine."

Will said, "We better make a page for this. Help us."

Nancy wrote dandelions on the A1 page and laid it in front of them, so they could make a copy. "Each letter has a sound. Do you remember the name of the first letter of this word?"

"You said that's a D," Matt answered.

"Right, what's the first sound of the word, dandelion."

Justin pronounced, "D."

"Yes. That is the sound the letter D makes, no matter where it is in a word."

Justin wrote dandelion on a new page. "I'm starting my picture, Nancy."

"I am too." Nancy drew her picture.

All of them put their new sheet into their pockets with the chickweed page, and the A1 page then continued their search. When they saw the cabins directly to their west, they closed the A1 section.

Nancy told the three men, "If you want to do the same tomorrow, come over in the morning."

Right away, Matt told her, "I'll be there."

"Me too," Justin assured her.

Will followed suit, "I want to continue tomorrow as well. Just remember what we said about not telling anybody."

Sarah and Fannie still sat outside. "Where is everybody?" Matt asked his wife.

Fannie wondered if Sarah would tell Matt about Morris spilling the tapeworm medicine. She herself, held her tongue.

Sarah answered, "They went to get a honey hive up on the north ridge east of the lower springs. I think they could use your help. They're chopping. You should be able to hear them."

"We'll try to find them." The five of them rode up to the north ridge then headed toward the chopping sounds.

When they got close, Matt called out, "Hello at the honey tree."

Morris answered, "Come on over."

Abraham instructed the others, "When we raise the top, you scrape off any honey and wax."

Morris, Lewis, Matt, Will, Justin, and Andrew took up positions on opposite sides of the tree.

"You pry up the edge, so we can get our hands under." Abraham stood on top of the tree and leaned down.

The men of Fletcher Creek pried up the edge. Lily, Abraham, Marie, Nancy, and Theo pulled up the top.

When he could see the inside of the top, Lewis said, "Just let it fall to the ground. It's clean."

They let it fall. Everybody looked inside. Several six-foot-long layers of honeycomb lay soaking in the honey that had flowed out. Abraham stood on top of the tree with Theo. "Let's try to pull these out."

They grabbed the outer layer of comb and pulled up. The rest of the people got a hold of it and pulled it over the edge and onto a tarp. They did the same with all the other pieces of the comb then dipped the honey out by the bucketful. They poured it into their twelve India rubber canteens and every bucket they had in their community. They divided all the combs between the six tarps, wrapped them, tied them so that the honey couldn't get out, and loaded them onto the donkeys. Either two canteens of honey were tied at the ends of a rope and hung across a mule, or they hung two buckets on a shoulder pole with their lids secured.

The hollow tree wasn't completely empty when Theo spoke up, "We've gotten all we can without getting rotten wood with the honey."

Morris looked into the log as he licked his fingers. "We can come back for the rest later. We already have more than enough honey and every bit of the honeycomb."

Twenty Seven

On the way home, Katie rode up to Lily. "Why don't you wear a dress?"

"Growing up I had to work like a man, and I couldn't do it in a dress. I never learned to want to wear one. They aren't practical."

"People will be able to track you because you're different."

"That's true. Thank you for pointing that out." Lily decided to talk to Nancy and Marie and explain why they should all wear dresses.

Because he needed to make amends for spilling Matt's medicine, Morris made an offer to Abraham, "I'll go to Little Rock to buy cloves and whatever you need. I know you can't go there, but I can. Although, I would have to use one of your animals. I'll buy what you want with your money. You know I'm coming back because my family is here."

Abraham agreed, "That's a good idea."

Morris rode over to Matt to apologize. "I tried to take your medicine. Sarah tried to stop me. It spilled, and it's gone. I'm sorry."

Matt replied angrily, "I need that medicine. Why did you do that?"

"I thought we all needed it, and you shouldn't have been hoarding it, but I want to make amends. I'll go buy what we need to make more."

Matt asked, "Did you know I have a tapeworm that's killing me?"

"I'm sorry. I'll go get what Abraham needs to make you more. I'll leave tonight."

Abraham was glad they would be able to get more food and any other things they needed, and he wanted to help the people of Fletcher Creek avoid more internal conflict, so he interrupted, "I'll give you a list and the money." Abraham told everybody in his family, "When we get back to the wagon, make a list of all the food or anything else you think we need for the next three months."

When they arrived at the cabins, the women and children at home came over to look. Sarah asked, "Are all those tarps and containers full of honey?"

"They sure are," Matt told her.

"The hive must have been gigantic," Fannie exclaimed.

Her husband, Lewis, told her, "It was. I wish you had been there to see it."

Fannie wiped some honey off the tarp and sucked it off her finger. "We don't need this much. We should take most of this to Little Rock to sell. We can buy crop seeds to plant and other things we need."

William jumped in, "Good idea. I want to go."

Andrew said, "Let's keep the biggest piece of the honeycomb for us. We should divide it equally because we'll all use the same amount of beeswax, but we should divide the honey proportionally."

Katie tasted the honey. "Agreed."

If Katie was agreeing and it was obviously fair,

nobody was going to argue. They put the biggest package on the ground then loaded the other five sections directly into the empty wagon. Andrew took two gallons of honey, William took two, Morris and Lewis each got four, and then Matt and Abraham took five gallons apiece.

Nancy pulled out six sheets of paper from her pack. "I'm glad to write your name and the list of what you want if you'd like me to do that for you."

Andrew immediately asked for her help, "Come to our cabin. We'll tell you what we want."

Marie offered, "I'll do the same." Lewis accepted.

Matthew knew she was literate, but he had decided to stay with their ruse of being escaped slaves, so he asked Lily, "Do you know how to write?"

"I can help you." Lily got a sheet of paper and a pencil. "Abraham, you, James, and Theo make our list."

After the men had their honey and their section of the comb in their cabins, they gathered with their lists. Abraham told Morris, "We should sell it and divide the money six ways. Each man can buy what he wants with his share of the money or put it together with others if they want."

Lewis said, "I found it. I should get more."

Abraham objected, "You found the live nest. I found the dead nest, and my family opened the tree. It's Theo's wagon and Theo's mules."

Will said, "Abraham's right. They should have the largest share."

"I don't want a larger share. I want us all to have an equal share."

"Why would you do that?" Morris asked.

"Because my God said to be fair, help your neighbors, and treat others as you want to be treated."

"I wouldn't have," Lewis confessed.

Abraham realized he needed to go to keep the transaction fair. "I'm going with you."

Matt piped up, "If you're all going, then I'm going."

"Then, I am too." Andrew then added, "And Abraham, just to be clear up front, if you're captured, we aren't doing anything to protect or save you."

"Fair enough. Let me tell Lily and the others." Abraham went to talk with his family. The other men also left to let their wives know they'd be gone for a few days.

As they walked to their cabins, Matt told Will, "Abraham is the same man who made me the medicine and those mules are branded with numbers like the others. I think they used the walnuts to dye themselves."

"I know. Maybe they were going to leave but decided not to go without their family."

"I think they're giving us a truthful way to describe the people who were here and not incriminate us."

"Maybe it's both. Meet you back at the wagon in a minute." Will stepped into his cabin.

Lily begged Abraham, "Please, don't go back to Little Rock."

Abraham assured his wife, "I'll be safe. I need to protect our share and get what we need. As their slave, nobody will even look at me."

Lily held Abraham to her heart. "I wish you

179

wouldn't. I'm going to be so worried. Please don't do what we did the last time. Don't help anybody; just come back to us."

Abraham kissed his wife. "Neither wild horses, nor Judge Daniel will keep me away from you. I promise."

Twenty Eight

As they traveled, for the first time since they had lived together in their small community, the men of Fletcher Creek planned as a group. They had hundreds of pounds of honey-filled comb to sell. Morris thought to himself: maybe we can make it out here if we work together.

They decided to travel the twenty-six miles to Little Rock without stopping, except to let King, Ace, Big Jenny, and Chief enjoy the new grass of spring while they ate the breakfast the women had packed.

Abraham pulled out his canteen. "This is parasite medicine. Everybody, take a drink." He poured out a dose into each of their tin cups. He didn't tell them that it was the original formula. He knew Matt needed the best he could get, and it would be good for all of them.

They arrived in Little Rock late in the afternoon of the following day. Abraham advised them, "I think we should try to sell directly to the inns and people because the man at the store doesn't give a good price when buying. I also think it will be better if all six of us don't go together to try to make a sale."

They went to Peabody Inn first. Since he knew how to read and negotiate, Morris went to speak with the innkeeper. Mr. Peabody had scurvy and was supposed to be eating new items. He was doing his best to

181

accomplish that. He had discovered how many good things there are to eat, so he went to the wagon, poked at the comb, and tasted the honey. It was full of flavor. Besides that, the inn went through hundreds of candles. His wife and daughters could use the wax to make their own candles and save him money. "I'll take a hundred pounds at thirty-one cents a pound. It looks like you have more than enough."

"Abraham, get a hundred pounds for Mr. Peabody." It worked out well for Abraham to be the slave; he was strong; he knew how to weigh correctly, and how to collect the correct amount of money.

Abraham carried in the innkeeper's purchase. "Please, pay Masa in six parts, all just the same." Mr. Peabody gave him thirty silver eagles, six ten-cent, six five-cent, six one-cent, and eight half-cent coins.

Abraham held out two of the half-cent coins. "Take them two back or give Masa four more."

"Well, I'll be. A slave who can count and divide. I'm not sure if that's a good or a bad thing, but here are four more half-cents."

To hide his blue eyes, Abraham kept his head bowed and respectfully looked at the floor, as a slave should. "Thank you, Masa, sir. Masa needs the wagon axle fixed, sir. Who can help Masa?"

"Are you staying in Little Rock long?"

"No, sir. Don't reckon so."

"Only person I know wouldn't be able to fix it very fast."

"Thank ya kindly for listenin', Masa." The slave left with the money.

182

Mr. Peabody watched to be sure the slave gave the money to his master. When he saw Abraham give the coins to Morris, he called for his family to come work on their new acquisition.

Abraham navigated the wagon through the narrow streets of Little Rock to the Hillcrest Inn. Before Morris entered the inn to attempt the next sale, Abraham asked for a favor. "Ask Mr. Hillcrest if he knows where we can get the wagon axle fixed."

Abraham, Matt, Will, Andrew, and Lewis waited in the wagon, ready to cut the next section. Mr. Hillcrest came to the wagon to look at the product.

"My Lord, where did you ever get this much?" He dipped his spoon into the honey pooled around the comb and drew up a large glob, which he ate with loud sucking and slurping.

Lewis spoke up, "I found it in the forest in a tree that fell down."

"Clark charges twelve cents a gallon for honey, and it's not nearly as tasty. The problem is that this is in the comb."

Abraham informed them, "I can get it out for Masa."

Mr. Hillcrest questioned him, "How much honey do you think you can get?"

"Two gallons or more, Masa."

"I'll take as much as you can get for twelve cents a gallon."

"We'll come back at the end of the day," Morris informed him.

"Where next, Abraham?" Lewis asked as he sat in the wagon seat.

"To Charles, he's the baker."

Matt informed the others, "I'm going to stay here and eat a meal then look around town."

Will and Andrew felt they weren't doing anything useful. "We'll stay with Matt."

"Fine, it's better for us to not overwhelm our buyers. Go ahead and do what you want." Morris went on with Lewis and Abraham.

Abraham flicked the reins. "We need to go to the end of Main Street then turn left on Markham. What did he say about the wagon?"

"Since we're going to stay at his inn and the wagon will be there, he will ask the Wainwright to come and look at the wagon tonight."

Morris went into the bakery. He informed the person behind the counter that he had honey in the comb for sale, and he would sell it at thirty-one cents a pound. A woman buying bread asked, "If I like it, may I buy some from you?"

"Of course, go talk to my slave." Morris continued negotiating with Charles.

Abraham stood in the wagon with his feet under the tarp ready to cut out another section with the long knife he always carried. He kept his eyes contritely focused away from the person approaching but glanced out. *Why her?* He twisted to face more toward the rear.

Mrs. Hall dipped her finger into the honey. "I wonder if honey would cause stomach problems?"

When he had been seeing patients as Dr. Luke Smith, Abraham had treated the woman's son for stomach pain. He wanted to know how the boy was doing, but he knew he couldn't ask directly. He spoke deeply to disguise his voice. "I'm sorry your husband has a bad stomach."

"It's my son, but he's doing very well now, and I don't want him to have a problem again."

"He needs ta eat lots a different things. Buy some an' let him try."

"That is what his doctor would say. Bless his heart. Every night, I pray that God is keeping him and his wife safe. How much is a quart?"

Abraham could have hugged the woman. He wanted to give her every bit of it. "Three cents."

"Do you have a jar?" she asked.

"No, ma'am."

"How long will you be here?"

"Ya has ta ask Masa."

Mrs. Hall went back into the bakery. "I want to buy some of the honey, but I don't have a jar. I can go home and get one. How long will you be here?"

"I'll let you use a pot, Mrs. Hall. Bring it back next time." The baker walked away. He returned with his son, two ten-gallon tubs, and a gallon pail.

"Abraham, this lady wants to buy a little honey, and this man wants 2 ten-gallon tubs of the comb full of honey."

Mrs. Hall said, "It's so tasty. I've decided to get more. Give me a pail full."

"Yes, ma'am." Abraham ran the pail along the side of the honeycomb. He scooped up almost a whole pail full then filled it the rest of the way by the handful.

"Forty-eight cents." Morris held his hand out toward the woman.

Abraham tried to clean the honey from the outside of the pail, but a glob ran down the side.

Plop.

The woman bent down to wipe away the honey on her dress and glanced up into the face of the man holding the pail above her. A smile lit up her face. "Praise be to God." The baker and Morris looked at her. "I don't think it's going to stain my dress."

She patted his hand as Abraham handed her the pail. "My son is doing wonderfully, and I hope he can enjoy this honey."

"I hope so too," Abraham replied.

Mrs. Hall spoke to the baker softly, "I'll send everybody to buy some if you buy it all."

Charles was doubtful. "I don't think I can sell that much."

She assured him, "What you don't sell, I'll buy."

Charles knew Mrs. Hall was as honest as the day is long. "I'll get more tubs and buy it all."

"First, we have to get some honey for Mr. Hillcrest." Lewis passed one of the tubs into the wagon.

"Then I'll take the two tubs now. What you have left after you've sold to others, I'll buy."

"Do you have scales?" Morris asked.

Charles replied, "Yes. I know how much these tubs weigh. Fill them up, and then we'll weigh them."

Lewis told Morris, "First, we should see how much a tub weighs empty."

They walked to the scales and weighed the tub while Abraham cut the comb into large pieces.

Charles stated the total after the second tubful of

honey sat on the scales. "Two hundred twenty-seven pounds."

Morris calculated. "Seventy dollars and thirty-seven cents."

Charles didn't want anybody to see where he hid his money. "Wait at your wagon. I'll bring it out to you."

Lewis followed Morris to the wagon. "We need to get some tubs, jars, pails, or something to hold the honey we're going to sell to Mr. Hillcrest."

Abraham overheard the comment. "Then we'll go to the store next. When Charles brings the money, ask him if they have a church and if the preacher ever misses a Sunday."

Charles arrived with the money. Morris asked, "Is there a church in town we can attend if we're still here Sunday?"

"Yes. Reverend Pratt's church is at the end of West Sixteenth Street at Park Ave."

"Does he have church every Sunday?"

"He's there every Sunday, rain or shine."

"Thank you. I'll see you later if we have anything left." Morris counted the money before he climbed back onto the wagon.

On the way to the store, Abraham advised Morris and Lewis. "Go in and buy first. If you don't, Clark will try to recover his cost for the honey in the price he charges for what you want."

The three men went into the store. Morris handed the shopkeeper their three sheets of paper. "We need to package and calculate the charges for each order separately."

187

"Get your slave to carry your supplies to your wagon," Clark instructed them.

Lewis issued the command, "Abraham, take our supplies to the wagon."

"Yes, sir, Masa," he followed Clark, took what he was instructed to take, and stacked it by the door. When they had paid for everything on their lists and Abraham had it all stacked by the door, Morris brought up the next item of business.

"I have honey in the comb to sell."

"I'll look at what you've got." Clark went to the wagon. "That is the biggest sheet of honeycomb I have ever seen. The bees must have been making that for decades. How many times did you get stung?"

"None," Lewis answered truthfully.

"How much are you asking?" Clark hoped what they had in mind was less than he would have offered.

Knowing the man would have to make a profit, Morris requested what he thought would be a reasonable place to start the negotiating. "Twenty-seven cents a pound for the comb with the honey in it."

"If I have to get the honey out, I'll give you twenty cents per pound."

Morris felt that Charles didn't really want to buy more. He feared that he would end up not selling all of it. He decided if Clark would buy it all, that he would settle for less. "How much do you want?"

"I'll buy it all. It would be best to be the only one with honey for sale."

Morris countered, "Twenty-five cents per pound, but I have to keep some of the honey."

"It's a lot of work to get the honey out. I'll buy what you have left for twenty-four cents a pound."

"Agreed." Morris was glad to be done with it.

Abraham saw an opportunity. "I'll get the honey out for three cents a pound."

Clark was his usual untrusting self. "Two cents a pound and you do it here, so I know you aren't taking any of it."

"Masa, can I?"

Morris replied, "Yes, but don't misbehave, or you'll regret it. Go get the honey we need to keep then bring the rest in here."

"Yes, sir, Masa," Abraham took the crates of jars and a pail to the wagon. He scooped honey from around the sides with the pail and filled six one-gallon jars. He smashed and squeezed the comb and freed honey until he had also filled four quart-sized jugs. He set the jarred honey aside. Then he pulled up the tarp edges into a sack and pulled it to the back of the wagon. He climbed out, took off the backboards, and then heard a voice behind him. "Hello, Dr. Smith. What on Earth are you doing back here in Little Rock?"

Abraham recognized the voice of his friend, Mr. Martin Harrow's stable hand. "Hello, Edwin. James is hurt, so we didn't get far. I have something for you but don't be surprised. I don't look the same." Abraham turned around.

Edwin saw the stained face of the man he knew as Dr. Smith. "That's for sure. You don't look the same at all, except I recognized the wagon and the animals and the shape of your body."

189

"That's because you're a very observant person. Right now, I'm Abraham, Morris' slave." He handed Edwin a quart of honey. "This is for your family."

Edwin looked in the wagon. "That's a big bee's nest."

"I know."

"Are you selling all of that?"

"Yes, to Clark. After he weighs it, I have to separate the honey from the wax."

"I can help you if you let me have some of the comb."

"You want the honey in it too?"

"No, just the wax."

"Is two pails full enough?" Abraham asked.

That was more than Edwin was even thinking. "That would be wonderful!"

"We have to get it first, so start squishing."

Edwin got into the wagon, grabbed a handful of honeycomb and squeezed the honey into the pail then set aside the mostly honey-free wax glob.

"How's my friend, Reverend Pratt?" Abraham asked.

"He's fine. I saw him in church last Sunday. I told Pa, 'Since we're working for God, we should be going to church.' He agreed, and the whole family went."

"That's wonderful," Abraham replied.

"What's taking so long?" Morris called out.

"I'm hurrying, Masa. We need a lot."

Morris didn't want to keep standing around in the store. He had looked at everything in the store twice already. "Yes, I know. Hurry it up."

Abraham got out his knife, cut the hive into sections, and filled both washtubs. "You keep working on it. I'll be back to get the rest." He got out and then pulled the tarp onto his back.

"Masa, weigh an empty washtub or two, so I can put this in 'em for ya. There's still more ta bring in."

Clark put two ten-gallon washtubs on his large scale. He, Lewis, Morris, and Abraham looked at the weight. Clark instructed the slave, "Put it in."

Abraham slowly filled the tub, so he didn't spill any, but mostly to make the task take longer. He filled the first one completely and part of the other. "I'll go get the rest." Abraham went back to the wagon with the tarp, another crate of jars, and another pail.

Edwin had crushed honeycomb as fast as he could. Abraham put the jars, the pail, and the tarp into the wagon. He opened up the tarp and pointed. Edwin moved a couple of pieces of comb out of one tub onto the tarp. Abraham took the tub, carried it in, and put the tub on the scales. "Can Masa trade the full ones for clean tubs?"

Clark agreed, "That's fine with me."

Abraham took two new clean tubs out to the wagon. Edwin had one of the pails full of wax and another jar of honey. Abraham took the last tub into the store and put it on the scale.

"Three hundred fifty-four pounds," Clark went to the counter and figured the amount due, "Eighty-four dollars and ninety-six cents." Clark counted out the money while Abraham carried supplies to the wagon. By the time Abraham had all the supplies in the wagon,

Edwin had two heaping pails of wax, and three gallons of honey.

"There are nine gallons of honey to sell to Mr. Hillcrest. Be sure everybody takes a dose of the medicine tonight." Abraham took a drink and handed the canteen to Morris. "Can we settle everything tomorrow?"

"We'll be at the Hillcrest Inn. Go there when you're done. We'll get the money right between everybody tomorrow. I'll tell Mr. Hillcrest to expect you and show you to your room in the stable."

"Thank you." Abraham looked around for Edwin, but he didn't see him. He walked back into the store and spoke with Clark. "I'll need more tubs, Masa. I'll leave 'em here when I'm done. Where should I work?"

Clark pointed. "Take the tubs, and work in the storeroom in the back."

Abraham knew Clark and wanted to have everything settled with no ability for further maneuvering. "Masa, you givin' me two cents for three hundred fifty-four pounds of honeycomb ta have the honey removed from the wax."

"I meant for the weight of the wax after the honey is removed." Clark assumed that the slave would agree to anything, now that his master wasn't there.

Abraham countered, "We weigh the wax an the honey after. I'll do it for two cents for the weight of the wax and honey together."

"That's the same as what it weighs now."

"Exactly."

Since Morris had told his slave to behave, Clark threatened, "That's not behaving."

Abraham kept his eyes focused on the ground as he negotiated, "I'll go get Masa ta arrange for ya ta use his slave's time."

"I'll pay your master two cents for the three hundred and fifty-four pounds, but I'll give the money to him."

"Agreed," Abraham finalized the deal just as Edwin came into the store.

"Who is this?" Clark asked.

"My helper."

"I didn't agree to an assistant."

Abraham pointed out the advantage of allowing Edwin to help. "Not changin' the amount, Masa, an you'll be done with us sooner."

"All right, take the tubs to the storeroom and get it done."

To the surprise of Clark, Abraham asked, "May we use a strainer? I wants ta get your honey real clean for ya. Do ya want all a it in quart jars?"

"You'd do that?"

"If you give both of us bread, cheese, ham, apples, an a gallon of clean drinkin' water, we will."

"I'll send it to you. Get a strainer, wax press, and jars off the shelf. You have to leave them when you're done."

Twenty Nine

In the morning, Abraham and Edwin had all the honey strained clean and packed into 80 quart-sized jars and 64 pint-sized jars. The wax had been washed and pressed into 61 quarter-pound blocks. All the tools were clean, and the product was ready to sell. Clark came into the storeroom and found Abraham and Edwin asleep on the floor beside the honey and the wax.

"Time to go," Clark stated loudly.

The slave woke. He kept his eyes looking down. "Be right back with Masa, so ya can pay him."

"Wait here." Clark came back with a tray holding two more meals exactly like those he had provided the night before and then refilled their water jars. He gave Abraham the seven dollars and eight cents. "You did a very good job."

"Thank ya, Masa." Abraham put the money in his bag. They ate the meal then left the store.

"Do you have animals at the livery to feed this morning?"

"We're taking care of five horses."

Abraham offered, "I'll help."

Edwin carried the jar of honey and the two pails of beeswax that he had hidden the night before. Abraham had the other three quarts of honey. At the livery, they put out fresh hay and water then shoveled manure. As Abraham rolled the wheelbarrow out, Martin walked into his stable.

"Good morning, Edwin."

"Good morning, Mr. Harrow," Edwin replied loudly, in case Abraham didn't want to be seen.

Abraham heard Edwin and walked back into the livery, looking at the floor. "Masa, sir, my Masa needed me ta work last night. I needed help an hired your man ta work all night. Can I buy him a few hours a sleep with this jar of honey?"

Martin said, "May I touch you?"

"Don't hurt me, Masa. I didn't mean no harm. I just had ta get the work done."

"I won't hurt you." Martin raised Abraham's face. "I thought so. What did you pay Edwin?"

"A quart of honey, two pails of beeswax, and another quart of honey to buy him sleep from you."

"And you helped him do his work this morning?"

"Yes, Masa."

"What's your name?"

"Abraham, Masa."

"Edwin, you can have the rest of the day off. Come back tomorrow morning. Use my bucket to take your wax home and then bring it back tomorrow. Give Abraham his pails."

"Thank you, Mr. Harrow. Can I stay until Abraham leaves?"

"Of course, I'm sure you're as happy to see Abraham as I am."

"Thank you, Masa. I'm very happy to see you both.

Is everything good with you and your wife since we last saw each other?"

"No problems. What about you?"

"James was hurt bad. He has broken ribs, a smashed-up back, and a badly sprained ankle, but he'll be fine when he heals. That's why I'm here."

"What happened?" Edwin asked.

"It's better not to explain. I'm glad to know that everybody here is fine. We've been worrying about you."

Surprised that a person running for his life would worry about somebody else, Martin and Edwin said, "You've been worrying about us?"

"Yes, and we're very sorry that we put you in a compromising position."

"Dollie and I think Judge Hall and that law are wrong. You and your wife have every right to love each other and to be married."

"That's what we thought. When we got married, we didn't even know about that law or that anybody would care about people they don't even know. It's created all kinds of problems for our family."

Martin expressed his feelings, "I hope your family finds a home where these things don't matter."

"Thank you, Martin. I also want to thank you for being concerned about my life enough to warn me about getting involved with another woman. I love my wife very much, and I don't want anybody else. Nancy is my sister-in-law. That was our connection, not anything else, but it's nice that you cared."

"Nancy is very beautiful." Edwin quickly added, "So are Isabelle and Marie."

"All three sisters are beautiful. Their mother was too. I've seen a picture."

Edwin told them, "I wish you could've stayed here. I'd marry Nancy when I grow up. She's the nicest person I've ever met," then he immediately added, "but you two are also very nice."

Abraham laughed. "Much obliged, Edwin. I understand that the charm of a woman is different than friendship between men."

Dr. Smith had just included him as one of the men that was his friend. Edwin beamed and stood up higher. "I'm glad to have you as my friend."

Abraham replied, "I'm glad both you and Martin are my friends, and Edwin, I'm glad we got to spend the night talking, and I really appreciate your help. I couldn't have done it without you."

Abraham turned to Martin. "Have you had any more sick animals to look at?"

"A few, but I haven't had time to look for those plants."

"If I knew somebody who would find them and sell them to you, would you be interested?"

"If the price was right, I would."

"Then, you'll probably be getting a visit. I need to be going. God bless you both."

"Get out of town, go far away, and be safe." Edwin hugged his friend.

"As soon as James can travel, we will. Remember everything I've told you, Edwin."

After Abraham was gone, Edwin asked, "Why doesn't everybody treat me like he does?"

"Abraham has the Holy Spirit directing him. He sees the true value of a man."

"I'm a man who has true value?"

"Yes, Edwin, you are! All three of us are."

"I want to be like him."

Martin replied, "I do too."

Abraham walked toward Reverend Pratt's home to leave a jar of honey with a note saying, "The man you care about so much is going to be fine." He believed Thaddeus would know that meant that Eli would be fine, so he wouldn't keep worrying. As Abraham walked past the Hillcrest Inn to the Reverend's house, Lewis stepped into the street.

"Abraham, we were wondering where you were. We need you to load up the supplies that Will, Andrew, and Matt are going to buy."

Judge Hall staggered out of the inn where he had spent another night, trying to drown his anger and unhappiness. He hadn't found Noah Swift Hawk or Ann Williams, his wife was barely speaking to him, and he didn't have one iota of patience. "Get out of my way." He pushed Abraham aside.

Caught off guard, Abraham stumbled. Lewis confronted the man, "Don't push my slave!"

In his deepest voice, Abraham said, "I'm not hurt, Masa." He didn't want to draw attention to himself. He had no idea why his path always crossed Judge Hall's path. He thought these would be his last moments on Earth. He knew Judge Hall would shoot him on sight. He kept his eyes focused on the ground. God, protect me. I promise I'll never come to Little Rock again.

Judge Hall screamed at Lewis, "I'll do anything I want!" He shoved Abraham and knocked him to the ground.

Mr. Hillcrest hurried into the street and tried to direct Judge Hall back into the inn. "Judge Hall, let me fix you a nice breakfast." He motioned for Lewis to get his slave out of sight.

Judge Hall ordered, "Get your hands off me!" He flailed and tried to push the man's hands away. He listed to the right, stumbled on the boardwalk, and fell onto Lewis who tried to catch him but only got a grip on his jacket sleeve. Judge Hall's head smashed into the post. The sound of ripping clothes filled the air.

Abraham jumped to his feet and took off. He ran as fast as he could away from imminent destruction. He left the two broken jars of honey and the note in the dirt road.

Judge Hall staggered away with blood trickling down his face from the gash on his forehead. His jacket sleeve that had separated from the rest of the jacket at the shoulder was bunched at his lower arm. Mr. Hillcrest instructed his oldest son, "Follow him. Be sure he gets home safely." He turned to Lewis. "I'm so sorry. I'd be glad to serve your party breakfast at no cost."

"Make it a good one. First, I have to find my slave."

"Yes, sir." Mr. Hillcrest sighed with relief that things hadn't gotten worse. He had no idea what was going on with the judge. He had never seen him act the way he had the last week.

Thirty

Judge Hall staggered into his home. Mrs. Hall exclaimed with concern, "Daniel, what happened?"

"You don't love me, and people don't respect me." He slumped into the chair by the door.

She had been sure Daniel had sent people to track down Dr. and Mrs. Smith and then kill them. Now that she knew he had honored his word to her and had let them go, she could love him again. "Of course, I love you. Let me get you cleaned up. Come to our room." She helped him get to the room, out of his clothes, and into bed. She cleaned his head and bandaged it. "Who doesn't respect you, Daniel?"

Captain Cornish refuses to look into the gap any more, and he won't send any troops to search for Ann Williams and Noah Swift Hawk. You're mad and upset with me. You barely speak to me, and you haven't shared my bed since those criminals left the Harrow's house. What Judge Hall told his wife was, "A slave is all."

"Don't worry about a slave. That's their nature."

Judge Hall felt his wife's tenderness as she cared for him. "I love you, and I need you to love me. Do you really love me?"

"I really love you. Now, go to sleep. I'll show you how much I love you later."

"Show me now."

"You're hurt."

"It doesn't matter. I need you."

"All right, my love. I need you too."

Thirty One

On the other side of town, Lewis, Morris, Andrew, Will, and Matt searched and hollered, "Abraham, come back!" They got no reply.

Abraham had decided to finish his other business, so they could get out of town. He went where his brother-in-law had told him he would find the tent maker. "I needs two big rubber wagon covers and one ten-by-ten rubber tarp that gots snaps. Do ya sell 'em rubber mattresses an' canteens?"

"Yes, how many mattresses and canteens?"

"Four mattresses an' twelve canteens."

"That's going to be eighty dollars."

Abraham had the money his family had put together and the seven dollars he had earned separating the honey for Clark. He had already spent a lot at Clark's General Store, but Roscoe had given him money specifically to buy the rubberized items they wanted, so he paid the man. "I be back ta get everythin'."

Next, he went to the gunsmith. They needed something better than the rifles and pistols they had. He knew they would not have survived the coyote attack if there had been more coyotes. The Butterfield Gang had taught them one thing for which he was grateful: there exists a gun with a lot of firepower and the ability to shoot many rounds in a short period. "I needs somethin' can fire real strong shots real fast."

202

The gunsmith joked but was seriously concerned about a black man who wanted a powerful weapon. "You're not planning on holding up the bank, are you?"

Abraham explained, "I needs to kill coyotes."

"This Lefaucheux 20-Round is the best I've got. It's French." He opened up the cylinder. "It's got two rows of chambers. Those in the outer ring are spaced further apart and fire out of the upper barrel. The cylinder rotates just enough, so the next shot comes from the inner ring through the lower barrel. Each shot switches back and forth between rings and barrels. You can fire twenty shots, and the barrels stay cool. The hammer strikes a pin into a 7.65-millimeter cartridge, which contains its own powder. You don't need to prime the gun. The barrels are four and three-quarters of an inch long, and it weighs only two and a half pounds fully loaded."

Abraham admired the revolver, "How much?"

"Twelve dollars."

"How many ya got?"

"Only three revolvers plus three 500 cartridge boxes. Forty dollars for all of it."

Later, Abraham would get thirty-one dollars for his share of the honey hive. Right now, he had only twenty-seven dollars on him. His plan of action was always to do the best with what you have because you can never be sure the opportunity will come again. That included information, and he wondered if these might be the kind of guns the Butterfield Gang had used to shoot up his wife's farm. "Anyone else ever buy any a these?"

A good salesman always promoted his product as

something people want, so he told the man about his previous sales. "I sold six of them already."

Abraham probed further, "How long they been using 'em? Maybe they ain't good an' they gonna bring 'em back."

"Not the last fall but the fall before."

That was what he suspected. "They buy up all the rest a 'em cartridges."

"They wanted all of them, but I insisted that I had to keep at least one box for each revolver left."

"Will ya sell two revolvers an' one box of cartridges for this twenty-seven dollars I gots?"

The man was only short one dollar, and he might never actually sell any of it, so the gunsmith agreed, "Without the gun belts."

"I hopes ta be back for the rest." Abraham put the two revolvers into his empty money bag, and the box of ammunition under his arm then started back to the inn. As he approached Clark's General Store, he saw Matt loading the wagon. Abraham whispered from around the side of the store, "Masa, is it safe?"

"Abraham, there you are. It's safe. Come load our supplies."

"Yes, Masa." Abraham put his purchase into the wagon, looked at the axle, and then carried all the new supplies to the wagon. When he passed Morris outside at the wagon, he whispered, "Give me twenty-four dollars of my share of the money, then buy me a gross of pencils, a dozen rubber erasers, and as much paper as possible."

Morris gave Abraham the money and then went

back into the store to make the purchase. Clark wouldn't sell less than a whole ream of paper. The remainder of Abraham's share wasn't enough. *Abraham did all the hard work, and he didn't even stay at the inn or eat a meal.* Morris added thirty-seven cents of his own money and bought the requested items while Abraham packed the last of the supplies into the wagon. Morris handed his slave the pencils, box of rubber erasers, and the ream of paper.

Abraham carefully placed them on top of his ammo box. "We need to go to the tent maker's shop." Three of them climbed up on the wagon seat. Two sat on the floorboards at the side with their legs dangling. Abraham walked beside the wagon. "I saw the axle had a metal strap around it. Did you talk to the wainwright?"

Lewis replied, "I did. He said he could tell that the brakes weren't working correctly. He installed a new brake before he worked on the axle. He said he couldn't accomplish more in one night."

Abraham assumed they had paid the man for him. "How much do I owe you for the repairs?"

"It was five dollars. I gave him the money from your share. He said he hated to ask for payment, but he thought it would be the wisest thing to do, given the circumstances. I have no idea what he was talking about."

"That's fine. Thank you." At the tent shop, Abraham loaded his wagon covers, mattresses, canteens, and the tarp. "One more place I need to go."

At the gunsmith, everybody examined the

Lefaucheux revolver. "That's quite a gun." William spun the cylinder.

"All three gun belts, this last revolver, the other two boxes of cartridges, a bullet mold, twelve horns of gunpowder, six of primer powder, four boxes of wadding, and all the lead I can get for twenty-four dollars." Abraham handed over his money.

The other men purchased ammunition, powder, and wadding for their rifles. Morris looked at Abraham. "Are we ready to go home now?"

"Almost." He pulled out the canteen of medicine and a tin cup. "Drink up." He poured each of them a dose before they left Little Rock with their wagon stuffed full of supplies but not a penny to any of their names. Abraham hoped it was the last time he would ever be in Little Rock. He was only sorry that he hadn't been able to give the honey and the message to Rev. Thaddeus Pratt, the man who had married Stephanie and Eli and had helped them escape Little Rock.

Unrealized by any of them, Morris drove the wagon past Judge Daniel Hall's house. At the time of day when the Judge would have been sitting outside on his porch drinking coffee, Abraham safely walked by.

Because she had seen Dr. Smith pretending to be a slave named Abraham, Mrs. Hall believed that Daniel cared more about her than anything else and was reassuring him that she loved him. Instead of capturing Noah Swift Hawk, Daniel Hall put his marriage back together.

Thirty Two

Abraham rode in the back and worked on the hard shoes that Matt had bought to straighten Elijah's feet. He attached them together at the heel and the toe with the metal rods that Matt had bought. At night, Matt could insert the rods to hold Elijah's feet in the correct position as they grew. During the day, Matt would remove the rods. Elijah would wear only these special shoes, so he would walk right in the future. Andrew watched and commented on the state of his wife. "Grace is so weak; it's hard for her to carry John all day."

Abraham offered to help, "I can show you how to make a cradleboard."

"What is it?"

"It's a backpack to carry a baby. It has hard wooden planks at the back and a loop of wood across the top to protect the baby's head if it falls over. We can make straps from duck cloth to hold John in and duck cloth shoulder straps to carry it on Grace's back. On the sides, two legs can be rotated to prop up the cradleboard on the ground."

Andrew asked, "Can we make the shoulder straps adjustable so either Grace or I can carry it?"

"Yes."

At noon, they stopped to eat dinner and let the mules graze. As William again inspected and admired

207

the revolver, a very malnourished elk came to the edge of the clearing to eat the new grass. Since he already held the loaded revolver, William whispered, "Can I try your revolver?"

After silently asking the spirits to allow them to have the starving elk to feed the starving people of Fletcher Creek, Abraham consented, "Go ahead."

William squeezed off all twenty shots. The shots riddled the Elk's body in only a few seconds. All six men were thoroughly impressed. Abraham told him, "Since you killed it, you should butcher it."

William disclosed his problem. "I don't know how. We always bought meat in town."

"What about the rest of you?" Abraham asked. They all shook their heads, no. "How did you think you were going to survive in the forest?"

"I thought we would farm and buy our food," William replied.

Abraham got an axe and his tarp from the wagon. "Follow me." He silently thanked the elk for giving its meager body and led the men across the field.

"First, you cut the hamstrings." He zipped his knife across the back of each leg just above the hoof. "Do you want the hide and antlers?" he asked William.

It was the first animal he had ever killed, so he told Abraham, "I want them and the meat."

Abraham demonstrated how to cut the skin up the insides of the legs and up the backbone, and then how to pull the hide off like a sweater. He showed them how to cut around the antlers, the eyes, and the inside of the mouth at the gum. He cut the tongue out of the head and put it aside, then folded the skin over on itself and rolled it up tightly. With the axe, he chopped the head from the rest of the body.

"If you're taking the whole animal, you would have to remove the insides, or they'd poison the meat. It's too heavy for us to take the whole thing, so I'm just taking the meat, and that's why I'm not opening him up to remove the guts." He cut the back strap from its back, removed most of the muscles from the rest of its body, and put it all with the four legs onto the tarp. Next, he peeled the flesh from the head. Then, he removed the brains, which he carefully packed separately to make sure he didn't lose any of it. He set aside the empty skull with the antlers attached. They left the bones and internal organs in the field but carried the tarp of elk meat, the elk hide, the brains, the tongue, and the skull to the wagon. Just under two hours later, they were on their way home again.

The sun sank closer to the horizon. Morris noticed the first full moon of spring rising. "Tomorrow will be Good Friday. I want to get home. Let's not stop." Everybody wanted to get back to their family, so they kept traveling.

When they arrived back at Fletcher Creek, it was fifty hours after they had left home and very late in the night. After the mules were grazing with the rest of the herd, Abraham went to his family's tent. Before entering, he whispered, "My wife, I'm back."

"Come in, my husband."

Abraham slid under the blanket beside Lily. "My beautiful one, I told you nothing would keep me away from you."

Lily snuggled against Abraham. "I'm glad you're back. I've been worried, and I've missed you. I hope wild horses didn't try to keep you away."

He replied, "No," but thought, *almost*, as he drifted off to sleep in the loving embrace of his wife's arms.

Thirty Three

Everybody helped unload the wagon and distribute the supplies to their owners. Once they'd finished their chores, Nancy gathered her group and went off to map the forest. Since they had tapped the trees the day before, Lily took a group, along with their shiny new buckets, to the maple trees.

James and Marie showed the people still at the cabins how to cut up the elk and harvest the sinew.

Rebecca declared, "I'm so proud of Will. He was the first of us to kill an animal for us to eat."

Will asked, "James, can we tan a hide full of bullet holes?"

"Since you brought the brains, we can if you want, but the holes are going to limit what you can do with it."

"So that's why Abraham brought the brains. I thought he planned to eat them."

Marie said, "Not the brains, but I think he brought the tongue to eat. It's very good."

Rebecca asked, "James, do you feel well enough to show us how to tan? I don't want to hurt you. It's just that it would be nice for Will to have the hide."

Even though he knew it was only a temporary condition, it bothered James that he wasn't able to be strong and capable. "I want to be helpful. This is something I can do that is meaningful, and I enjoy it, so I'll tell you how."

Before going off to hunt crayfish, freshwater mussels, fish, ducks, or anything else they could find, Andrew, Morris, Lewis, and Abraham stacked the bricks that Lily, Nancy, and Marie had formed then heated in a very hot fire. They made a two-foot high, four-foot square, three-sided fire pit, just like the one that had been in the sugar shack at the Williams Farm. They got the crate with the utensils needed to make and mold maple sugar and lay a flat, shallow pan across the top of the fire pit.

At the maple grove, Carmen raised the cover over the tube and the bucket. "Look how much we got!"

Lily explained, "Cold nights like last night and warm days like today make the sap flow."

"Mine has a lot too." Freeman quickly swapped the full bucket with an empty one.

After they had swapped all the sap buckets, Lily said, "Let's go make syrup!"

Once home, they made a fire in the newly built pit and got started. While they stirred and condensed the maple sap, they boiled the jars purchased in Little Rock, and since they now had the equipment they needed, they dealt with the honey as well. They crushed the comb and poured the honey through their new strainers into the sterilized jars and used washed wax to seal the honey jugs. With their new contraption, they pressed the rest of the wax into blocks.

By the end of the day, all the honey had been stored in jars, and all the wax pressed into blocks. As well, all their first batch of maple sap cooled in sugar block molds for long-term storage. They ate roasted elk back straps for the evening meal, along with chickweed, dandelions, onion grass, and dead nettle brought home by Nancy, Matt, Will, and Justin.

In clouds of hickory wood smoke, the rest of the meat cured on newly built racks beside the four ducks brought home by Morris, Lewis, Andrew, and Abraham.

To celebrate Good Friday, after the meal, James read the story of Christ's crucifixion. He closed the Bible. "That's how much God loves us. He let His Son pay the price for all our sins."

Matilda expressed her opinion, "God didn't love His Son very much. My paw would never let somebody do that to me."

Matt agreed with his daughter. "I could never love the people who are against me and my whole family, and certainly I wouldn't let them hurt my children. I wouldn't even let people I love hurt them."

Stephanie explained why. "It's not that God didn't love Jesus. God, Jesus, and the Holy Spirit all got together at the beginning of creation and made a plan. They were going to make the world and everything in it, but They wanted Their creation to love Them of their own free will, so They made us with the ability to choose. They knew that some of us would not choose to love Them and would get all of creation messed up because of wanting to do everything our own way. They agreed that They wanted to be fair, so They decided there would be consequences if somebody broke the one

213

and only rule which was not to eat the fruit of the Tree of Knowledge of good and evil. If they broke the rule, the consequence was that they wouldn't live forever. The three of Them wanted the people They made to be able to live with Them forever, so They decided there would be a penalty that could be paid to redeem them, but the penalty had to be equal to the crime. The problem was that the cost was too high, and the beings They created weren't able to pay the price. Jesus decided He would pay the price for Their creation. When the time was right, He would become a human filled with the Holy Spirit, live the perfect life required, then pay the penalty of death. The necessary consequence to have justice would be paid, and Their creation would be able to live forever and love their Creator if they chose to. That's why God let His Son be crucified. He knew that Jesus wanted to do it because They all loved Their creation."

Carmen pointed out, "James did read that Jesus said, 'You don't take my life, I give my life freely.'"

Lewis and Fannie's daughter, Pearl, stated her opinion, "God, and Jesus, and the Holy Spirit are so smart."

Her sister Edna told them, "I think so too."

Katie's son Caleb said, "It's just too bad that He's dead. I would have liked to have met Him."

Morris told him, "That's where another miracle happens. You'll find out about it this Sunday on Easter Day."

Caleb replied, "I hope it's something good and not so sad."

The next day after they got the maple sap for Sarah, Grace, and Fannie to cook into maple sugar, they started to build the food storage and animal shelter for the animals that were going to stay at Fletcher Creek. To keep the children out of the construction area, James, Katie, Rebecca, and Marie taught the children how to make letters. Sarah, Fannie, and Grace came to watch the children and to help. Sarah requested of Katie, "May we help the children practice?"

"Please do," Katie happily encouraged them. That gave them the opportunity to learn but not feel that the women already capable of reading and writing thought they weren't good enough. By helping their children write letters, say the letter names, and make their sounds, they all started becoming literate.

Easter morning, as the sun rose above the horizon, everybody gathered to eat eggs, bacon, freshly baked bread, stewed apples, and honey washed down with goat's milk and hot coffee. James read Matthew 28:2, "Suddenly there was a violent earthquake; an angel of the Lord came down from Heaven, rolled the stone away, and sat on it."

Matilda jumped up and informed them, "They're in trouble now. They're going to get a spanking like you wouldn't believe."

James continued, "His appearance was like lightning, and his clothes were as white as snow. The guards were so afraid that they trembled and became like dead men."

Matilda whispered to her sister Elizabeth, "They deserve it."

James read on, "The angel spoke to the women, 'You must not be afraid,' he said. 'I know you are looking for Jesus, who was crucified. He is not here; He has been raised, just as He said. Come here and see the place where He lay. Go quickly now, and tell His disciples that He has been raised from death, and now He is going to Galilee ahead of you; there you will see Him! Remember what I have told you.' Therefore, they left the tomb in a hurry, afraid, and yet filled with joy, and ran to tell His disciples. Suddenly Jesus met them and said, 'Peace be with you.' They came up to Him, took hold of His feet, and worshipped Him."

Matilda was overjoyed. "I knew it! Jesus loves them so much He let them do just like they did to my Uncle Will, but He still wouldn't leave them."

Will corrected his niece, "What they did to Jesus was much worse. They hit him so many times with a whip that had pieces of metal in it that you couldn't even tell he was a human."

"That's horrible. I wish I could kick those men." She ran over to Will and hugged him. "I'm sorry they did that to Jesus and to you. Can I kick those bad men for you?"

"Honey, remember what Jesus said, 'Forgive them. They don't know what they do.' The person who did this didn't know what he was doing either. Let's forgive him just like Jesus did."

Matilda thought about it. "If Jesus could do it, I guess I can. Can you?"

"I'm trying," he replied truthfully.

Rebecca said, "I guess I should try as well."

216

They rested, talked, and enjoyed the beautiful Easter Day. As the children played, the community continued to get to know each other and discovered that they liked each other.

The first half of the next day, the women and children learned together. Even though they were still weak from starvation and they had to rest often, the men worked side-by-side on the animal shelter. After dinner, they decided that was all the heavy labor they could accomplish for the day.

Matt, Will, and Justin decided to spend the latter part of the day mapping the forest and learning with Nancy. That evening, Abraham looked at the pictures of what they had found in the forest and marked the plants they could gather and sell to Martin.

Thirty Four

They worked on the barn in the morning. After the mid-day meal, Matt said, "Come on, Will and Justin."

Abraham said, "I can go with you too and help you find other things."

Matt looked at Nancy. Nancy loudly declined, "I think we can do fine by ourselves," then whispered to Abraham, "I'll tell you later."

Then, curiosity changed everything. "See you later. Anybody want to go hunting?" Morris, Lewis, and Andrew all went for their saddles. Abraham knew which section of the forest Nancy would search, and he wanted to know their secret. As they rode away, Noah explained, "If you want to find out what somebody is doing, and you know where they're going, get there first, and hide. Let's move quickly and find out what they don't want us to know."

Morris agreed, "All right, I doubt they want to find out what's in the forest so badly that they have to go every day. I think they're up to something."

The four men found a high knoll that gave them a view of a large part of section G7 where there was a low waterfall in a narrow stream of water. He knew Nancy would stop to eat at this kind of place.

Andrew whispered, "Here they come."

Just as Abraham had assumed, Nancy said, "Let's

stop here." They got off their mules. Nancy got out five binders, five pencils, and several sheets of paper. She opened a binder, looked inside, then passed it to Justin. She did the same with the next binder and handed it to Matt. The third binder she moved to the bottom of the stack, handed the next to Will, then the next to Theo. Nancy put a blanket on the ground, they all sat down, and then she passed out the food.

Justin said, "What letter comes after F?"

"After F is G. You make it like this." She wrote the letter G then Matt, Justin, and Will copied it.

Between bites of food, Matt repeated, "G," and wrote the letter repeatedly.

As they practiced the letter G, Will asked, "What sound does this one make?"

"You remember this word?" Nancy pointed to a word on several of the pages.

"That's green, but it starts with a different letter."

"Every letter has an upper-case and a lower-case. This is the same letter, but lower-case."

Justin stated with assurance, "So it makes the sound." He made the first sound of the word 'green.'

Andrew whispered to Abraham, "I want to learn too. All the children and women are learning. Matt, Will, and Justin are learning, Morris already knows. It will be only me and Lewis, who don't know."

Morris offered, "I'll teach you if you want me too."

"I do, but don't tell Grace."

Lewis stated, "I'm not going to be the only one who doesn't know how to read or write."

Abraham told them, "You don't really have to hide to learn."

Andrew explained, "Yes, I do. Maybe I can't learn."

Morris replied, "Andrew, you're a very smart man. You'll be able to learn, but I'll teach you the same way Nancy is teaching them. Out here, just the three of us, making a map, but we'll make ours about where to find animals."

"Thank you, Morris." Andrew felt good; Morris thought he was a very smart man.

That night, Abraham made another set of drawings like the set he had created for Martin and then gave it to Nancy so that Matt, Will, and Justin could make copies. "Morris is going to be doing the same thing with Lewis and Andrew: hiding in the woods to learn because they're afraid they can't, and somebody will find out."

"Are you like that?" Nancy asked.

"Maybe about certain things."

Matilda, Matt's youngest daughter, hurried over to Abraham. "Come look. It's horrible."

Abraham thought, what happened now?

"It's huge." She led him to whatever was horrible. Nancy followed.

Abraham looked at the dead body. "I thought so."

Matt asked, "Am I all right now?"

"You're not parasite-free yet. There are eggs still in there that will hatch. You have to keep taking the medicine to kill them, and there may be more adults."

Matilda ran off to get everybody else to come and look. In a few minutes, everybody stood around the dead tapeworm.

"Should we measure it?' Justin stared with fascination at the very long but flat creature.

Matilda ordered him, "It's in his poop. Don't touch it." It was too late. Justin was already stretching it out.

Morris said, "Probably ten feet."

Matt measured the creature that had left his body by stepping toe to heel beside it.

Abraham told Matt the bad news, "There's no mouth at either end. This isn't all of it. It shed part of its body, but part is still holding on inside you. Keep taking the medicine until you see the mouth. Until you pass the whole tapeworm, keep eating plenty of eggs and crayfish, so the parasite doesn't sicken you as it dies."

Matilda exclaimed, "Paw, you can't be that long inside. How did you do it?"

Matt picked up his little daughter. "Next time we kill an animal, I'll show you how long we are inside."

"You promise to show me?"

"I promise."

Matt's other young children, Elijah, Elizabeth, and Agnes didn't want to be left out. Elizabeth informed her father, "We want to see too."

Thirty Five

It had been twelve days since James had driven the wagon with bad brakes over the cliff. He was able to sit and stay awake all day with only willow tea, so he decided it was time to tan coyote hides, the hide and intestines of the elk that Lily and Abraham had shot at Pine Bluff, and the elk hide William had shot with the Lefaucheux revolver.

Andrew and Abraham finished the cradleboard. Andrew demonstrated how to use it. He picked up John, hugged him, and kissed him. He told Grace, "Lay John, bundled tightly in his blanket, onto the cradleboard. I packed it with moss, so it's soft. Pull these straps tight to hold him in. You can pull these legs out to prop him up, or put them in and wear it like this." He put the contraption on his back. "You want to try it?"

Grace told him, "This is really nice. Put it on me."

Andrew adjusted the straps to fit Grace and helped her put it on. "Do you like it?"

Grace was thrilled. "I love it. I feel like I'm free. Thank you, honey."

The next day, Grace asked Marie, "Show me how to milk Snowflake."

Marie demonstrated how to squeeze the teat from the top to the bottom. Grace said, "I used to eat goat
222

cheese. You wouldn't know how to make it, would you?"

Before her mother had died, they had made cheese every year. "I do. We can make cheese and butter. Let's milk all the goats and try to make some." Twelve hours later, they added milk from the evening's milking to the morning's batch and then heated four gallons of goat milk to start the butter and cheese.

Justin strolled over to Nancy. "I was wondering if you would give me special lessons."

Nancy thought it was unusual for him to change his mind. "I'm glad to help you. I thought you didn't want anybody to know that you're learning."

"I don't. I want it to be just me and you."

"Here in camp, I will."

"That's fine. I'll come over after the others have gone to sleep."

"What is that you want to learn?" Nancy asked.

"Arithmetic."

"All right. I'll be awake at the fire."

Justin came every night to learn how numbers work but mostly, to be next to Nancy. He talked to her about being there in the middle of nowhere. He told her about what he wished for his life. Nancy told him that she as well wished her life was not hiding in the forest or going to live in the west far away from everybody on the planet, even though she did very much want to be with her family.

Nancy had an idea. "You can leave with us."

Justin whispered, "It would be nice to be around you."

"You want to be around me?" Nancy wanted somebody to want her.

Justin replied, "Yes," as he sat beside Nancy and looked into her eyes. Nancy got up and walked away. She was afraid to make her heart available.

Carmen stood in the cabin and watched Justin sit next to Nancy, doing something on paper. Tonight, he had held her hand. Carmen turned away. She didn't want to see what would come next. She didn't see Nancy walk away.

Carmen lay in her bed. How am I going to make Justin love me? She thought she needed to know what Nancy, Theo, Justin, Will, and Matt were doing in the forest and decided to follow them. Shortly after the sun was up, Nancy and Theo rode directly into the rising sun, followed by Carmen on foot. Abraham, along with Morris, Lewis, and Andrew, went out to execute their own plan.

Katie and Lily innocently went to get maple sap. Katie poured maple sap from the bucket into one of the India rubber canteens and said, "She would have been ten today. She would have loved to make maple sugar."

Lily understood how much you miss the ones you love, who have passed on. Lily hugged Katie. "I know how you feel, and I'm very sorry about Ann. I wished we had gotten here sooner. We never stop thinking about those we've lost or stop loving them."

Katie didn't think Lily understood. "Thank you for saying so, but you don't really know how it feels."

"I lost both of my parents a few years ago."

"They were your parents. Ann was my child." Katie

wept bitterly as she thought of the daughter she would never hold in her arms again.

"I know it hurts. Every day there is an empty place in your heart, and three years later, it's still there. I know there are things inside you that you didn't resolve with them, and you will never get a chance to change it. I know that in the midst of that pain, you can also have happiness and joy." They stood in the maple grove. Katie held onto Lily as she cried out her loss.

When her heart had returned to a place of manageable sorrow, and her tears had subsided, Katie said, "Thank you. May she look down on you from Heaven and keep you safe."

As they rode back home, Lily brought up the subject Katie had mentioned going home from the beehive. The three sisters had decided to follow her advice if they could. "I wonder if any of you have extra dresses we could buy or trade. Maybe we have something you would like."

"Ann's dresses might be able to be altered to make one dress that would fit you. We would have to cut them apart and use the material of all four dresses."

"How much can I pay you for them?"

"I'll help you make the new dress. That way, I'll help make Ann's life continue in your dress. That will be pay enough."

"If you change your mind, I'll be happy to pay for the dresses and your time."

Thirty Six

Morris knew Will planned to ask to go to the beehive. He wanted to have their papers out, so Matt, Will, and Justin would find them learning. Then maybe he could continue teaching them after Nancy left. He told nobody about his plan. "Abraham, can we go look at the beehive?"

"I've been wondering if the bees got back into the log. I heard you talking about the lower springs. That would be a good place to look for wildlife. How close is it to the beehive?"

Lewis answered for Morris, "It's close enough to go there in the morning and get to the beehive by noon."

"To be healthy, you have to eat fat. The early spring and the fall are the best time to hunt bears for fat. You have to find them quickly in the spring because they use up their fat looking for food. Geese and ducks are also good for fat, and they'll be going north soon."

Lewis remarked, "I've seen the sky completely full of those white geese."

"Maybe they'll come through before we leave." Abraham hoped they would because Lily, Marie, and Nancy loved roasted goose.

Will walked over to Nancy. "I want to map the North Slope and look at the beehive again."

"All right. So we know these sections are on the

north side, let's name these sections with lower-case letters. Just east of the cabins, the sections would be in which range?"

"I think it would be two," Matt answered.

Justin rode close to Nancy. "If I guess which section has the beehive, can I win a kiss?"

"I'm not a game," Nancy replied with a smile.

Loudly, Justin said, "Just asking. I think the beehive is in lower-case d2. What do you think?"

William guessed, "It's going to be in two, but I think it's in section e."

Theo guessed and suggested, "I think it's at the corner of four sections because it would be a good marker to designate the division of sections. It will probably be at the corner of d4, d5, e4, and e5."

Matt rode up closer. "So, let's ride east about the same distance as from the creek to home and look for a landmark. Then, we can turn north."

At a tree that had fallen and then ran horizontally for some ways before it turned and grew toward the sky again, making a great bench and obvious landmark, they stopped and made a sheet for sections a1 and a2. Nancy showed them how to write living, fallen tree. They already knew how to read and write: cabins, green, yellow, purple, white, tree, rock, creek, dandelion, chickweed, onion, grass, dead, and nettle, and a lot of small words like: I, a, the, to, and, ride, north, south, east and west.

Will wrote, a2 - RIDE EAST FROM CABINS TO THE FALLEN LIVING TREE. "Is this right?"

His brother Matt read what he thought was on the

paper. "I think it is. You wrote, 'Ride east from cabins to the fallen living tree.'"

Theo looked. "Yes, you did! Very good!"

"This isn't too hard," Will remarked.

Justin said, "It helps that you're writing and reading something that's meaningful."

On the page, they wrote chickweed, which was on every page along with dandelions. They rode east and came to a landmark. They stopped, sat on their mules, and made new pages in their binders for a3 and a4. Even though it wasn't quite as far as the other sections, they decided to make the trail up to the lower springs the division between a4 and a5. As they rod the trail and passed each section's landmark, they made pages for the 4th and 5th sections from b up to d. The springs were on the west side in section d4. They rode back west for several yards to get there. The springs were already in use.

Theo whispered, "Halt. This is very good food. Even though Abraham is searching and mapping hunting areas, we shouldn't let this go." Before he could pull out his rifle, Nancy already had out the revolver Abraham had given her to use when she was in the woods. She shot the black bear in its chest, right between its front legs where she believed she would hit its heart. The bear didn't go down. Instead, it reared up and charged. Theo slid his rifle out of the scabbard. Matt, Will, and Justin untied the straps from their rifles as they galloped away from the bear that was coming toward them with a mindful of retaliation. Nancy continued to fire at the bear. Even with all twenty bullets inside, it continued its furious roaring approach.

Justin yelled at her, "Ride away!" He rode in front of her and shot the bear. Justin's round sunk beneath the fur. The bear's roar filled the forest.

Twenty-one shots still did not stop the bear. It was invincible and persisted in its pursuit of Nancy. She wheeled Jumper around and flew away with the bear hot on her heels. "God, help me, and save us all."

Theo, Matt, and Will shot as the mass of fury focused on Nancy charged past them. Its belly and its rump absorbed the lead. It mindlessly chased Nancy as if it didn't already have twenty-four bullets in its body. The men re-loaded and pursued from the rear.

The other group out surveying heard the roaring. Abraham exclaimed, "That's a mad bear." He urged Eyanosa to run toward the bellowing.

Nancy remembered that Abraham had told her bears couldn't run downhill very well. She directed her mule in that direction. Jumper understood that the roaring, charging bear behind meant death, and ran for its life. Nancy gave it complete control to weave between the trees as it chose.

Abraham, Matt, Andrew, and Lewis charged up the hill. They immediately understood the problem. Froth flung from the mouth of a giant, suffering, and furious bear determined to rip Nancy to pieces. It roared its hatred and desire for revenge. As she raced down the hill, Nancy tried to refill the chambers of her revolver. As she bounced, she dropped the rounds.

The bear had too much fat. The rounds weren't reaching its vital organs. Abraham knew how to reach one of them. He drew his knife and rode alongside the bear. He squatted on his feet on his horses back, put his foot against Eyanosa's side, and thought, this is something I would have liked to have tried before Nancy's and my life depended on my success. Great Spirit, help me speak to the bear spirit and grant me permission and success to stop this bear. Just as determined to take a life as the bear was, Abraham sprung from his horse.

The ferocious bear felt something land on its back. It reared onto its hind legs to remove the hindrance as a knife went through its eye. Noah rotated the knife inside the bear's skull and scrambled its brain. The monster fell backward. Abraham started down with it. He pushed off to the side just in time to prevent three hundred pounds of bear from squishing him.

Nancy didn't hear the roaring anymore. She looked back and saw tiny figures on their mules standing around a black lump. She pulled the reins to signal to go right. Jumper didn't hear the bear either, and Nancy was telling it to go right, so it did. They made a half circle and rode back up the hill at much less than their previous break-neck speed. Everybody was thoroughly impressed by Abraham's leap from his horse onto the bear and implantation of his knife into the bear's brain.

Justin explained to Abraham, "We all shot it. That didn't make one little bit of difference."

Morris added, "Except to make it madder."

As Nancy joined them, Justin told her, "You should have seen him."

"I'm sure he did something daring and wonderful." Nancy hugged Abraham.

230

To bring up the point of appearing vulnerable in front of others, Abraham purposefully said, "That was something I wish I didn't have to do for the first time with everybody watching me, and your life depending on my success. Not to mention my own life."

Nancy turned to Justin, put her arms around him, and laid her head against his shoulder. "You tried to put yourself between that bear and me. You were very brave. Thank you."

Justin returned the hug. "You're welcome."

Nancy stepped away after a few seconds. "What happened?" she asked. "Why didn't I kill it? I shot it right in the heart twenty times."

Abraham wasn't sure. "Let's get him home and find out." Eyanosa had previously had a monster on his back when he had carried a large, dead alligator from the Cypress Swamp to Cadron Creek. He didn't like the heavy bear, but he let Abraham, Morris, Lewis, and Andrew raise the bear by its legs while Will, Theo, and Justin held up its belly and slipped it on from the rear. They canceled their plans to go to the beehive and took the bear home.

Justin whispered into Nancy's ear, "I guess I'll have to win that kiss another day."

"I think you already did," she replied.

Nancy was a very sweet and beautiful girl. Right then, the whole group was together, so he couldn't receive his reward. Justin looked forward to that kiss.

Thirty Seven

When they arrived at their little community, everybody was outside. The maple sap cooked over the fire while they practiced writing. Matilda was the first to see them coming. She jumped up. "They have something."

Everybody turned to look at the large black mass that rode on Eyanosa. When the people returning got close enough, those at home could see that they had a dead bear. Matilda reminded her father, "Paw, don't forget, you promised to show me how long we are inside."

"When we butcher it, you can watch and find out."

The men went inside their cabins and got the butcher boards they had made when they cut up the elk. They tried to leave all the fat attached to the carcass as they skinned the bear.

Abraham knew Matt was under orders from his daughter to show her the inside of an animal. After the hide came off, with the feet and the head still attached, Abraham said, "Matt, cut open the bear's belly."

With Matilda close beside him, Matt slit the bear open. Its intestines spilled out. Elijah said, "So that's how we got to be so long inside."

As if she had known all along, Matilda stated, "Of course, that's how. You didn't think we were longer inside than outside, did you?"

They already knew about back straps, so Morris and Lewis cut them out as Abraham removed the scent glands and Andrew cut off slabs of the precious fat.

Abraham directed them, "Cut the fat into small pieces." He examined the bear's chest, found all twenty-four rounds, and discovered not one had penetrated through the fat and muscle and gone into a vital organ. "Here's the reason why you couldn't kill it."

Nancy said, "Something's wrong. If this revolver is able to shoot a bullet through a wooden shutter, it should have been able to go further into that bear."

Andrew stated what they had all realized, "We all need to work on our guns. I agree with Nancy; the rounds should have gone deeper."

Everybody worked on butchering the bear. Some cut the fat into half-inch pieces. Others cut off the silver skin then cut the meat into cubes, slabs, or strips. The upper part of the legs they left whole to smoke like a ham. They ground bear fat and the scrap pieces of meat in a meat grinder with spices, using one of Theo's recipes.

When they had all the fat cut into small pieces, they added a small amount of water and a lot of the fat into their cast iron pots. Abraham explained the next step, "The fat needs to melt slowly. Put the pots beside the fire cooking the maple sap."

It took six hours to melt the first batch of fat. "Strain the liquid through your cheesecloth into your jars and keep the cracklings."

Since the whole community prepared and ate every meal together since their guests had been there, all the women learned how to make Theo's barbeque ribs as they made several pans of barbequed bear ribs to take into their cabins to cook while they melted another batch of fat in the pots around the fire.

Nancy reminisced, "I remember Mama put pig cracklings into cornbread."

Lily said, "Let's make some with these bear cracklings."

Katie told them, "I'm also going to make some."

Then, all the women decided to make bear crackling cornbread.

Much to the unhappiness of Matilda, everybody old enough was asked to clean a portion of intestines. She insisted she was one of the babies and couldn't. Lily, Marie, and Nancy did help, even though they had vowed that they would never again clean intestines.

When the bear guts were completely clean, with the outer and inner membranes removed, they stuffed them with the spiced, ground bear meat and rendered fat. They tied off the end, stuffed a section, and made another knot to end that section, then another knot to start the next section until they had long strings of bear meat sausages.

They marinated other pieces of meat in vinegar and different spices and made pickled bear meat cubes. In the smoke from the fire cooking the maple sap, on the racks they had built when they'd smoked the elk, they hung the bear sausages, the four bear leg hams, as well as slabs of bear bacon. While the meat hung in the maple-sap-laden smoke, they ate barbeque bear ribs, bear cracklings cornbread, and dandelions cooked with amaranth leaves.

234

Morris reached for a piece of cornbread. "I think we should build a smokehouse."

"We already have so much to do," Andrew remarked.

Lewis ignored him and asked, "Can you draw us a diagram that shows how to make a smokehouse?"

James answered, "One of us will before we leave."

Matt shared his idea, "I think we need to plant. We can explore more or build a smokehouse later." He brought this up because he hoped they could use Theo's mules to plow a large plot for a vegetable garden, and the many small fields in the valley around them to plant their cash crops. "Can we use your mules to plow?"

Theo wanted to know how many mules they would need. "How many plows do you have?"

"Only four."

Nancy remembered how much it had meant to her when the people of Harmony had come to help them plow and plant the previous spring. She quickly said, "I'll plow for you."

For the same reason, and because they had plowed their fields with their father for years and knew how it should be done, Lily told them, "We'll plow. You keep learning what's around you."

Because he wanted to learn as much about how to read and write as he could, Matt said, "But we won't have Nancy. She needs to go with us."

"You can go with Theo," his wife Sarah told him.

Matt insisted, "We need Nancy."

Sarah didn't like Matt insisting he had to have another woman around. "And just why do you need to have that woman with you, Matt?"

Matt immediately realized his mistake, but he had promised Will and Justin he wouldn't tell anybody what they were doing. "I'm not telling you. Just trust me."

"Matthew, you had better tell me what's going on this very instant."

Rebecca thought, "Will is out there with them." She fixed her glare on him.

Will felt her eyes boring holes into him. "What?"

"What are you doing out there?" Rebecca asked.

Justin gave his permission to spill the beans, "We better just tell them, Paw."

With much irritation that his wife didn't trust him, Matt stated, "Since you have to know, Nancy is teaching us how to read and write."

Sarah questioned her husband, "Why on Earth would you think you have to hide that from us?"

Matt explained, "Because I didn't know if I would be able to do it."

"Since you're insisting that she continue to teach you, I guess you've been able."

"Want me to show you?" Matt was proud of what he had learned.

"I would love it, and I'm sorry I thought you were doing anything wrong."

Matilda said, "Paw, show me too."

"All right."

Nancy had already looked through her pack and found Matt's binder. She handed it over. Matt said, "I know every letter and its sound. I know both the upper and lower-case." He wrote them each as he said their names and the sound they make.

"Paw, can you help me make mine?" Agnes asked.

"I would love to help you, honey." Matt looked back at his paper.

"These are whole words I know." He wrote all the words he knew as he said them.

"What about you?" Rebecca asked her husband.

Nancy handed him his binder and then gave Justin his. While Will showed Rebecca what he knew, Justin joined in with his father and showed his family all his pages as he read them.

"I have a confession," Lewis told them.

"What?" Fannie asked.

"I saw what they were doing, so I asked Morris to teach me."

Andrew joined them. "Since everybody else has revealed that they're learning, I am too." Abraham handed over the binders that he had been concealing.

Grace said, "I think we'll have a one-hundred-percent literacy rate in this town."

"We aren't a town," Sarah pointed out.

Grace felt proud of them all. "Why not? Someday, we'll have even more people than we do now, and they'll say, 'Everybody who started this town could read and write.'"

Fannie said, "I'll show you what I've learned." Marie gave her paper and a pencil. They all showed each other what they could do, including the children.

As they stood side by side, looking at the people of Fletcher Creek, Lily whispered, "Isn't that beautiful?"

"Yes, it is!" Marie replied.

Nancy hadn't said anything. They looked around.

"Where's Nancy?" Marie asked.

"Justin isn't here, either," Lily replied.

While they were eating, Nancy had told them how Justin had tried to protect her from the bear. The sisters had an idea why Nancy and Justin were gone. Marie took Lily's hand. "Let's go find them."

Lily said, "I don't think we should draw attention to this. We need to leave camp quietly."

"I think I know where they might be." Marie walked toward the creek with Lily beside her. They saw the two standing together as one.

Marie talked loudly to be sure Nancy and Justin heard them before they came into view. The two kissing in the light of the rising moon heard and moved apart.

"What are you doing out here?" Nancy asked.

Marie said, "Just enjoying a walk." Protecting you from yourself. I know your heart aches from losing Melvin, and Justin just risked his life for you.

Lily politely ordered them to return home, "It's possible that there are coyotes out here. The other pack wasn't that far from here. You two should come back home." None of them made any comment about their rendezvous in the night, but they all knew that everyone knew why they were all there.

When they arrived back at camp, Matt questioned his son sharply, "Where have you been?"

Before anybody could answer, Lily said, "We had to get out of the smoke and breathe some fresh air."

Matt ordered his son, "Tell us before you go off like that. Your mother was scared to death."

Justin quickly said, "Yes, sir," but he didn't like

238

being ordered to report to his parents in front of everybody, especially in front of Nancy. I'm old enough to know what I'm doing.

They rejoined the group and made plans for the days ahead. Abraham wanted his friends at Fletcher Creek to be able to help his friends in Little Rock. He decided to verify that they had everything right. "Which are the plants you can sell to Martin in Little Rock, and where will you find them?" They all knew the plants, showed Abraham each picture, and explained everything they knew about the plant. They assigned the task to Morris because he could read, write, and cipher numbers.

Abraham said, "I think you're ready."

Thirty Eight

The plan was formulated for Morris, his son George, and his brother Lewis, to make the trip to Little Rock on May 3rd. That would give them time to collect plants and be in Little Rock on the first Monday in May. Since they hadn't recently been starving, Nancy, Lily, Marie, and Abraham planned to plow the fields, starting with the vegetable plot. The women and older children's task would be to plant the vegetable seeds. Theo, Andrew, Will, and Matt were to plant corn and cottonseeds. Grace would be responsible for all of the young children. James would help her by also watching the children and notifying Grace if any of them did something they shouldn't be doing.

The following day, as they prepared to plow, they heard a sound rising from the south. Elizabeth asked, "What's that, Paw?"

Matt looked at Abraham. "It almost sounds like a pack of dogs."

Morris cocked his head to hear better. "I hear honking, like geese."

Abraham looked into the sky. "If that flock of geese is coming this way, you better stuff something in your ears, and get your rifles ready."

The cacophony of sound increased until they could barely hear themselves. In the distance, they saw what

240

looked like a huge thunderhead approaching. It filled the sky and turned it completely white. The lead ganders led an enormous flock to the creek and the open fields ahead. All along Fletcher Creek, they descended to eat the abundant rushes and grasses. Like the snow of the blizzard that had swept across Arkansas in the early spring, tens of thousands of snow geese swirled around them. They could see nothing but white.

As the mass of white descended around them, Morris called out, "Get the children inside." The women hurried all the children, except George, Justin, and Freeman inside. Outside, the adults took advantage of their near inability to miss, due to the sheer numbers of geese that flocked around them. They shot geese on the ground. They shot geese as they took flight and as they landed. The deafening sound of thousands of geese prevented the small sounds of the rifles from traveling beyond the immediate vicinity. The geese nearby rose, only to have others settle down into their places. They repeated the cycle continuously. The people waded through the blanket of white, covering every inch of ground. The geese retreated as they walked among them to pick up the fallen.

Freeman hollered, "I feel like Moses parting the Red Sea, only this is a white sea."

As he walked through his own sea of geese that moved aside, Matt told his second oldest son, "It sure does seem like that." They gathered the bodies and piled them in the empty wagon.

Nancy told James, "I doubt if we're even going to find them all. I don't even know how many I've shot."

James replied, "Me neither, but I can't go get any, and I have to stop shooting. It's making me hurt."

Concerned that her husband would go back to his previous level of pain, Marie told him, "Stop shooting. I'll go look for them."

"Thank you, honey." James kissed her.

Marie looked at Nancy then Lily. "Let's go together."

Lily nodded her head. She was happy that the three of them were a team again. They all felt the same. It had been difficult to work separately. The way they did things had always been together. Not only did they miss each other, but they also felt awkward and broken without the three of them together.

They slung their rifle straps over their heads and across their chests and then waded together into the field in section A1 to retrieve the geese they had shot. As she carried geese to the wagon, Nancy knew she had made the right decision to go with her family. She couldn't have lived without her sisters. None of them could.

Abraham and Theo worked with Andrew in the fields of section B1. Matt, William, Justin, and Freeman went to the creek in section A1 then went upstream. They stacked their quarry in piles along the creek bank. Morris, Lewis, and George moved along the creek in section a1, going downstream.

Abraham called out, "There's going to be more than we can process. Let's stop shooting and carry home the geese we already have."

Andrew and Theo had come to the same thought.

They also started gathering the fallen. They had only shot the geese inside the field, so they worked from the four sides to the center to bring the geese to a common pile then shifted several yards and searched from the edge to the center again. After repeating the search until they had covered the entire field, they started moving the birds toward home.

Andrew raised a concern, "I wonder if predators will come and try to steal these while we're gone."

"There are so many. I don't think they could steal enough to be a problem," Theo replied.

Abraham suggested, "Let's just carry as many as we can now then come back with a tarp and a carrying stick."

When they got to the wagon, the others had also decided they had shot enough and were bringing the geese home. Theo gave each group a tarp with the stake-down ropes attached. "Find a stick to use as a carrying pole."

Even using that method, they had to make several trips, due to the weight of the plump birds. The wagon held hundreds of geese. When all the hunters were at the wagon, Abraham said, "Everybody, take as many as you can carry home, pluck them, gut them, hang them, then come back and get more. After you're tired, let other members of your family take a turn. We have to get them cleaned as quickly as we can. If you want, keep all the little down feathers to make pillows. It takes about twelve birds to make one."

"We don't have a place to hang them," Andrew informed him.

Theo remembered how the women had strung rope all around the trading post to hang their clothes to dry. "String this rope around inside then tie the feet of two birds together with a piece of this twine and hang them over the rope." He gave each family a rope and a ball of twine.

Morris told his brother, "Lewis, you and Fannie bring Edna and Pearl over to my cabin."

Matt told Will, "Brother, I've got a whole herd in my house. You go work with Andrew."

Andrew said, "That would be nice. Bring Rebecca over to my place. It'll be easier for Grace to stay in our cabin."

Everybody worked through the night to the sound of the honking geese. Elizabeth helped her mother, older brothers, and father. "Paw, can I try to skin some? I want to stuff them and sew them back together."

"If you want to, you can. We certainly have plenty of them for you to try." Her father had given her permission, so she carefully skinned her geese and put aside the skins she liked the best.

"Paw?"

"Yes, Elizabeth?" Matt replied.

"Am I big enough to stay up all night to help while the babies sleep?"

"I'm not a baby!" Agnes and Matilda objected together, now that there was no advantage to being a baby.

Matt looked at his wife. He didn't need to say much. They knew each other. She nodded her head slightly up and down.

Matt put his youngest daughters one on each knee. "You are definitely not babies, but you need to go to bed when your mother tells you." He hugged and kissed them both on the cheek.

"Can I sit here and help you clean one?" Matilda asked.

"Of course."

"Me too. Let me help too," Agnes requested.

Matt put Agnes down. "Right after Matilda because she asked first."

Matilda told her older sister, "I'm first," then stuck out her tongue at Agnes.

Sarah directed Matilda, "Apologize for being mean, or your father won't be letting you help."

Matilda did so because she wanted to help her father. "I'm sorry, Agnes."

Matt told Elizabeth, "You, however, may stay up as long as you want and help."

Elizabeth wanted to clap her hands, but she knew her mother always insisted they be kind and respectful of each other's feelings, so she only clapped inside.

Matt instructed Matilda, "Put your hand on mine right here. You have to hold on tight. Are you ready?"

Matilda placed her hand on the back of Matt's. "I'm ready!"

Matt pulled the feathers off the belly of the bird. That was the easy part. Having to keep Matilda's hand on his to pluck the bird made things much harder, but he had told her she could help and knew it would mean a lot to her to help her father. After all the feathers were off, he took a knife and opened its belly.

"Can I pull out the long part?"

"It's going to be slimy. Are you sure?"

Matilda had decided to be brave enough to touch them and assured him, "I'm sure." She stuck her small hand inside, held onto one part of the intestines, and pulled it out like a very long spaghetti noodle. She kept pulling and pulling until she finally had the whole thing out.

"Is there anything else in there?"

Matt helped her take out each part and told her what it was. "Do we have all these things inside?" Matilda asked.

"We don't have a gizzard, but we have the rest."

When they finally finished removing all the innards, Matt put her down. "Thank you for helping, Matilda. I love you."

"You're welcome, Paw. That one had a horribly long inside. I hope it doesn't have a tapeworm." Her whole family laughed.

"It wouldn't matter, now that it's dead," Freeman informed her.

Sarah had a ten-gallon tub of water ready to wash her daughter, who had spread the goose blood and guts pretty well across herself and her father.

Matt held out his hands to Agnes. "You're next, honey." He put her in his lap and again did the difficult task of pulling out the feathers with Agnes sitting in his lap, helping. Elijah and Matilda were already in bed asleep when Agnes was ready for her turn in the bath. Agnes put her blood-covered arms around her father's neck and hugged him. Agnes informed her father. "I'm glad you're our father. Mother picked you out very wisely."

"Thank you, Agnes. I'm glad she picked me out, so I could have all of you as my children."

"I'm ready for my bath now, mother. I think I'm quite a mess." Agnes hopped off her father's lap.

Freeman looked at his father. "Those marks Agnes left on your neck with her arms make you look like your neck's been cut."

Elizabeth got up and got a warm, wet towel. "I'll wipe them off." She cleaned the blood from her father's neck. "She's right, you know. We are lucky that you're our father." She kissed his cheek and sat back down to finish the goose she was plucking.

"Thank you, honey. I don't know how I ever got so blessed." He looked at Sarah. "But I am."

Sarah knew Matt was saying she was the reason he felt blessed. He was a good father and husband, which made her respect and love him more. That was one reason why they had so many children.

Matt said, "Justin, get more geese."

Justin only heard an order to comply. "I'm going." He forcefully chopped through the neck of the goose in front of him then went out the door. *He could stop treating me like a child, ordering me around like that.*

In the other cabins, and at the tables outside, everybody was doing the same by the light of lanterns that burned bear fat oil.

Thirty Nine

Flocks of geese spent a day or so feeding and then continued north, only for more to arrive from the south. The people of Fletcher Creek roasted, smoked, salted, and pickled the brothers and sisters of those swarming around them. Carmen didn't want to learn how to shoot geese, but she did have an objective. While they had thousands of targets, Carmen requested, "I need to learn how to shoot. Justin, will you show me how?"

Justin agreed, "Let's all go to the creek and shoot geese."

Nancy, Justin, George, Freeman, and Carmen had become friends and did most things together, so Nancy suggested an alternative. "If we go to one of the fields, we'll get a clear shot."

Freeman thought that was a good idea. "I agree. Let's go to the field."

George carried his rifle. Nancy had the Lefaucheux revolver, just in case, but brought her bow to practice shooting geese. When they got to the field, Carmen asked for help again, "Justin, show me how to aim."

Justin stood beside Carmen. He showed her how to aim, hold the rifle, and breathe when shooting. "Go ahead and try again."

They all aimed at the constant swirling mass of geese taking flight or landing at the other end of the
248

field. Carmen squeezed the trigger as Nancy released her nocked arrow. Nancy missed. Carmen missed. The two victims of George and Freeman dropped into the field. They reloaded and shot again. Two more dropped. The sky was so full, they didn't have to aim to hit a bird.

It was a wonder how Carmen continued to miss and need more instructions. "Show me again."

Justin explained and helped her shoot, repeatedly. Carmen totally monopolized Justin. Freeman rolled his eyes. He, George, and Nancy knew what Carmen was doing. She was focusing Justin on herself. Freeman told his brother, "Justin, let her miss. Shoot some geese."

"Carmen needs my help. I don't need practice." Carmen drew Justin in. He knew none of the others needed him, but Carmen did.

The boys didn't plan to carry any home, just to take advantage of an opportunity to practice hitting a moving target while Nancy practiced hitting a sitting goose. When she was successful, she tried hitting one farther away. Each time her quiver was empty, she went to gather her arrows, which mostly were not in a goose. "I'm in the field," she called out before she made another trip to gather arrows.

Nancy looked at all the dead geese they were going to leave on the ground. Abraham wouldn't like it. "Justin, will you walk home with me?"

Since they were no longer shooting geese, and Carmen didn't need him anymore, he replied, "I'd love to, Nancy."

Justin put his arm around Nancy's waist, so she

slipped her arm around him. "We need to carry them home," she told him.

"Why? We already have enough."

"It's wasteful and disrespectful to nature. I wish we hadn't done it."

"You're making a big deal of nothing. I'll help you get them if you feel you really need them, but you'll have to do what you want with them yourself." Justin thought, what an idiotic idea.

Carmen voiced her alignment with Justin's opinion, in order to point out that Nancy was not in agreement with him. "I agree with you, Justin. We don't need them. I'm not going to help carry them."

Abraham saw Nancy and Justin get a tarp and pole, so he followed them. Dozens of dead geese lay among the live birds. He watched to see what they would do. They gathered up the dead.

"I think we found them all," Justin told her.

Nancy made a suggestion since she didn't want Abraham to know they had wastefully taken so many lives. "We don't need them. It would be more respectful if we buried them than just leaving them in the field to rot."

Justin refused, "I'm not digging a hole big enough to bury all these geese."

Nancy decided she would confess and face the consequences. "Let's take them home."

Abraham hurried home to be there before they arrived. When they got there, Nancy went directly to Abraham. "I've done something wrong, and I want to apologize to you and nature."

250

Justin stood silently. She's making a big deal over nothing.

"What did you do, Nancy?" Abraham asked as if he didn't know.

"I allowed my friends to slaughter dozens of geese, and I participated."

"Why?"

"We were using them for target practice."

"Did your skills improve?"

Justin informed Abraham, "Mine didn't because I only shot one of them. I'm not guilty."

"I think my ability to hit a sitting goose with an arrow improved, but that's not a good enough reason. I don't know if George and Freeman got any better. Carmen can't hit a barn right in front of her. What can I do to make it right?"

Justin defended Carmen, "You didn't have to say that about Carmen. Just because she's not like you, who can do everything under the sun and doesn't need anybody, that doesn't mean you have to talk about her like that. She was trying to learn."

Nancy snapped back, "The only thing she was trying to do was keep you away from me!" She saw the realization spread across Justin's face. "You're right, Justin. I'm sorry."

Lily had been sitting beside Abraham when Nancy had confessed. She gave her opinion, "We don't need any more goose meat."

Abraham said, "Pluck the birds, get all the down, the skin, and all the fat. Don't let any of the meat get in with the skin and fat. You can render goose fat."

251

Justin said sarcastically, "I hope that makes you feel better." He walked away.

Abraham stood up to tell him to get back over there and help, but Nancy put her hand on his arm. "I'll feel better if I do it myself. It's my conscious that's convicted not his."

When they woke in the morning, Nancy was still plucking geese. She had all the down in a bag and a large amount of skin and fat in one pile on the table and breast fillets and legs in another. "I'm going to help her," Lily told Abraham.

Abraham replied, "If you want her to forgive herself, you won't."

Freeman came outside in the morning and saw Nancy sitting at the table with feathers attached everywhere by the sticky fat. "What are you doing?"

"I'm making amends for killing these geese for reasons other than food," she explained.

Freeman unknowingly said what she should have known and what Abraham had tried to get her to realize. "Wouldn't target practice be necessary, so you can shoot your food in the future?"

Nancy thought about that. "I can practice shooting at a target."

Freeman continued on his train of reasoning, "But not a moving one."

"Freeman, you're a smart person. I like you. But I'm still going to finish what I'm doing." Nancy appreciated that he saw what she hadn't.

"I shot some too. I'll help. What are you doing?"

Nancy explained, "We really only needed to get the

fat and skin, so we can render the fat like we did with the bear. I hate to lose all the meat, but there is only so much space, so I thought I could salt the breast fillets and legs and then wrap them in a cloth. I'm going to add the down to my feather pillow."

The two of them were plucking geese when Justin came out. He walked over to Morris's cabin and knocked. Even though Carmen was sitting in the small cabin looking right at him, he loudly asked, "May I speak with Carmen?" She walked over to him. "Carmen, I want to teach you how to shoot a rifle. Do you want to learn?"

Carmen didn't know what had happened, but she was thrilled. "Pa, can I use the rifle again?"

Morris told him, "Be careful with my daughter, Justin."

"Sir, I promise I will very carefully protect Carmen." Holding Carmen's hand, he walked back over to his cabin and opened the door. In an even louder voice, he said, "Maw, since I have to report everything I do to you and father, I'm telling you, I'm taking Carmen out to shoot geese, so she can learn how to shoot a rifle." He closed the door and escorted Carmen away.

Freeman looked at Nancy. Nancy told him, "I don't care what he does anyway."

Inside the cabin, Sarah asked Matt, "What was that about?"

"I'm not sure, but I'll try to find out," Matt replied.

Lily asked Nancy, "May I have the wings?"

"You can have any of it you want. What are you going to do?"

"I'm going to make a collar."

Freeman wondered how she would make a collar. "How are you going to make it?"

"I thought I could cut a piece of buckskin that would fit like a collar about eight-inches-wide all the way around then sew a wing to it starting at one side and then overlap the bone with the next one, keeping the bone ends close and spreading them out at the primary feathers."

Justin stood beside Carmen with his arms around her to help her hold the rifle. He asked, "Were you trying to get me to pay attention to you yesterday?"

Carmen wasn't sure if she should say yes or no but decided it was always best to tell the truth. "Yes, Justin, I was."

"I'm sorry I wasn't observant. I think my eyes are open now, and they see you."

Over a hundred geese still needed to be preserved. They built several fires to get as many as possible into the smoke. A very large column of smoke rose out of the forest. It looked as if they might start a forest fire. They decided they did need to build a smokehouse when they had the time.

When all the geese were north for the year, they had left behind fields deep in goose dropping. Lily, Marie, Nancy, and Abraham each harnessed a mule to a plow and turned over the rich forest soil and goose droppings.

Abraham told Morris, "The fields were well fertilized by the geese. Do the same next year. Wait until after the geese migrate to plow."

When the fields were ready, Theo, Andrew, Lewis, Freeman, and George planted corn and cottonseeds. Meanwhile, Abraham, Matt, Will, Justin, and Morris searched for plants to sell to Martin Harrow.

After they planted the fields, Abraham, Lily, Marie, and Nancy decided to build the smokehouse and let Theo lead the forest exploration. Abraham and Lily cut cedar trees the same way they had when they had built the Cadron Ferry.

Abraham asked Lily, "Does it seem as hard to cut these trees as it did at Cadron Creek?"

"I still get tired, but I don't feel miserable."

"Me too. It's because I can do this." He walked over to Lily, took her into his arms, and gave her a long kiss.

Lily replied, "That certainly changes how I feel about everything, but I think we should test your theory again."

"I think so too, my wife." With another kiss, Abraham again tested then confirmed. "That definitely changes how I feel about everything."

They went back to sawing the tree. "My husband, it's too crowded around our camp all the time. We could start making the trip up the creek to look for travelers."

"I agree. I'll talk to Theo and get him to show me the procedure."

As they felled the trees, other people used the mules to drag them to the cabins and split them into planks. James saw the growing pile of planks that didn't split correctly. He asked Marie, "Do you think it would be good to teach these people how to make a cart like

255

those we made at Cadron? We could make another one for us as well."

Marie wanted James to heal as well as possible. "I don't want you to do that kind of hard work." She saw the look James was trying to hide. "Not yet, anyway. I'll make ours while you direct us. I mostly remember what we did, but I need you to make sure we do it right."

James knew that Marie never forgot anything she had learned, but she had given him a way to not feel so bad about being mostly useless. "I'll be glad to supervise."

Forty

Over the next weeks, during the mornings, they built the smokehouse, a corral, and carts. In the afternoon, along with their other plans, Abraham and Lily took the trip up the creek to look for people to move safely to the west. Nancy and Theo led literacy training and surveying of the forest with the men. James, Marie, Katie, and Rebecca taught the women and children at the cabins. In the mornings, Justin worked with Carmen on whichever project she was helping to complete, stuck close to her in the afternoon to learn, and avoided Nancy.

April passed. The people of Fletcher Creek learned how to live in the forest. James healed. Lily and Katie made a dress for Lily from Ann's small dresses. When May 3rd approached, James implored Marie, "I feel like I'm trapped here. Please give me parole to go exploring as a birthday present."

"Are you sure you feel up to it?"

James pulled Marie into his arms. "I think we should test how good I feel when everybody leaves today."

"I've been missing you. I'd like that, but not if it hurts you."

"I'm sure I'll be fine." After a month of waiting for his chest, ribs, and back to heal enough to be able to move, James didn't care if it hurt a little.

"I want Abraham and Lily to explore with us. If a giant bear or something attacks, we'll need help."

"That's fine with me. I want to see the beehive and the lower springs. If we have time, and I still feel good enough, we could try to find the upper springs."

"I'll ask them if they want to go." Marie went to find the rest of her family before they left for the day. Nancy and Theo said they had seen the beehive and lower springs enough and would skip the trip that day. Abraham and Lily agreed to go exploring, as long as James would tell them if he started to hurt, so they could go home. Because birthdates make it easier to identify a person, Nancy and Theo planned to secretly bake one of Theo's delicious birthday cakes and then serve it when they were all alone in the tent.

On James' birthday, Morris, Lewis, and George left for Little Rock after breakfast.

Abraham wanted to fill the day with something special for his brother-in-law. "James, you want to go a new way to the lower springs?"

"You mean something nobody else has done yet?" James asked.

"Exactly. We could go straight north from here then ride east along the ridge to the springs and the beehive."

"Let's take our binders, so we can map what we find." James was happy to not only do what the others had already done but also to go into a new area and still get to see the lower springs and the beehive. The four packed dinner, canteens of water, paper, pencils, erasers, spy glasses, bags for plants, a few sheets of duck cloth, and blankets to sit on when they ate their mid-day meal. Abraham had sheets of paper already labeled for the path he planned to take. a2, b2, c2, d2, d3, and d4

James excitedly told Theo and Nancy, "See you when we get back!"

As they rode away, James disclosed what he thought was a gift he had received the previous year. "When I first came to the farm, I hadn't been anywhere except to get supplies with Pop, and we never left the road or looked around much. The world is such an interesting place. I can't imagine going somewhere and not trying to see everything. I have you three and Nancy to thank for giving that to me."

Stephanie took the credit. "I'm glad you're happy I did that, darling."

Lily knew she was the one who had introduced James to exploring, but it didn't matter. They looked as far as they could see with the spyglasses then talked about and notated what was in each section.

Abraham sat up tall and pointed. "It looks like wild grapes over there." They rode to the vines strung from tree to tree and then marked the location on sheet c2. "The grapes won't be ripe until August."

They went on. On the ridge, in section d2, they found a rock outcropping. James stopped Ace. "I want to climb up there and see what we can see."

James seems to be doing fine. "Sure," Abraham agreed. Lily jumped down from her mule. She and Marie followed them to the top where they sat on the rocks and looked down at the cabins with their spyglasses.

Marie said, "I can see somebody walking to the wagon."

"They're so tiny," Lily observed.

Abraham turned and looked into the valley on the other side of the ridge. "This is a great observation place. We have to tell everybody about it."

After six weeks of thinking seriously about herself, Marie wondered if anybody else felt like she did. "Do any of you feel different?"

"Different than what?" Lily asked.

"Different than yourself." Marie explained, "I felt different back on the farm. I felt like a child. Even though I worried, the farm somehow helped me feel like things would be all right. Now, I feel like I'm floating in the wind, going wherever circumstances take me. It leaves me feeling... I don't know... maybe unsettled and agitated. Wherever I go, there will be consequences, and I don't know if I'll be able to handle them."

"I don't feel like the same person who lived in my father's store. I was so naïve, but I didn't worry about anything, and I was happy. Now, I understand so much more. I feel worried too. In some ways, I'm extremely happy, but in some ways, I'm not."

Abraham thought about it and realized he also felt different than he had a year ago. "I felt like I was only a piece, and something was missing. I didn't feel complete. As early as I can remember, I knew the missing parts were not where I lived. I didn't know who I was, but I knew in my village that I wasn't allowed to be what I ought to be. That's why I left. All of you, this family is what I was missing, and now I'm becoming who I am. What about you, my wife?"

"I've always felt like I'm a million different things that I'm trying to figure out how to fit together."

Abraham didn't know that Lily felt un-reconciled with all the aspects of herself. "I want you to know I love and like you exactly the way you are. However, as you're trying to fit everything together for yourself, I'm here for you."

Marie hugged Lily. "Me too. I mean that. I want you to always be one of three sisters that nothing could ever separate. I couldn't live long without you and Nancy, and I'm sorry for being upset with you and Abraham."

"Then the six of us are one, no matter what!" James felt joyful because the tension between Marie and Lily was gone.

"Exactly." Abraham squeezed them all together.

They sat a while longer and looked into the valley below, happy in the moment. They marked the location of the rocks on the map and designated it as the dividing marker for sections d2 and d3, and on the other side of the ridge, e2 and e3.

"We'd better move on." Abraham stood up.

They climbed down the rocks and rode on into section d3, then on to d4 until they were close to the lower springs. Because they didn't want to encounter any bears, they scanned the area carefully before riding down to the water at the bottom of d4. They ate dinner and watched the water flow down the mountain, eventually to join Fletcher Creek. After enjoying the lower springs, they went to the beehive at the far end of section d4.

Marie pointed. "That big tree on the ground had the beehive."

Abraham warned them, "We should approach cautiously. We haven't been back since we took their hive, and we don't know what the bees are doing now." They looked with their spyglasses. Bees swarmed around and covered the smaller nest in the living tree.

Lily reported her observations, "Looks like they're still in their new nest."

They went to the fallen tree, Abraham and Lily put on their gloves, climbed on top, put their hands in the holes at each end, and raised the top. Bees swarmed out. They dropped the lid. It crashed back into place and sent even more bees out to defend their reclaimed nest.

The four invaders made a desperate dash for their mounts and attempted to outrun the angry bees.

When they were far away, Lily called out, "I think we're safe!"

James looked around. "Where are we?"

Abraham said, "I think we went east and up the mountain. Seems like we went pretty far. We're almost back up to the ridge."

"I hear water," Marie told them.

James stated with anticipation, "Must be the upper springs."

"Did any of you get stung?" Lily asked.

Everybody replied, "Yes."

They stopped and counted the bee stings on Eyanosa, Redeemed, Honor, Ace, and themselves.

"Three on me," Marie stated.

"Only one," James informed them.

Abraham said, "I have a lot."

Lily told them, "Me too. I guess they got us more because we were the one's removing their roof."

"James, did that mad dash away from the beehive hurt you?" asked Marie.

"Jumping on Ace made my ankle hurt."

"Should we go home?"

"Let's look at the springs first."

Forty One

The four of them looked at the overgrown pool full of leaves. Abraham cut four branches from the trees to use to clean it out.

Marie said, "It doesn't look good for drinking."

Lily watched pollywogs swim in the water turned dark brown by the tannin of the leaves and by the sediments that they had stirred up. "I assure you that I'm not going to drink any."

James squatted and peered into the water. "It's not much to look at. It's rather disappointing."

"I agree. Are you ready to go home?" Abraham asked.

James said, "I am. We can map as we go home and try to determine what section this should be." James pointed at something in the water. "What do you think that is?"

Lily tried to use her branch to seize the slightly glittery object. The other two came back over. "Can you get it?" Marie asked.

"It's heavy." Lily tried to raise it.

Abraham joined the retrieval attempt. "James, let's me and you try to get our branches under it. Lily and Marie, you push it onto our branches then try to hold it on."

The branches snapped when they tried to raise the

264

long object. James told them, "We need stronger branches." They got much stronger branches and tried again. Unfortunately, they couldn't keep them level. The object slid back into the murky water.

"I think it's something man-made." Marie tried again to snag the object at the bottom of the pool.

"Abraham." Lily pointed. "Try to put the smaller stick into that hole to help hold it."

As they started to raise the mysterious item up, Abraham slid a thin stick into the loop at the end of the long, slender object.

"Got it!" They carefully backed away from the pool with the bumpy brown object. When they had it over the land, they lowered it and gathered close to examine their find.

"I think it's a very old sword." James held it at both ends, dipped it back in the water, and tried to brush the mud and leaves off. A compound hilt protruded from a scabbard.

Marie said, "I would love to see it, but if we try to pull it out, we may break it."

"I bet there's a skeleton in there," James remarked.

They felt around in the muck at the bottom with their sticks until Marie said, "I touched something."

James instructed his wife, "Keep your stick there and let me see if I can feel it from the other side." He jabbed around into the pool. "I feel it too." He tried to dislodge the second artifact from the mud. "Try to dig around it."

Lily dug beside the object, but her stick kept losing it. "It's small. It may be a skull." Lily and Abraham dug around what seemed to be a ball.

James exclaimed, "I think I see a hole! Everybody stop digging and let the mud settle."

An eye socket peered out of the water. Abraham gave his advice, "Like we did with the sword, we'll use the smaller stick to poke into the eyehole." He got the stick. James slid the stick into the eye of the long dead skull, pulled it up, and resurrected it from centuries of rotting leaves. Suddenly, the stick slid out of the eye socket. The skull plopped into the mud. Both eyeholes stared at them.

Lily looked at the empty eye sockets peering at them from the bottom of the pool of brown water. "He looks so creepy."

James told Abraham, "Get another small stick." Abraham hacked a long and slender but strong living branch, then handed it to Marie. James said, "Push toward my stick, and I'll push toward yours."

Marie inserted the stick into the skull's other eye. They returned the skull to the air it hadn't breathed since it had found its place in the pool of the upper springs. Now that they possessed it, Marie told the others, "It'll be perfect with the bone necklace I made."

Abraham commented, "James, you got two very nice birthday presents. Let's take them home and see what we can do to get the sword out."

Lily thought it was curious that Stephanie didn't particularly like Noah's Indian ways and had never made a medicine bag, but now she wanted a human skull and an animal bone necklace.

James carefully wrapped the skull, then handed it to Marie to carry. He wrapped the sword in another

266

square of duck cloth, got on Ace, and put the sword in his lap. They left the upper springs and followed the stream from the spring down the mountain.

At the distance they thought would be one section, they came to a small waterfall. They designated it as a boundary then rode west about as far as they believed would be a section and came to a dry rockslide covered with a large stand of plants.

"Prairie sage!" Abraham exclaimed. "This is just like mugwort." He pulled a pouch with a tobacco plug from his saddlebag. "Mother Earth, I offer tobacco in exchange for this sage." Because sage was so valuable, he crumbled the whole thing and scattered it on the ground. The other three laid out both pieces of duck cloth. "Cut the oldest, tallest plants a few inches from the ground. Lay them all going the same way."

They harvested a very large amount and still left a good patch that would flower in August. Abraham also made sure that every plant they cut still had a root ball in the ground that would grow into a new plant. He wrapped the duck cloths around the plants, folded in the ends, then tied one onto Eyanosa behind his saddle, and put the other behind Lily's saddle. They rode down the mountain another section then went west again and came to the trail to the lower springs.

Lily said, "The lower springs are right over there. We're at the junction of 4 and 5 between c and d."

James calculated, "So, the upper springs are in f7. The ridge is higher there."

Abraham identified the page with the upper springs as f7, and the page with the prairie sage stand as d6. The rest of the ride home, they went through areas already mapped, so they didn't bother documenting anything and just enjoyed the ride through the forest. They got back home in time for supper. While they ate, they told the others about the new sections they had explored and mapped. After the meal, they put out the new pages so anybody who wanted to could copy them.

Abraham gave half the sage to the people of Fletcher Creek. "Divide this however you want." Abraham and his family tied their half into small bundles and hung them inside the empty wagon to dry. They put the sword in the sap-cooking pan, covered it with vinegar, then added salt, and left it to soak.

Later, after the people of Fletcher Creek were in their cabins, Nancy and Theo brought out the cake they had baked. They cut the cake, covered half to save for the next day, and then divided the rest into six pieces.

"Happy birthday," the whole family whispered.

"Excellent." James savored his birthday cake.

"Was it a good birthday, darling?" Marie asked.

"Very good. Even considering the bee sting."

After the evening prayer that Theo spoke that night, they lay in their tent, contented and happy as a family once again.

Forty Two

Morris, Lewis, and George stopped part way to Little Rock and slept in the tent made from Theo's tarps. In town the next afternoon, they showed Martin the plants they had brought. He bought everything. "I'll buy as much as you can bring. I have customers who already want these plants. How soon can you come back with more?"

"It's a long way. Not too soon."

Edwin jumped into the conversation because he had recognized the mules. "I can ride halfway and get the plants."

"If you'll do that, exactly two weeks from today on May 18th, we'll meet you in Maumelle.

Before anything changed, Edwin said, "Agreed."

"Do you know of a good mule for this much money?" Morris held out the money Martin had just paid them.

Martin told them, "Come back tomorrow morning. I'll see what I can find tonight."

Lewis informed him, "If we have to spend the night, we'll have less money for the mule."

Martin repeated, "I'll see what I can do."

"Thank you. We'll see you in the morning." Morris appreciated that the man was going to help him.

"Want to stay at the Hillcrest Inn again?" Lewis asked.

Morris agreed, "Mr. Hillcrest will be glad we came back after what happened the last time."

George was excited. He was in Little Rock. Justin didn't even get to come with them. Now, they would spend the rest of the day looking around, eat at the Hillcrest Inn, and spend the night there. Nobody had reported anything George would have considered as something important. He asked, "What happened the last time?"

"You have to swear to never tell anybody," his father told him.

"I swear." George thought, *Oh my! I'm going to be in on an adult secret!*

As they walked to the Arkansas River to look at the lower ferry, Morris told George what had happened. "Abraham pretended to be our slave. The judge in this town was at Hillcrest Inn, being very drunk and belligerent. When he came outside, he attacked Abraham." Morris wanted to make an important point to his son. "You understand that you have a lot of power over a man when you can ruin his reputation?"

"Yes, father."

"Don't use that power unless absolutely necessary, or even let the person know that you have that power. Most importantly, don't ever do something that will give others that kind of power over you."

"Who knows about him?" George asked.

"Mr. Hillcrest, his oldest son, the men of Fletcher Creek, and Abraham."

George wanted to be sure that he understood correctly, "I'm one of the men of Fletcher Creek?"

"What do you think, Lewis?"

Lewis affirmed his nephew, "I think so."

Morris told his son, "I do too. Welcome to the adult world and your first lesson for adult life." He had wanted to find a way to welcome his oldest son into manhood. This may not have been the best way possible, but he could tell by the way his son stood that George felt he had come of age. Others saw him as a man. He walked proudly as they continued to explore the town. They looked at all the shops, but when they got to the gun shop, they stepped inside.

The gunsmith recognized them. "Howdy. How are those revolvers holding up?"

"William shot an elk on the way home. Quick as a whistle, he filled it full of twenty shots. It was something to see," Morris passed on the report.

George added, "Twenty shots from that revolver didn't kill a bear. Abraham had to stab it in the eye."

The shopkeeper doubted the story. "That couldn't have killed it."

"It's a long knife, and Abraham is very strong." George held up his hands to show the length of the knife.

"I guess one story is as good as another. I wouldn't want to tangle with Abraham. Anyway, what can I do for you gentlemen today?"

Morris said, "Nothing, we're just looking."

Lewis asked, "What can a person do to make their rifle have more power?"

"Are those the rifles?"

"Three of them," Lewis told him.

"Let me take a look." The gunsmith checked them over. "How long are you going to be here?"

"Until the morning," Lewis replied.

"I can have all three fixed by morning for one dollar."

Morris pointed out their problem to his brother, "We may not have enough to buy a mule if we get the guns fixed."

George voiced his take on the subject, "How are we going to be able to kill anything if we don't get them fixed?"

His father respected his son's opinion as an equal man. "Go ahead and fix them." They left all three rifles then continued to explore the town.

George knew they needed more money. They had learned useful plants often live in a wet environment. "I wonder if we can find any plants by the river that we can sell."

Since they were already on the south side, they walked the edge of the river along the road toward Pine Bluff. Morris pointed. "Look, willows." They walked to the water-loving trees. Abraham had taught them to always have a way to harvest a plant because you never know when you'll come across something you want, and you may not be able to go back later. Therefore, they had a hatchet, three sharp knives, and several small storage bags. They hacked pieces of bark off the trees and scraped the inner bark into their pouches. When they had a large supply, they went back to Harrow's livery. Edwin was the only one there.

Morris strolled over to the stable hand. "Would you

be able to tell Mr. Harrow that we have more willow that he can buy?"

"When I'm done here, I'll tell him, if you'll tell them Edwin said hello."

Not knowing there was any connection between the boy and anybody he knew, Lewis asked, "Tell who?"

Edwin said, "Your slave and his family."

Morris paused as he wondered to himself. *Should I tell him I'll pass the message and let him know they're still there?*

When Morris didn't reply, Edwin resolved the problem he knew he had placed on the man. "Let me see how much you have." He looked into the bag. "He'll probably give you three dollars for this much."

Morris negotiated, "We'll sell it for three dollars and twenty-five cents."

"It shouldn't cost that much to stay at the Hillcrest Inn," Edwin replied.

Morris didn't want to tell the boy they were unarmed, "Something else came up."

"I'm done here. I'll take you to Mr. Harrow. You can work it out with him."

"Much obliged."

Martin answered the door. Edwin disclosed the reason for their visit, "They have willow bark. I have to get home. See you tomorrow, Mr. Harrow."

"Let me see what you have." Martin stepped outside and closed the door behind him.

Morris opened the bag. They had spent quite a bit of time getting the pink inner bark. The bag wasn't very large, but it was bulging.

Martin knew they must have found a place close by, and he could probably get some himself, but he never had time to go around searching and gathering. "How about three dollars and fifty cents?'

"Agreed." Morris handed him the bag of bark. "Please give us back the bag."

Martin went into his house.

"Who's there?" Dollie asked.

"My medicinal plant supplier."

"You have one?!"

"Yes."

"Good for you. You're such a good businessman. I'm lucky to be married to you."

"Thank you, Dollie, my love. I'm lucky to be married to you." That day Martin realized he really did feel lucky to have Dollie as his wife.

Martin got out another bowl and poured in the willow bark. Earlier, he had put the other herbs and plants he had bought into bowls. Now, the table was covered. "I need to get something to store these, and I need to look into buying a mule. I'll be back later." He kissed the woman he loved and left with the money he needed. He handed Morris three dollars and fifty cents and the bag.

Martin said, "See you tomorrow," then left in search of a mule.

Morris had an extra bit piece. "Let's go to the bakery!" He had seen and smelled the baked goods when he had sold Charles the honey, and he looked forward to trying some. He decided they should have an extravagant treat. "Charles, three of your finest pastries and three hot chocolate drinks."

As Charles prepared the hot cocoa, he said, "You never came back with more honey."

Lewis confessed, "We didn't think you wanted to buy more."

"I would have."

"I know, and we appreciate that."

"I saw that you sold most of it to Clark. Your slave did a fine job separating the honey from the wax."

"Much obliged. He's a good slave."

Charles served them the pastries and hot chocolate. George took a bite. "What is this?"

"It's called an éclair. Do you like it?"

"I sure do!" It was a great day. He was with his father and uncle, eating a very special treat. They had the money they needed, plus some extra because he had suggested looking around at the river. They had considered his opinion, as they would have done with any adult. They had even accepted it as a good idea and had acted on it. That day, George felt he became a man. He ate slowly, savored every bite of his éclair, and sipped the chocolate to make it last as long as he could.

In the morning, they got their rifles then made their way to Harrow's livery. The mule that Martin had found for them had the number 15 seared into its flesh. The previous owner had bought the injured mule from Arnold for five dollars. He thought it wasn't healing up right, so the previous night he had sold it to Martin for ten.

Buying the mule would help Martin's friend. Just like Edwin, Martin had recognized the mules, and he knew the mule he had just bought would be going to a person who could care for it properly. Morris would end up with a good strong mule after it received care from Dr. Smith. He thought everybody, including the mule, would benefit.

Morris, Lewis, and George looked over Mule 15. It didn't look as well healed as the mules with Abraham.

"She's injured. I'll give you twelve dollars, and I want a bill of sale."

Martin would still make two dollars, so he wrote out the sale and gave the paper to Morris. "She's all yours."

As they left Little Rock, George asked, "Why did you take it, Pa?

"I think Abraham can help her, she's a very big mule for twelve dollars, and I think she's pregnant."

"It can't be. Mules are sterile," Lewis told him.

"I know, but I'm sure I felt one in there."

Forty Three

The other mules from Russell French's team immediately recognized Mule 15. They brayed a greeting when she walked into the corral. George called out, "Abraham, come look at Mule 15."

Abraham and James had just poured the vinegar and salt out of the sap pan in which the sword soaked and then added saleratus and water. Abraham walked to the mule. "How much did you pay for her?"

"Twelve dollars. I don't think she healed as well as the others. Is there anything you can do for her?"

"You could rub honey into her scars, but this injury should be reopened to remove this lump of scar tissue and then let it heal again with proper care. In addition, you're going to have two mules before long."

"I told you!" Morris looked at Lewis.

Lewis reported his understanding of mules, "I thought mules couldn't have babies."

"This one is pregnant, so I guess it can happen. I don't know if she was with a horse or a donkey. Do you know, Theo?" Abraham looked at his friend.

Theo told them what he thought was the answer, "I think he only has horses that aren't castrated."

Lewis came to a conclusion, "We need to build a shelter for Snowflake, Mule 15, and their babies."

"It's been ten minutes." James was more interested

277

in what he had been doing and went back to the pan holding his sword. Abraham helped him dump the water. They put on gloves, held the sword over the pan and then each took a handful of ground walnut shells and scrubbed at the dirt and corrosion. To try to get the solvent inside, James tried to wiggle the sword during the process.

It moved. Abraham asked, "Did the sword move?"

"I think it did. Should we try again?"

"Let's try heat. Theo had a forge at Pine Bluff; let's ask him."

James went over and asked Theo, "Would fire help us get the sword out?"

"Probably." Theo explained, "We don't want to get it too hot and melt anything. We just want the scabbard to expand." The three of them built a hot fire and then held the sword in it with the blacksmith's tongs. Every minute he took the sword out of the fire and tried to pull the sword with pliers while Abraham held the scabbard with another pair of pliers. They tried several times. Every time Theo removed the sword, it cooled and contracted slightly. When the sword was in the fire, the scabbard expanded. They hoped the two pieces separated slightly as well.

They tried again. James told the men pulling, "I think it's moving!"

"Not too hard. We don't want it to break. We need to heat it again." Theo put the sword back into the fire.

After a few more times, they were all sure that the sword was breaking free. Since they wanted it to slide out whole, they were gentle when they pulled. Once again, Theo put the sword back into the fire.

Pop.

"Did it break?" James asked.

"I don't know. It might have, or it might have broken free. Let's try to pull it out again."

Abraham held the ring rod of the scabbard and planted his feet. Theo pulled the sword. With a scraping sound, the sword moved toward Theo and then slid out. "Hurray!"

James examined the mostly corrosion-free blade. "This mark looks like a little dog."

They passed the blade around. Everybody looked. Theo examined the sword last. "I know the basics of blacksmithing. I'm sure we can easily burnish this back to perfection."

Abraham tried to look inside the scabbard. "Can we clean this out? Will you teach me how to work with metal?"

Theo agreed, "I'll show you what I know as we restore these."

The next morning, Abraham said, "I should work on Mule 15. Anybody want to learn what to do?"

The very first hand up was Matilda's. "I do." Abraham looked at Sarah and Matt. Sarah nodded her head, "Yes."

"All right. Anybody else?"

"Can I learn with you, Matilda?" Will asked.

"Abraham has to give you permission," she whispered.

"What do you say, Abraham? May I watch?"

"Of course. You two, help me get set up."

They made a batch of the sedative and then gave

the mule the least amount that would be effective because of the little one it carried. Matilda had asked to watch, and Sarah had given her permission. Therefore, while they waited, they made a stable platform of crates where Matilda could stand. When the mule slept, Abraham cut open the injury. He removed the bunched-up scar, cut apart, and then sewed back together the improperly aligned muscle.

Matilda observed intently. She informed the others of something else she had seen since she had become interested in how things work. "I watched a chicken lay an egg."

"You did?" William asked.

"I've been looking at a lot of things. Did you know that all kinds of strange things happen to animals and people?"

William told his niece, "I agree with that."

Matilda informed them of an important matter that had come to her attention, "Those eggs come right out of their butts. We shouldn't be eating them."

William and Abraham smiled and tried not to laugh. Abraham told Will, "Go ahead and explain."

"It's not a butt like ours. It's a different part. The eggs don't exactly come out of the part that poops."

"It looks like it does to me. You can eat them. I'm not going to do it."

Abraham brought them back to the current matter of concern. "I'm ready to show you the next step of this mule's treatment. Push the needle through the skin, but not so close to the edge that it will rip through the skin and not too far, so the skin won't roll up. Move over a little and do the same again." He handed William the needle. "Just keep sewing like I showed you."

Matilda requested, "I want to try one. Let me."

Abraham agreed conditionally, "All right, but if I tell you to stop, you have to stop."

"I will."

Will gave Matilda the needle. She repeated the instructions as she started. "Move over a little. Push the needle through not too close to the edge, so it won't pull out and not too far out, so the skin doesn't curl up in the middle." She calculated where to put the stitch to meet the requirements, put the needle under the skin, and looked at Abraham to see if he agreed.

"Looks right to me," Abraham told her.

She pushed the needle through the skin and pulled the sinew through. "Pull it snug, but not too tight, so the skin doesn't rip." Matilda stopped when she thought the sinew was tight enough and repeated the instructions again. "Not too close to the edge and not too far out." She placed the needle and paused.

"Just right," Abraham stated.

Matilda pushed the needle through the skin and pulled the sinew snug. "Did I do it right?" she asked.

Abraham said, "Perfect."

Matilda passed the needle to her uncle and asked, "What does the meat part do?"

"That part is a muscle. It attaches to the bone. When the brain tells it to squeeze, it moves the bone, which moves the hand or foot or leg or whatever part it's connected to."

Matilda didn't believe it. "I've never heard my brain tell my muscles to squeeze."

"It doesn't talk with words you can hear."

"So, the brain writes." Matilda deduced.

"Good logic. But it sends a signal through a nerve that connects to the muscles."

Matilda, being a very curious and intelligent girl, said, "I wish I knew all about how it works."

Will said, "When we learn how to read, we'll get some books, and we'll read all about it."

"You promise, Uncle Will?"

"I promise."

Will put in a stitch. "How did I do, Abraham?"

"Perfect. Change the cedar poultice twice a day."

"Also, I wonder if you'll show me how to make one of those cradleboards." A big smile spread across Will's face.

"Rebecca's pregnant?"

"We may have a Christmas baby."

"Congratulations! I surely will show you how to make a cradleboard."

Matilda jumped off the crates, "I'm telling Maw." She ran to her cabin and slammed open the door. "Maw, I helped fix the mule, and Uncle Will is having a baby."

"I guess there's not going to be any breaking it to everybody slowly," Will remarked.

"I think not. That girl should be a doctor. If there's a way to do it, somebody should send her to college."

After that day, to anybody she could get to look, Matilda pointed out the stitches she had put into Mule 15.

Forty Four

Nancy and Lily had worn dresses for the last few weeks, and Lily had told Abraham that Marie was going to wear a dress when they could get another. Therefore, Abraham asked Will, "I wonder if Rebecca would sell any of her dresses. That would give you money to buy a maternity dress."

"I'll ask."

Later, Rebecca went to talk with Lily, Marie, and Nancy. "Abraham said you want dresses. I'll sell you three dresses for ten dollars."

"Do you have that many?" Marie asked.

"My family had money, but I made all my own dresses. I took them all when I left. I have several."

The three women went with Rebecca. "These are very nice. They're much too nice to wear for everyday use."

Rebecca brushed her hands across the bodice of the dress she was wearing. "This one used to be nice. I decided I would only use one and keep the others nice. I don't know why."

"You're going to need new dresses from what I heard Matilda yelling."

"Do you think ten dollars will be enough to buy material to make a dress to wear while I'm pregnant?"

Nancy buttoned the back of the blue dress Marie

had put on. "Congratulations on the upcoming baby, Rebecca. Let's go ask Theo. He'll know what you should be able to get with ten dollars."

The sisters walked toward the wagon in their new dresses. Nancy called out, "Theo, we need your help."

"You ladies look very beautiful," Theo exclaimed.

Lily informed Theo, "We're probably going to buy these dresses. Rebecca made them."

"What help do you need?"

Marie told him their question. Theo asked, "Rebecca, would you be interested in making dresses to sell?"

Rebecca said, "Do you think people would buy them?" Theo knew the answer. He left to get a piece of paper and a pencil to make a list.

Lily told her, "I'm sure people would buy a dress like this in Little Rock."

Lily asked for her husband's opinion. "Abraham, do you think anybody would buy a dress like this?"

"I would buy it for you because it shows off your incredible beauty. Then I would stroll all around town with you on my arm, so everybody could see what a gorgeous wife I have."

Rebecca whispered into Lily's ear, "I see why you married him."

"Seriously," Lily replied.

"I amserious. I want to buy that dress for you right now."

Lily's beautiful smile graced her face. "See? I told you people would buy them."

"Three dollars thirty-three and one-half cents."

Abraham counted out the money and handed it to Rebecca. James walked over and gave Rebecca the same amount. "I'm going to go walking right beside Abraham to show off my beautiful wife."

"I guess I'll have to be gorgeous by myself." Nancy gave Rebecca her share of the ten dollars.

"That's an extra half cent." Rebecca tried to hand her back the half-cent piece.

"You keep it. This way, it's equal."

Theo came back with a list.

20¢ - 100 needles @ 4¢ per pack of 20
40¢ - twelve 200-yard spools of various
  colored thread.
4¢ - 9 dozen small white agate shirt buttons.
1¢ - a dozen medium hooks and eyes
$2.10 - 14 yards cotton cloth @ 15¢ per yard
$2.00 – 10 yards fancy calico cloth @ 20¢ per
  yard
$5.25 – 15 yards flannel @ 35¢ per yard
(Get two different complimenting colors
  of each type of material)
10.00 TOTAL

Rebecca took the list. She would give it to Morris, along with the money to get the items in Maumelle when they went to sell the plants. Lily, Marie, and Nancy decided to pack their dresses and keep them for special events and then buy dresses for ordinary use when they could. Lily continued to wear her dress made from Ann's dresses.

In two weeks, they had planted the fields and built the smokehouse and corral. Freeman and George had both built a cart. Morris and Matt had harvested a large supply of plants from the forest. When May 17th arrived, Morris was ready to meet Edwin in Maumelle. They hadn't arranged the time of the day to meet, so they decided to go, stay in town that night, and be there from the dawning of May 18th until Edwin arrived.

Matt had an idea about what was going on with his oldest child. This trip gave him an opportunity to fix the problem. "Justin, I want to go with Morris. You're a man now, and I believe you can take care of our family. I want to leave all the people I love very much, including you, in your hands. I know you can keep everybody safe. Do you want to take this responsibility, so I can go?"

"I thought you didn't think I was smart enough to do anything."

"Son, I've never thought you aren't smart enough. I think you are very capable. I'm sorry that I gave you that idea. I want you to know one thing. I love you so much that I worry about you, just as I do about all my children. I will never stop loving you or being concerned about your well-being. That doesn't mean I don't believe you're capable."

Justin accepted his father's acknowledgment of his abilities. "Go with Morris. I'll take care of everybody. You'll find us all safe and happy when you get back."

"Good. I appreciate you doing this. I'm going to tell Morris I want to go with him." Matt wanted to hug Justin, but he didn't know if he should. Justin hadn't

286

wanted him or his mother to hug him in a long time. He held open his arms. Justin stepped over and put arms around his father, then patted his back.

"I love you, son."

"Love you too, Paw." Justin stepped away.

Before he left, Matt told Sarah about his conversation with their oldest son. "I knew you'd figure out what the problem was and then fix it." Sarah always believed in Matt. That was how he knew how much it meant to a man to be respected and appreciated. It made him love her even more. That was the other side of why they'd had so many children.

Forty Five

Morris and Matt were already in Maumelle when Edwin rode into town with Mr. Harrow's money, the authority to determine how much he would pay, and what items he wanted. Martin had come to trust Edwin to know what he was doing and to make a good deal. When he found Morris and Matt, Edwin was surprised that they had such a large supply of so many different types of plants. He didn't have as much money as he needed, but he knew Martin would want all the plants, especially the plants that could only be harvested this time of the year. Edwin made a proposition, "I don't have enough money to pay for all of this, but I want it all. Would you trust us to pay you the rest next time, or you can come to Little Rock to get it?"

Matt told Morris, "We do need to go to Little Rock again to get the rest of the rifles fixed. If Martin owes us money when we get there, we won't have to worry about being robbed on the way."

"Good point." The two men held out the plants toward Edwin. Morris gave him their answer, "We'll let you take it all. Give us what money you have now. In about two weeks, we'll bring what we have at that time to Little Rock, get the rest of what you owe us for this and whatever you pay us for the next batch."

"Deal." Edwin shook hands with both men. It was

late in the day because his mother hadn't let him leave until daylight and it had taken him the whole day to get to Maumelle. He planned to spend the night inside, also under the orders of his mother. "You two staying here tonight?"

"Yes. Coyotes were in the woods yesterday."

"My mother says, 'Coyotes come on four legs and on two legs.'"

"Smart woman," Morris remarked. He and Matt walked with Edwin to the boarding house. Edwin went in to get his room. The other two stepped into the parlor. "Before it gets dark, let's look around for plants." Matt got out a paper and pencil. He started a page to chart the area around Maumelle. Matt drew a circle in the middle of the page. "How do you spell Maumelle?"

Morris said, "M, A, U, M, E, L, L, E."

Matt wrote Maumelle in the circle, divided the paper into four quadrants and marked them A1, A2, A3, and A4. In section A1, he wrote, "START AT CABIN," then stopped. It's not really a cabin. I wonder how to write boarding house. He erased cabin. Matt reasoned out what letters would make the sounds they needed and came up with "BORDEN HOUS."

"I think I have it." He showed the paper to Morris.

"Very good guess, but there are some minor changes to make. You know if I say; talking, walking, reading, sleeping; they all end with the 'ing' sound."

"Like boarding."

"Exactly. That 'ing' sound is always spelled with the letters I, N, G."

"Let me fix it."

Matt erased the en and added the 'ing.' He had BORDING.

Morris said, "To make writing more complicated, somebody came up with silent letters."

"What's a silent letter?"

"For example: the word house sounds exactly the way you wrote it, but there is a letter E at the end that doesn't make a sound."

"That's one of the stupidest things I've ever heard of." Matt added the letter E. "Any other silent letters?"

"There can be K or G at the beginning of a word that doesn't make a sound like knife." Morris wrote the word.

Matt said, "That word only needs the three letters in the middle, but it has a silent k at the front and a silent e at the end."

"Exactly."

Matt stated with conviction, "This isn't going to be easy, but I'm not giving up."

"One more change. There's a letter A here." He pointed between the O and the R. "When two vowels are together, they sound different."

"What's a vowel?"

"Write it there, and I'll explain as we go."

Matt erased the B and the O. He made the letters smaller, so B, O, and A would all fit and then continued with GO WEST ON THE ROAD TO THE.

"We'll fill it in when we get to whatever we'll make the marker." Matt showed the paper to Morris again.

"Perfect." The two men left the boarding house and walked across town, heading west.

Edwin had listened to the conversation while he secured his room. He thought; they're mapping something, so he slipped along behind them.

When Abraham had been in Little Rock as the veterinarian, Dr. Luke Smith, he had told Edwin to always be aware of what was happening around him, so Edwin tried to be very observant. Abraham had also told Matt and Morris the same thing. That was why they saw each other, and then noticed a couple held at gunpoint in the alley.

Morris signaled Edwin to go through the shop and come out into the alley. He indicated that he and Matt would do the same on the other side of the alley. Edwin opened the shop door very slowly, so that the bell didn't jingle. He crept behind the counter, crates, and barrels to the back of the store, and then into a windowless storeroom. The only light in the room came in from the store. Dr. Smith said to wait until I can see before I move. Edwin waited just inside the door until his eyes had adjusted. When he saw the exit to the alley, he carefully made his way across the room and tried the knob. It didn't turn. He applied more force. It still didn't budge. He told himself, of course, it would be locked.

Edwin remembered, in Clark's General Store when he had helped Abraham bottle the honey, the door key had been hanging on a nail. He glanced around the dingy room. He could barely see, so he ran his hand along the wall. Spider webs wrapped themselves around his fingers. He jerked away from the wall. I hate these things. He wiped the sticky cobwebs on his pants. Before he felt around again, Edwin picked up a wooden spoon from the stack on the shelf and removed the rest of them. I found it. He took the key off the hook and tried it in the lock. It rattled much too loudly, but the cylinder did turn. He cracked the door and peeked out. I'm not far behind that evil varmint. Across the way, a door opened. Edwin locked eyes with Morris.

"Don't shoot us. I'll give you my wallet."

Lewis held up one finger, two fingers, three fingers. They threw open the doors, charged up the alley, and flung their bodies onto the bandit.

Four men crashed to the cobblestones. An explosion made their ears ring. Acrid smoke stung their noses and made their eyes water. The gun sailed from the purse-snatcher's hand and skidded to the feet of the man who had just handed over his money.

The man picked up the gun. "Are you all right, my dear?" he asked his very pale wife.

The woman put her hand on her belly. Blood poured over her fingers and dyed her dress red. "Shoot him, Horatio. He's murdered me!"

The gunslinger got up on his knees and pleaded, "Don't kill me. It's their fault."

Morris ordered Edwin, "Get a doctor!"

Edwin took off running.

At least I have enough life left in me to see him die first. "Give me the gun!" The woman jerked the large revolver from Horatio's hand and pulled the trigger. The recoil flung her dripping blood onto the men around her. Her assailant remained on his knees, but his life had ended. The second impact knocked the body to the ground. As her life ran out her gut, she discharged round after round into the body of the man she believed had killed her.

Edwin returned with a man, along with the woman who operated the boarding house. As they looked over the scene, Edwin tried to get his breath. Blood spatter covered the clothes of all the people in the alley. The gun and ammo belts were on the dead man who still held the moneybag that had cost his life. Clearly in shock and out of her mind, the woman bled profusely as she pulled the trigger again and again. When she sank toward the ground, her husband swept her into his arms.

"I'm a midwife, but I know how to get a bullet out. Bring her to my place."

Horatio carried his wife away in his arms. Morris, Lewis, and Edwin started to follow. "Hold on, men. I'm Sherriff Norman Sweeting. Tell me what happened."

Morris explained then added, "She shot that footpad more times than possible with one revolver."

The red-haired fellow operating as Maumelle's lawman looked strong enough to throw the body over his own shoulder and lug the culprit on his own. He ordered Morris and Matt, "You two, carry the body." Edwin helped them. Leaving behind a trail of blood, they more or less carried but somewhat dragged the body to the boarding house. Norman opened the door and then called out, "Lucy, I'm renting the parlor for the body and investigation."

Lucy spoke from an upstairs room where she had undressed the woman and was examining the wound. "I thought you would. The tarp is in the cabinet."

The lawman went into the parlor. He put the tarp on the floor before he went to the desk and got a sheet of paper and a pencil. "Put him on the tarp. What are your names?"

I can't give my real name. If they find me, they'll find Will and the family in the Railroad. Morris looked at Matt with panic in his eyes. *If he finds out I'm lying, he might arrest me.* He decided to take his chances. "Henry Parker."

Matt also knew Will was wanted for the death of his sister-in-law's father. His brother hadn't killed the man, and Will's safety came first. "Charles Woolsey"

Edwin didn't know the men hadn't given their real names. He gave his: "Edwin Snow."

"Wait here." Norman left the room and went upstairs.

"Is she going to live?" Norman asked.

"I don't know. The bullet went clean through, but I can't stop the bleeding."

"Sir, come out here and talk with me." In the hall, Norman questioned the man. "What are your names?"

"Horatio and Esther Knapp."

Norman wrote the names on his paper. "Tell me what happened."

"We were walking back to Murray's house when that man came out of the alley, grabbed Esther's arm, and pulled her in. I chased him into the alley where he pointed his gun at me and demanded our money. I told him I would give it to him and had just handed it over when those other men ran up and jumped him. He shot Esther when they knocked him down. I picked up the gun and shot him twice. Esther took the gun and shot him repeatedly after he was already dead."

"The other men didn't say anything about you shooting the gun."

"I don't know why they didn't. I killed him."

"It's self-defense either way."

"I'm the one who shot him," Horatio insisted.

"What about those other men? Is it their fault the gun went off?"

"He was going to shoot us one way or the other. I could see it in his eyes when I handed him my wallet. He was probably already pulling the trigger. That may be why the gun went off. He had the gun pointed at my heart. I think they saved my life. I hope they've saved Esther's too."

"Go back to your wife and stay there."

Horatio went back into the room and begged his unconscious wife, "Please don't die, Esther."

Norman proceeded back down the stairs and then stood in the doorway. "You're under house arrest."

"For what? We tried to help!" Morris exclaimed.

"When you pushed the man, you may have caused the gun to fire. If Esther dies, you'll be guilty of murder." He backed up and locked the door.

Edwin fretted, "Now what do we do? My Ma is going to be worried out of her mind if I'm not home tomorrow."

Morris looked around. There were bars on the windows that looked decorative, but they were substantial. "My wife and children will be worried too."

Matt tested the bars. "We aren't getting out, we

don't know how long we'll be locked up, and we can't send a message." He looked at the body locked in the parlor with them. "I think we should search the body and see if we can find anything to help us."

Morris looked at him. "Go ahead and do it."

To which Matt replied, "I'd rather not be the one."

"But you suggested it." Morris thought, therefore, Matt should search the body.

"I'll do it." Edwin had been in the blood and puss-filled infections of Russell's mules, he had been in blood when animals at the livery gave birth, and he'd been in manure twice a day for years. He searched the pockets of the pants and found them empty. Edwin slipped his hand into the dead man's inside vest pocket, found a pocket watch, and handed it to Morris. When he got to the pocket with a hole made by the round that had gone into the man's heart, he could see a folded paper. Edwin pulled it out and handed it to Matt, who unfolded the bloodstained sheet that had a perforation in each quadrant.

Matt didn't have to try to figure out everything on the paper. He'd seen some of the words before. He said, "Wanted dead or alive," then tried to read the name, "Roy Butterfield."

Edwin, Morris, and Matt looked back and forth between the paper and the face of the dead man. "Looks like him, only skinnier," Edwin commented.

Morris agreed, "I think it's him."

As they scrutinized the man's face, Roy's eyes popped open. All three shrieked. Edwin screamed, "He's alive."

They heard the thumping of someone running

down the stairs. Morris slipped the watch into his pocket. Matt quickly folded the paper, then stuffed it out of sight as Norman flung open the door.

With more calmness than he felt, Morris said, "His eyes opened."

Norman went to Roy, pushed his eyelids down, pulled two pennies out of his pocket, and put one on each eye. "He's dead. They do that sometimes."

"My daughter's eyes didn't open like that."

Norman walked to the door. "A child's body doesn't usually have rigor mortis like this. I'm sorry you lost a child." He stepped out of the room, closed, and locked the door again.

Matt commanded, "Don't ever tell anybody I screamed like that."

"I won't if you don't," Morris replied.

"Same for me; it might interfere with getting a woman when I get older." The three made a pact to never mention anything about any of them screaming.

"What does the watch say?" Edwin asked.

Morris pulled out the watch and read the inscription, "To Jasper, my beloved husband on our first anniversary, Candy."

"He's not Jasper," Edwin pointed out.

Morris said, "Put it all back. Mr. Sweeting is sure to search him."

Matt folded the paper, being sure to align the holes, and then slid it back into the pocket. He wiped the blood from his fingers on the dead man's clothes. Morris put the watch back into the man's vest pocket.

Morris, Matt, and Edwin still stood beside the body when the door opened, and Norman entered.

"How's the woman doing?" the three of them asked together.

"Probably going to bleed to death."

The three standing over the body all said, "We have a treatment for bleeding."

"What do you have?"

The three of them once again spoke in unison, "It's shepherd's purse and yarrow."

Norman looked at them, "Do you say everything together?"

To which they all replied, "No."

"I don't know if the woman's husband wants to let you put plants on his wife. I'll go ask." Norman left them locked in again.

They heard him walk up the stairs. It wasn't long before he was back. "He said to try." Norman thought it wasn't likely for the boy to overpower him. "Can the boy do it?

Edwin assured him, "I can make it. The plants are in my room." They walked to Edwin's room. "Why are there bars on the windows of a boarding house?"

"Lucy thinks it's safer. When her husband died, she had bars put on all the windows and on her bedroom door."

Edwin got all his plants. He assumed they didn't have time to cook them. "We need to get a bowl." In the kitchen, Edwin told Norman, "Bring a couple of sharp knives as well." Norman quickly retrieved the items before they hurried back to the patient.

Norman knocked on the door. "Are you ready?"

"Yes."

Edwin walked toward the bed that ran red with the blood that still spilled from the woman. She wore her husband's shirt tied closed below her breasts but above the entry point of the bullet. The sheet pulled up from her feet, hid the woman's lower body and most of the blood that had covered the bed.

Edwin put the proper plants into the bowl. "Cut these up together." He looked around the room but didn't see any water. "We need a pitcher of clean drinking water, a cup, and cloth strips."

Lucy left the room to get the items Edwin requested. After Norman cut up the plants, Edwin added a little water and then put them on the hole in the woman's belly.

"I need to get to her back." Horatio raised his wife and held her to his body. Edwin was shocked at the much larger size of the exit hole. He put the plants on her back. "It's best that the bullet isn't in her." With the plants inside the cloth, he wrapped it several times across her back and around her waist. "We need to replace the blood she's lost. Start dripping water into her mouth. Get as much into her as you can."

Horatio sat beside Esther in the blood. He put a glass of water to her lips and tried to pour some into her mouth. Most of it went down her front, but she swallowed some.

"Keep it up," Edwin told him.

It had been barely a minute since Edwin had applied the poultice. Horatio didn't see the cloth bandages rapidly turn to crimson. Only a small amount of blood had seeped through. "I think that worked." He continued to trickle water into his wife.

"She's got to be bleeding inside as well. I'm going to send up some yarrow tea. She needs to get a full cup twice a day. I'll make a whole pot since she's not really swallowing much."

The man on the bed said, "I'm Horatio. This is Esther. Thank you."

"I'm Edwin." He told the man, "I hope she'll be all right," but he doubted that she would be. He picked up his plants. "Come on," Edwin called Norman out of the room. They went back into the kitchen.

Edwin asked, "May I look for honey while I cook the tea?"

"You can't leave the kitchen," Norman informed him.

Ten minutes later, the tea was cooked. Edwin poured it into the teapot and added lots of honey. "Give it to her when it's cool enough to drink."

"I'll search the body then take her the tea after." Norman took Edwin back into the parlor, locked the door, slid the key into his pocket, and then knelt down beside the body. He found the pocket watch. He read the inscription then said, "I don't think he's a married man." He put the watch into his own pocket. Next, he pulled out the paper in the dead man's upper shirt pocket and unfolded it. "He's Roy Butterfield. I'll check into why he's wanted." He left the room with the wanted poster and once again left Matt, Morris, Edwin, and Roy Butterfield locked together. After delivering the tea, Norman came back down the stairs with Lucy. "Don't open that door no matter what." They heard the door close when Norman Sweeting left.

Forty Six

Roy hadn't smelled good when alive. He smelled worse as the night wore on. Since he was the only one small enough to fit, Edwin tried to sleep on the sofa. Matt and Morris slept on the carpet as far away from the body as they could get and remain positioned, so they could keep an eye on the body.

Roy Butterfield lay on the tarp that Norman had laid out to protect Lucy's floor from the blood. "ahhhh," the sound came from the direction of Roy.

"Did you hear that?" Edwin whispered.

Another sound came from the vicinity of the body, "grraa."

"I'm just saying; I'm not making any noises." Edwin got down on the floor beside Matt and Morris who were both sitting up against the wall, staring at the body. Screams again flew out of their mouths when Roy sat up. Edwin ran to the door and pounded. "Let us out."

After several minutes of pounding and begging to get away from the body, they heard, "I can't," from the other side of the door.

The body said, "Nuuu."

Matt begged, "We won't leave. We swear. Just let us out of this room."

They heard the soft footsteps of Lucy going back up

the stairs. All night, the three locked in the parlor huddled in the corner of the room and stared at Roy as the gases moved inside his decomposing body, causing it to moan and groan. Then, they heard a different kind of sound. As if he didn't want the dead man to hear him, Edwin spoke very softly, "That sounds like he's pooping."

Morris asserted, "He's dead. He can't do that."

Matt smelled the results and pinched his nose shut. "I think he did."

In the morning, they really wanted to be in another room. They pounded on the door and pleaded for mercy until they heard the footsteps of more than one person leave the house. The exiting people left them locked in the room of death without food, water, or acceptable air. Due to the stench, they couldn't have eaten even if they'd had food.

"I don't think I can stay in here," Edwin told his fellow inmates.

Morris knew he couldn't continue to stay with the body either. "Let's see if we can find some way to get out."

Attempting to make their escape, they searched the desk. Edwin found a letter opener. He gave up trying and handed the tool to Morris. "See if you can unlock the door."

All three of them tried. There was no way to get to the action in the lock cylinder. The door hinges were on the outside, so they couldn't get to them either. Matt worked the letter opener under the window and pushed down. The tip of the blade snapped off. "D@%#*@#%!"

There was no way Morris was giving up. "Try again."

Matt took off his shoe and used it to hammer the letter opener farther under the window. He gently pushed down. It didn't budge.

Morris ordered, "You're going to have to push harder, so do it!"

Matt refused, "It'll just break again."

Edwin encouraged Matt, "At least we'll have done our best. Try again."

Matt pushed down hard. The window didn't budge. "It isn't going to come open."

"I'll scrape the paint off the edges of the window." Morris pulled the letter opener. "I can't get it out. We need to find something else."

As they searched the room again, Edwin reported his state of dehydration, "I'm really thirsty."

After a long, exhaustive search, Matt said, "I wonder if there's something on Roy that we missed or maybe on his gun belt or ammo belt."

Morris refused to get close, "Whatever's on him is staying there."

Matt countered, "But maybe we missed something. We have to get that window open. These fumes are going to kill us."

"Since he's sitting up, now is the time to get the gun and ammo belts." Edwin held his nose and edged over to the corpse. Very carefully, and touching Roy as little as possible, he got his fingers under the ammo belt and pulled it up. When he had it high over Roy's head, Edwin held his arm over the body, walked behind it, and drew the belt over Roy's head. Once the whole thing was on one side, he lowered the belt and then pulled it out from under his arm. He dragged it to Matt and Morris. "Let's see if we can find something on this before I do anything else." They found nothing that would help them, so Edwin went back, unbuckled the gun belt, and pulled it away. Nothing helpful was there either. Edwin searched the clothes again. He noticed something. It looked like a small metallic circle inside Roy's boot. He pulled on it. A shiv slid out from the inside seam of the boot. "Perfect."

As he scraped the paint away, Morris gouged the wooden window frame and the sash. Matt held out his hand. "Give it to me. You're ruining the window."

"I don't care. They shouldn't have left us locked in with a body." When the paint that had sealed it shut had been removed, Morris hammered the shiv under the window. "Let's try pulling them up."

"All right."

"Ready. Pull." Morris pulled up on the shiv as Matt pulled up on the letter opener. The window broke free. They put their hands under the sash and opened it wide. The bars prevented them from exiting the room. Before they even tried to get to the screws that held the obstruction to their escape, the three of them sat beside the window and sucked in deep breaths of breathable air. Unfortunately, when they tried to reach through the bars to the sides, they discovered every screw was under the clapboards.

They sat in front of the opening and talked about what had happened in the alley. Was there anything they could have done differently so that there wouldn't be a decomposing body in the room with them and possibly another dead person wherever they had taken Esther Knapp?

As they looked out the window, Matt attempted to get their minds off the death that lay in the room behind them and asked, "Tell me about vowels and how they work together."

"I want to learn reading." Edwin requested, "Teach me too." Morris explained how vowels sounded in different words and showed Edwin how to make letters. They scattered their practice papers across the floor as they concentrated very hard on learning to read and write.

Much to their dismay, the body of Roy Butterfield constantly drew their attention. Morris asked, "Does Roy look like he's leaning back more?"

"I think he looks flatter," Edwin replied.

Matt looked but stayed on the far side of the room. "He can't move. He's dead." Two hours later, Matt admitted, "Roy's definitely lying down again."

Edwin saw a woman approaching the house. "Let us out of here." She moved to the other side of the road and hurried past.

Morris decided that people would help if they understood the situation. "If somebody else comes, I'll explain why."

An elderly man came into view. "Sir, they have us locked in this room with a body. Please, let us out."

The man walked over and looked in the window. "There sure is a dead man in there, but I can't help you.

This room is the jail. If you're locked in there, you did something wrong." He backed out of the bushes beside the house.

Edwin begged, "At least bring us some water." The man mercilessly left them to their fate. The day wore on, but nobody else passed the window. At the end of a very horrible day, they watched a beautiful sunset from the room of decay. Edwin sighed. "At least God gave us something beautiful, even though there's something so horrible beside us."

It was the longest day of their entire lives. Every second was an agony of wanting to be out of that room. Now, they were going to spend another night with Roy as he rotted, groaned, stank to the high heavens, and slowly sank to the floor. They sat beside the open window and held under their noses the plants that Edwin blessedly had brought into the room.

Forty Seven

In Little Rock, S.R. and Mary Snow were very concerned. "Edwin should have been home. We need to go find him," Mary told her husband.

"Edwin has our horse. It's gonna take a long time to walk to Maumelle, and I don't know how long it'll take to find him. You stay here. I'll go."

"I'm not sittin' here. I'm gonna find my son. If he's hurt, I might never see him."

S.R. knew his wife. "We'll go ask Mr. Harrow if we can use some horses."

They walked to the Harrow's and knocked on the door. Dollie Harrow opened the door. "What's wrong? Is Edwin back?"

S.R. replied, "No, and we need to borrow horses to find him."

Dollie stood in the doorway and tried to decide if she should.

"Please," Mary begged.

"Martin is out. I shouldn't decide for him, but I will Go to the ivery, and get what you need."

"Thank you! God bless you!" Mary took S.R.'s hand, and they hurried to the stable.

S.R. saddled two horses. "If we ride through the night, we should be in Maumelle tomorrow morning."

Forty Eight

At Fletcher Creek, they were concerned as well. "Where's Paw?" Matilda asked. "Paw promised he'd be home to kiss me good night."

Sarah assured her daughter, "He's just a little late. He'll be home when you wake up in the morning." She whispered to Justin, "After Matilda is asleep, go tell your uncle that your father isn't home."

When he heard Matilda softly breathing, Justin sneaked away. He knocked on his uncle's door. "Paw isn't home."

"Then something is wrong. There is no way he wouldn't come home unless something prevented him from coming. I'll go talk to Katie."

A few minutes later, Will came back with George. "We're going to Maumelle. You ready?"

"Almost." He walked to the tent beside their cabins and spoke. "We need to borrow mules."

"What's happening?" Abraham asked.

"Paw and Morris aren't home. We're going to find them."

"I'll come with you," Abraham offered.

"No. We'll go. Just let us use the mules."

"You can take some of mine." Theo left the tent to show the young men which mules to take.

After they rode out of town, Lily kissed Abraham and said, "Go on and follow them."

"I love you very much, my wife." Abraham got up, dressed, saddled Eyanosa, packed a first aid kit of bandages, sutures, scalpels, and plants, and then he followed.

Forty Nine

The sun came up. Norman returned to Maumelle and walked into Lucy's parlor. Morris immediately demanded, "Put us in a different room. There's no reason to make us stay in here with him."

"Come on." Norman waved them out of the room.

Morris insisted they receive what they needed desperately, "Before we go anywhere, we need water and the outhouse."

Norman escorted them to the Johnny House and stood guard while they took turns taking care of the business they'd been holding in for two days. Afterward, he took them to the kitchen, poured water into glasses, and handed them out. They gulped the water and then requested more. "I'm sorry about keeping you locked up with the body. I didn't know what was what, and we don't have a jail. I've been to Little Rock and back. Roy Butterfield is wanted for the murder of Jasper Daniels, and the attempted murder of his wife, Candice Daniels, as well as some people named Ann Williams, Stephanie Williams, Sally Williams, and Eli Yates.

"After Mr. Butterfield cornered Jasper and Candace Daniels in an alley, he got their moneybag and a pocket watch, and then he shot them. A man, who had talked with Roy at the saloon, saw and recognized him when he crept out of the alley. They immediately got the Daniels to the doctor. The doctor couldn't work on both of them at the same time. Mr. Daniels insisted the doctor first help Mrs. Daniels. He died before the doctor could get back to him. The doctor did save Mrs. Daniels.

"Mrs. Daniels described the pocket watch and the inscription. I think having this pocket watch on him proves his guilt, but she's being escorted here to verify that this body is the man who shot her and killed her husband."

"How is Mrs. Knapp?" Edwin asked.

"She's healing and awake. They want to talk with the three of you."

Justin, George, and Will arrived outside Maumelle. They climbed into the trees at the edge of town and secretly observed a man with a gun escort Matt, Morris, and Edwin across town. When they were out of sight, the three men stealthily made their way to the house their family had just vacated. They looked in the open window. A very smelly body lay on a tarp. All the plants Matt and Morris had taken into Maumelle lay on the floor. The scene inside the room made them fear the worst.

George looked at Will with much distress. "We need to break them out."

"Before we do anything rash, let's find out what's happening." Will told George, "Remain calm." They followed the tracks of the four men the same way that Abraham had trained them to track animals.

Upon arrival at Maumelle, Abraham also climbed a tree and saw the three he was following looking into the window of a house close to the edge of town. They left, clearly trying to not draw attention. Abraham wrapped Eyanosa's reins several times around the tree branch so that the horse would stay but also be able to pull loose if he needed to do so, or if Abraham called for him.

Abraham also looked through the window. It can't be. He couldn't see the dead man's face clearly. This was something he needed to know for sure. Abraham knocked on the door. Nobody answered. He tested the door. The knob turned, so he gently pushed the door open and silently made his way into the parlor. He stood over Roy Butterfield, dead on the floor with pennies on his eyes. It couldn't have happened to a more deserving person.

The plants Matt and Morris had taken to Maumelle, a shiv, a letter opener, pencils, and papers covered with letters and words also lay on the floor. Abraham touched nothing. Unseen, he cautiously slipped out of the house.

Norman knocked on the door of a house across town. "Are they ready?" he asked the man who let them into the house.

The man replied, "Go on up."

A female voice inside the room said, "Come in."

Mrs. Knapp's husband sat on the edge of the blood-free bed on which she lay and held her hand. Her very pale face and the dark circles under her eyes bespoke of her recent ordeal. She looked at the men who had just entered. "Mr. Sweeting told us that Mr. Butterfield has murdered as well as attempted to murder. We're sure we would be dead if you had not intervened. We want to thank you."

Edwin replied, "You don't need to thank me. Just get better."

She held out her hand. "I'm Esther Knapp. I'm very pleased to meet you, Edwin Snow. I understand you stopped my life from running out of me, and then told my husband to get yarrow tea and water into me."

"Yes, ma'am."

"I recall waking up very wet, but alive."

"I'm sorry, ma'am."

"Don't be. We want to do something for you that will change your life forever for the better. We want to send you to school and college."

"That's too much," Edwin told her.

Esther ignored the comment and continued, "You, Mr. Woolsey, and Mr. Parker gave us our lives. Please let us have this privilege to provide all three of you or a family member to go to school and college."

Matt accepted. "I need to talk with my family. I would like to send one of my children." How am I going to do this? I gave the wrong name to Mr. Sweeting.

"Same here," Morris had the same concern.

Edwin declined, "I would go, but I have to work to help my family, my boss, and God. They need me."

"You can start learning your letters in Little Rock and work at the same time."

"Then, if my folks let me, I will."

Somebody knocked on the house's front entry door. Murray Strong, who was the brother of Esther and the owner of the house, went to the door.

"I'm Candace Daniels. This is Captain Cornish."

"Come in. They're all upstairs. I'll take you to them." Candace entered the room, followed by her escort, Captain Cornish.

"I'm Esther Knapp, my deepest condolences on the loss of your husband."

"Horatio Knapp." He shook Mrs. Daniel's hand and then the hand of Captain Cornish. Edwin introduced himself correctly. Morris and Matt stuck with their false names.

"I understand that I have the three of you to thank for bringing down my husband's murderer, and you, lovely lady, for dispatching him to Hell."

Horatio looked at Norman. "I shot him."

"I don't believe you. No charges will be pressed. It was clearly self-defense."

Mrs. Daniels had no choice but to change the subject. "I don't mean to be rude, but you three need to take a bath before we talk further."

Edwin informed her, "We were locked in a room with the rotting body for days. It was cruel torture."

Mrs. Knapp confirmed, "They were locked in there when we left."

Norman tried to defend himself, "It's the only room in the town that can be secured."

Edwin continued his report, "And we didn't have food or water for two days and two nights."

"I'm sorry, but I had to find out what's going on, and the only place to do that is Little Rock. I haven't slept since the night before Roy Butterfield was shot because I've been trying to do that as fast as possible."

Morris assured him of their gratitude. "We appreciate that very much, Mr. Sweeting. Thank you."

314

Mrs. Daniels issued instructions, and she expected them to be followed. "While I go identify the man, provide a meal, water, bath, and new clothes for all three of them."

"Follow me." Murray led Edwin, Matt, and Morris to the kitchen.

Will, Justin, and George crossed paths with Mrs. Daniels, Norman, and Captain Cornish on their way to the boarding house to view the body of Roy Butterfield. They didn't realize one of the men was the person who earlier had escorted their family away at gunpoint.

In order to figure out what was happening, Abraham had decided it would be best to stay close to the boarding house. He hid at the side of the house, observed, and listened. He heard people approaching, dropped to the ground under the bushes, and peeked around the corner. A woman and two men entered the house. Abraham listened intently through the open window.

"That's the man who killed Jasper and shot me."

Norman had no doubt that would be the case, but he had needed to confirm his deductions. "Thank you for identifying the guilty party."

Mrs. Daniels wanted no respect to be given to the man who had murdered her husband, tried to kill at least six other people that she knew about, and had probably committed many more atrocities. "Can we throw him to the wild animals?"

"No, Mrs. Daniels, we can't." Even though he believed the man deserved nothing better, Norman denied her request.

Abraham thought, too bad. He hated Roy having anything. Especially because Roy was wearing Ben's boots and vest, which meant he had either murdered Ben or forced him to give up his clothes. Either way, it was wrong. Abraham did not want Roy to have one single thing with him in the grave.

"Oh well, no harm in asking. It is horrid in here. I don't know how those men are even sane after being locked in here for two days and two nights. They deserve more than my reward money."

Norman told her, "I think the Knapps have a plan." He also didn't want to endure the smell a second longer, so he hurried everybody out of the house.

Abraham now knew that Matt, Morris, and Edwin had been confined in the house, but they weren't in danger, and they were even going to receive a reward. I'm sure it was bad being locked in there. I hope they get something very good.

Fifty

Abraham made sure nobody was looking and then slipped back into Lucy's home. He took a piece of paper and a pencil off the parlor floor, wrote something, folded the note, and then put it in his pocket along with the pencil. He cautiously followed the trail of the seven people he had seen leave the house.

S.R and Mary found no sign of their son on the road between Little Rock and Maumelle. They rode into town. "Where do we start looking?" Mary asked.

"We have no idea what's going on. We should take the horses to the livery then walk around town and see what we can find out without asking."

As Abraham walked away from the house, he saw S.R. and a woman. He assumed she was S.R.'s wife. Abraham picked up a small pebble and threw it at S.R.'s arm. It gently struck him and bounced to the ground. S.R. looked in the direction from which the stone had arrived. Abraham stood at the corner of a building with one finger over his lips and waved him over with his other hand. "Let's go this way," S.R. told Mary.

Even though Abraham was dark-skinned, S.R. recognized Dr. Smith. "What's going on?"

"I'm Abraham, the slave of one of the men with your son."

S.R. acknowledged that he now knew how to address him, "I understand."

317

Abraham reported his findings, "Edwin is in the house two streets back. Turn left. It's the third house on the left. Give him this note without anybody knowing. Tell Edwin to give it to the sheriff secretly. What's your last name?"

"Why?" S.R. didn't know what had happened, and he didn't think it wise to give out his name to a man in the Underground Railroad.

"It's a request for the belongings of the dead man."

Highly upset and concerned, Mary asked, "What dead man?"

"Don't be alarmed. He deserves to be dead. I'm sure whatever got him shot, as well as things I know he's done in the past, have been very bad."

Mary wasn't going to take a chance with the life of her son, so she asked, "Will it get him into trouble if he asks for these things?"

"I don't think so, but just to be cautious, give it to Edwin, and tell him to give it to the sheriff privately, but only if it's not going to cause him a problem. Edwin is very smart. He'll know if it's safe or not."

"What does it say?"

"It says; I Edwin," He stopped reading, turned the paper around, and pointed. "I'll write your last name here." Abraham resumed reading, "place a claim for the personal belongings of Roy Butterfield. Anything was found on his body or known to belong to Roy Butterfield, his horse, saddle, bridle, and any other tackle that is found on or is known to belong with the horse of Roy Butterfield, only excluding any items that are known to be stolen property of another person with

318

known identity." Abraham stopped reading. "Also, I want you to tell Edwin to strip Roy Butterfield naked and take every single thing, including the shiv, and also to recover all his plants."

S. R. gave Abraham the previously requested information, "The name is Snow."

Abraham wrote Edwin's last name in the space, then handed the note to S.R. "I'll find you later. Leave your horses at the stables then go to the house. If I need to talk with you again, I'll notify you the same way I just got your attention."

As directed, S.R. and Mary rode on to the stable before going to the house. "How did that slave know you?" Mary asked.

"Never mind how he knows me."

Mary knew that S.R. had secrets, and she knew that he was a good man, so she dropped the subject.

Abraham went directly to the house where he knew Edwin, Morris, and Matt were located. He approached carefully. He wanted to secretly discover where Justin, George, and Will were hiding and to determine what they were doing. When he found them, he circled around behind them and listened.

"How can we get them out?" George asked.

Will again tried to restrain George. "I told you, we are not going to go in with guns blazing to try to rescue them. We don't know if they even need to be rescued. If we don't know who, what, or where people are, there's no telling who may get hurt. Be patient."

Abraham decided he needed to get another message to S.R. He didn't want any of the people of

Fletcher Creek to know he was involved, but he wanted to relieve the concern in the minds of Will, Justin, and George. He stayed out of view of the men he had just overheard contemplating plans that were highly likely to go bad and circled back toward the stable. When Abraham saw S.R., he threw a pebble at him again. S.R. and Mary walked over.

"Anything change?" S.R. asked.

"Ask the two men with Edwin to walk outside and say, 'Aren't you happy everything is going so well,' then get them to walk around the block out of view of the house. They can go back into the house if they want to. Don't waste time, but don't make it obvious that you're trying to get them to do it."

"How on Earth will we be able to do that?" Mary asked.

"You might be surprised to discover how smart and capable your husband happens to be."

S.R. stated confidently, "I'll make it happen." Abraham concealed himself behind the men hiding outside the house as S.R. and Mary knocked on the door.

Edwin wanted to eat before taking a bath. Morris agreed to bathe first. When Matt bathed, Morris smelled like roses and wore the new set of clothes and the new boots that Horatio had purchased at the town store. Morris loaded his plate with the very generous meal that Murray had laid out for them. As Matt got out of the bath, somebody knocked on the door.

Thinking it was Norman, Mrs. Daniels, and the Captain, Murray called out, "Come on in."

Outside, Mary told her husband, "I don't think we should walk in. Knock again." S.R. knocked again.

"Oh, for pity's sake." Murray put down his fork, then walked to the door and opened it. "Norman, I told you…" He realized the people at the door were not who he had expected. "I'm sorry. Who are you?"

"I'm S.R. This is my wife, Mary. We think our son may be here."

Murray asked, "Is your son Edwin?"

Edwin heard the voice and flew across the house into his mother's arms. "Ma, you're here!" He hugged his father. "Pa, you found me!"

Mary couldn't help herself. She told her son, "My word, child, you smell awful."

"I know. I'm going to take a bath in rose toilet water. You will not believe what happened."

Murray told his new guests, "No need to stand at the door. Please, come in." He led everybody to the dining room. "Join us for breakfast."

Mary had never seen so much food laid out all at one time. "Thank you." She and S.R. sat at the table. Murray handed them each a fine china plate, a linen napkin, and a real silver knife, fork, and spoon.

"Coffee?" he asked.

"Yes, please," S.R. answered.

From the cabinet, Murray retrieved two delicate cups on small saucers that matched the fine china plates. He filled the cups with freshly ground French Roast coffee and brought it to his newest guests.

Edwin whispered to his mother, "Isn't this a fine meal?" He smeared Dulce de Leche on another croissant.

Upstairs, Mrs. Knapp heard Edwin call out Ma and Pa. "Horatio, help me get into something I can wear to go downstairs."

Horatio attempted to reason with his wife, "Esther, you're in no condition to get out of bed."

"We must meet Edwin's parents and get everything arranged for his education."

"At least, don't wear a corset. I don't know why you wear one at all, but I won't let you do it today."

"I agree to your terms. Now, help me." Esther put on a loose dress and housecoat, put her feet into slippers, and motioned for Horatio to help her walk. He got her to the door of the dining room before Edwin saw her.

"Mrs. Knapp, you shouldn't be out of bed!" he exclaimed.

With much fondness, Esther said, "I want to meet the people who raised such a fine, intelligent, young man."

"This is my father and mother, S.R. and Mary Snow. Ma, Pa, this is Horatio and Esther Knapp."

"Pleased to meet you." S.R. shook their hands.

Horatio told his wife, "Please sit down, Esther."

Esther moved very slowly and with a lot of pain.

"Are you all right?" Mary asked.

Esther told her, "I will be, thanks to these three fine men."

"Let me tell the story, so you can eat and not strain." Horatio put what he knew were his wife's favorite things on a plate for her and then narrated the story for Mr. and Mrs. Snow as the two partook of the

322

most elegant meal they had ever eaten. Matt joined them before the story was over.

S.R. stood up. "Since you two were in that room with my son, I need to ask you something privately." He looked across the table. "Would you mind if these two men step outside with me?"

"Of course, I don't mind," Mrs. Knapp replied.

S.R. asked, "Would you speak with me?"

"What do you want to know?" They were fathers and knew how they would feel if their child had been in this situation. They followed S.R. out of the house.

As he walked out the door, as loudly as he could without being conspicuous, S.R. said, "I'm happy everything is going so well." He started them around the block.

Matt said, "What do you want to talk about?"

Loudly S.R. informed them of what he wanted to know. "I need to know you and Edwin are really free. Walk around the block, so I can see what happens."

"I believe we're free, but it's a good idea to test it. Let's go, Morris." Matt and Morris started their stroll. S.R. walked back into the house.

"Where are Mr. Parker and Mr. Woolsey?" Esther asked.

"They wanted to see how those new boots feel. They're walking around the block."

Esther hoped he wasn't still worried about his son. "Did they answer your question?"

Everybody sat calmly and continued eating. Nobody seemed to care that the two men were gone. "I hope you don't mind, but can I speak with my son alone?"

Murray said, "Use the library. It's down the hall."

"Thank you." S.R. motioned for Edwin to follow him. When they got to the library, S.R. verified that no one had followed then closed the door. "Is everything all right? Do they think you killed that man?"

"Everything's fine, Pa. Everybody knows Mrs. Knapp killed him after he shot her."

"Dr. Smith told me to secretly give this to you and to tell you to give it to that lawman secretly, but only if it's safe." S.R. passed on the rest of Abraham's instructions then said, "And don't tell anybody he is or was here. One more thing, his skin is dyed, and he goes as Abraham, the slave of one of the men with you."

"All right, Pa." Edwin took the note and put it in his smelly pocket. He strongly did not want to have to undress Roy's body. They returned to the dining room.

Morris and Matt started around the block. "Pa." George hurried over to them. "Is everything all right?" George probably would not have hugged his father in public, but he had been afraid that his father was dead, and then he had feared that he was captured. He was very relieved that his father was none of the above, so he hugged him tightly. Since George hugged his father, Justin felt free to do the same and happily hugged Matt.

Morris wanted his family, S.R., and himself to know that they were free. "Let's walk around the block."

"I'm glad you're both all right," Will told his brother and brother-in-law.

Matt and Morris recounted what had happened while they sauntered around the block. They opened the door of Murray Strong's house. "We're back. We have some family with us. Can they come in?"

Mr. Strong stood in the dining room doorway and waved them over. "Bring them to breakfast."

Matt touched each one as he named them. "My son Justin and my brother Will."

Morris added, "My son, George. We should have been home yesterday, and they were concerned."

Fifty One

Just as they sat down at the table, Mrs. Daniels, Norman Sweeting, and Captain Miles Cornish returned. After introductions, they joined the others at the table.

As if Edwin had not realized that he had failed to complete the assigned task, Candace told him, "Edwin, you haven't had a bath."

"We were telling our families about what happened, and I wanted to wait until after the story came to the part where we were in the room with Mr. Butterfield."

Norman still felt it best to gather as many facts as he could. "We haven't heard the story either, so please tell us."

True to their pact, not one of them mentioned any screaming in the story but explained everything else in disgusting detail.

Esther said, "I had no idea dead bodies did all those things. I'm sure I would have passed away from fright."

Very matter-of-factly, Candace stated, "Long before he did any of those things, I would have used that letter opener to chop Roy Butterfield into small pieces, but you were very brave."

Esther held her dainty coffee cup with her little finger out. "I did shoot him nineteen times for us, Mrs. Daniels."

326

"Everybody, please call me Candy, and thank you very much, Mrs. Knapp, for killing him thoroughly."

"All of you call me Esther."

"I've posted a thousand-dollar reward for Mr. Butterfield alive or dead. I believe it should be divided between Edwin Snow, Charles Woolsey, Henry Parker, and Mrs. Knapp."

Esther spoke right up, "We don't want any. Please divide it among the others." She switched subjects. "Mr. and Mrs. Snow, Horatio and I want to provide an education for Edwin. Please don't say no. We have no children. Now I will never have any. It would be a great privilege for us to be able to do this. We would like to keep in touch with you and Edwin."

S.R. refused, "We don't take charity."

Horatio disputed S.R.'s opinion, "Sir, there is no way this would be charity. Your son deserves more than a mere education for saving the life of my wife. An education is a mere pittance of what is owed for what he has given Esther and me."

S.R. thought about what his family meant to him. Nothing could ever have more value to him. "I understand. I know how much Edwin and Mary mean to me. If he wants to get educated, we'll allow you to do that for him, and we'll be grateful."

"Thank you, Mr. and Mrs. Snow. I look forward to communicating with Edwin through the post when he can do so. We'll remain here until everything has been arranged for Edwin's instruction."

Matt knew there was no way he would ever be able to pick between his children as to who to educate, but he had an idea. "I know some teachers for us."

327

Esther replied, "That's wonderful. Who is it? How do we get in touch?"

Matt told them, "One is here now, the other two can be here it two days, but I'd like for you to hear my proposal now if you're up to it. I know you should be in bed and not here."

"Do you feel able to sit a while longer?" Horatio asked his wife.

Esther replied, "What do you propose?"

"Since you would like to provide for one education for each of us, I thought maybe once you have determined how much that education will be for Edwin, that you might give us twice that amount to purchase educational materials that we would use to educate all our children. It wouldn't be any more for you, but it would be extremely more for our community."

"I think that would be wonderful! What do you think, Horatio?" Esther looked at her husband.

"Who is the teacher here?" Horatio asked.

"Henry. The others are his wife and Will's wife. All three are well-educated."

Horatio walked to the library. He perused the books, pulled one off the shelf, and then carried it back into the dining room, along with a handful of papers and some pencils. "Please read this book." He handed the book to the man posing as Henry.

Morris read, "The Narrative of Arthur Gordon Pym of Nantucket. Comprising the details of a mutiny and atrocious butchery on board the American Brig Grampus, on her way to the South Seas, in the month of June 1827. With an account of the recapture of the vessel

328

by the survivors; their shipwreck and subsequent horrible sufferings from famine; their deliverance by means of the British Schooner Jane Guy J, the brief cruise of this latter vessel in the Antarctic ocean; her capture, and the massacre of her crew among a group of islands in the eighty-fourth parallel of southern latitude; together with the incredible adventures and discoverys still further south to which that distressing calamity gave rise. New-York: Harper & Brothers, 82 Cliff-St. 1838. Shall I keep reading?"

"Yes, please," Edwin requested.

"You don't need to keep reading. What about numbers?" Horatio asked.

Edwin said, "But I want to know what happened."

Esther explained, "That is why you must learn to read, Edwin."

Edwin wasn't giving up, "Can I use that story to learn?"

Horatio stopped the thread of discussion, "Possibly, Edwin. Henry, what about arithmetic?"

"I can do your books right now if you'd like."

Horatio wrote out some problems and handed the paper to Morris who sat down and worked them all, except one, then handed the paper back. "You didn't complete this one, and you didn't even try."

"It's not solvable."

"How do you know? You didn't try."

Morris explained how the rules of arithmetic made the equation unsolvable.

Horatio had not intended to make an unsolvable problem. He simply made up something randomly, but he was impressed that Morris had realized immediately that the problem didn't conform to the rules.

"Is your wife as good as you?" Esther inquired.

"I think I'm a better mathematician, but she is very good at reading, writing, and arithmetic, and so is her sister. My wife and my sister-in-law also know how to read music, and they play the flute and the violin."

Horatio calculated the practicality. "How many people live in your community?"

Morris replied, "Twenty-three," then corrected the number, "I'm sorry, it's twenty-two. Also, some of the children are too young for school right now."

Edwin gave out more information than Matt would have liked. "They're all trying to learn. We practiced yesterday. Our papers are on the floor over at the boarding house. Charles is getting good. I saw him write a whole bunch of words."

"May we look?" Candy asked.

Edwin realized he had the answer to the problem presented by Dr. Smith's request. "If I can talk to Mr. Sweeting about it, I'll get the papers."

Norman sat behind his plate. "What do you want?"

"Can I talk to you outside, like my Pa did?"

"Yes." Norman slowly walked out the door. Edwin pulled the door shut.

Fifty Two

"Please keep this just between us." Edwin handed Norman the paper requesting Roy Butterfield's possessions.

"The law does say you can do this. I'll have to check on the horse and see what other things Roy Butterfield had with him."

"Can we walk to the stable and look? After you check it over, I'll go get what's at the boarding house. You already know what's over there in that room."

Norman was very tired, so he agreed. "After we go to the stable, I'm going home to get some sleep."

Roy's slender horse stood in the stall, enjoying hay and oats. His saddle sat on the stall wall, and the bridle hung on a peg with a saddlebag. Norman looked in the bag. He only found a bundle of letters addressed to Hank Butterfield. Roy also had a box in the corner of the stall. Norman opened it. Inside were rounds for the revolver. He saw no stolen items, and none of it seemed important.

"You can have it all, but you'll have to pay for the horse's board. Come over to my house. I'll write you a paper of custody and give you the gun."

"Wonderful." It pleased Edwin to have his own horse, saddle, saddlebag, bridle, gun, and a box of ammunition. He didn't care about the letters. He couldn't even read them. Edwin definitely did not want to undress Roy and started thinking about how to get out of it.

At Norman's home, they went inside while Norman wrote the paper that gave all the possessions of Roy Butterfield to Edwin Snow. Norman handed Edwin the paper and the gun. "I guess you'll come to Maumelle frequently to buy those plants. Make sure you come and let me know how you're doing."

"I will if you promise you'll never lock me in a room with anybody dead again."

"Fair enough, I promise."

Edwin took the paper and the gun, then headed to the boarding house. Abraham joined him on the way.

"Hello, Dr. Smith."

"Hello, Edwin. I'm still going as Abraham. Did he do it?'

"Yes, but I'm not taking those clothes off that body. If you want them, you do it. Do you want to see what's at the stable?"

"I do. Let's go." They walked into the stable and examined the horse.

The stable owner came in. The people touching and looking over the horse were not its owner. He pulled out his gun. "You don't own that horse. Move away from it."

Abraham and Edwin quickly moved away. "Show him your paper," Abraham whispered.

Edwin said, "Actually, I do own this horse." He handed over the paper from Mr. Sweeting.

The stable owner asked, "You're Edwin Snow?"

"I am. This horse, the saddle, bridle, ammo box, and saddlebags are mine now."

"I guess I'd better bring you the rest of his things."

"There's more?"

"Yep." The man holstered his gun and left. He came back with a locked wooden box one-foot square and two-feet-long. He put it down and put the strap to bind it to the horse on top.

Edwin took out the letters. "You want these?" He searched the saddlebag. There was nothing else in there. Definitely not a key, so they searched the saddle and bridle but still found no key. Edwin decided they had looked long enough. "We can come back later to get these. I need to get some papers from the boarding house."

Abraham picked up the letters. "I'll take the letters." They headed over to Lucy's.

"Mr. and Mrs. Knapp are going to pay for me and the people at Fletcher Creek to get an education. I wish Mrs. Knapp would go to bed; she's badly hurt. Maybe you can come see her."

They knocked at the boarding house. Nobody answered, so they let themselves in. Edwin picked up all the papers. "They want to see these papers." He stacked them up on the desk then gathered all the plants he had purchased.

Abraham put the gun belt, ammo belt, and shiv together then tried to pull Ben's boot off the very repulsive, stiff body of Roy Butterfield. The foot resisted letting the boot slide off. Abraham didn't want to touch the body either, but he was determined Roy wasn't keeping Ben's clothes. To hold it in place, Abraham pushed Roy's leg down with his foot. The body had not flattened out completely, so Roy's head rose. "That's creepy. It's like he's watching me." Abraham held Roy's leg and pulled the boot.

"Crack." Roy's foot broke as the boot came off.

"I sure am glad that Roy has on socks. I don't want his toes that just detached in the boot." Abraham moved over to Roy's other leg. The same problem occurred with the other boot, but Abraham got them both off. "Use the boots to hold his legs down. I want to get his vest, shirt, and suspenders."

Edwin held his nose and pushed Roy's legs down with the boots. With repulsion, he watched Abraham unbutton the shirt and the suspenders.

The suspenders came off easily and with no problem. Abraham pulled the shirt and vest over the body's head, bunched them together, then wrestled them down the arms. The arms pulled together slightly, but there was no further damage to the body.

"Leave his pants on him, Dr. Smith. He messed in them after he was dead."

"I don't think the pants belonged to Ben anyway. I'll leave them. Don't forget to call me Abraham."

"You know this man? Who is Ben?"

"It's better if you don't know anything. I don't want him to have anything or any dignity." Abraham thought about everything the man had taken from his family and, he was sure, from other families as well. Roy had even taken Ben's clothes after Ben had saved Roy's life. "Actually, I'm not going to leave them." He pulled his knife and started to slit the pants leg up the front.

334

Edwin was surprised. He knew Abraham as Dr. Smith, a very caring, loving man. Edwin didn't want his friend drawn into something disgusting by anger or hatred. "It's too nasty. He would be getting at you one last time by making you deal with his stuff. Roy Butterfield must be a very horrible man for you to have such strong feelings against him, but don't let him control you."

Abraham stopped. "You're a wise person, Edwin. He was a very terrible man, and you're right about the pants, but the key to that box must be in them."

"I checked his pockets before he got so rotten. I didn't find a key."

Abraham slid the shiv into its place in the boot then crammed the suspenders, shirt, and vest into the boots. Since they legally belonged to Edwin, he asked, "Do you want these?"

Edwin picked up the plants, papers, gun, and ammo belts. "Only these, you can have the clothes."

"Thank you. I want to show them to my family."

"Come look at Mrs. Knapp. Mrs. Daniels may also need you to look at her. She doesn't move her arm right."

"I don't want anybody who brought you these plants, or those with them, to know that I'm here."

"You could come after they leave. I think they're leaving soon."

"I'll wait at the stable. If the women want me to help, come get me right after they leave."

"I'm getting you no matter if they do or not. Mrs. Knapp is missing half her back."

335

"All right, I'll be waiting with a first aid kit. Do you want me to take anything to the stable?"

"You better take the gun, and the belts or the others will ask questions."

As they parted, Abraham reminded Edwin, "Don't forget; I'm Abraham now."

Edwin went back to Mr. Strong's house and cracked the door. "It's Edwin."

"Come to the library." Mr. Strong called out.

Candy stopped him in the hall. "Give me the papers. Get in the bath, RIGHT NOW!"

"Yes, ma'am." Edwin handed her the papers. He felt extra defiled and was more than ready to get into the bath. He was sure he would have to soak in rose water for hours to get the smell off.

Esther looked over the papers. Matt explained, "We map where we find certain plants and hunting areas. We also learn how to read and write."

Esther became sure that there was a good and creative teacher in their group. "Charles, I think your proposal is a wonderful and workable plan."

Horatio agreed, "We'll be here for some time while Esther heals, so bring your families to meet us when you can, and we'll work out all the details."

Morris told Mr. and Mrs. Snow, "Edwin won't need to come here in two weeks. We'll go to Little Rock. We have other business there as well."

Matt and Morris waited to say goodbye to Edwin. When Edwin strolled into the library after his long bath, Mrs. Knapp had gone back upstairs to bed. Mrs. Daniels had decided to stay in Maumelle with Esther, so they could comfort each other. Captain Cornish had already started back to Little Rock alone.

Matt and Morris decided to make some purchases with the reward money before they went home. Edwin shook the hands of the men with whom he had forged an unbreakable bond while locked in the boarding house with Roy Butterfield's body. "I guess things ended up good for everybody." Edwin stepped out with his friends.

"Except for the dead and injured," Matt added.

Morris replied, "It will be very good for us, but I don't want to ever do it again."

"I don't either. Are we going to meet here again in two weeks?" Edwin asked.

"In a few days, we're going to bring our families here to meet the Knapps, but we'll bring the next batch of plants to Little Rock. We'll probably be buying educational materials in Little Rock. I remember seeing some things in Clark's store, plus we want wagons."

"Go see Reverend Pratt. He's the best wainwright this side of the Mississippi."

Matt teased Edwin, "You know that for a fact?"

"Well, I think so."

Morris assured him, "We'll talk with him. See you again soon, Edwin. Goodbye." They left with the rest of their family and went to the store to get the items on Rebecca's list, along with whatever else they decided they wanted.

Fifty Three

Edwin went back into the house and told Candy what he had on his mind. I have a good friend who is a very good doctor. I saw him in town when I was out. I asked him if there is anything he can do to help Mrs. Knapp, and I noticed you aren't moving your arm right. He said he would come. I just have to fetch him."

Candy spilled out her heart, "I know there's something wrong with the way I'm healing. It's my fault, and I don't deserve anything better. I don't even want to be alive. I don't know how to go on without Jasper. I don't think I should be alive when he isn't. If the doctor hadn't been taking care of me, Jasper wouldn't have died. It doesn't seem fair, so I don't do any of the things the doctor told me to do. I can't speak for Esther, but I want to suffer because Jasper is gone." Candy started to cry. Mary Snow stepped over and let Candy cry on her shoulder.

Murray knew both women needed a doctor. He issued the orders, "Go get him."

Edwin immediately ran out the door. His new boots slowed him down pretty quickly. By the time he got to the stable, he walked barefooted. "It's going to take some time to break in my new boots."

"So, they want me to help?"

"Mr. Strong told me to get you."

Abraham picked up his first aid box. "Let's go."

Edwin opened the door. As they entered Murray's home, Edwin notified everybody, "I have the doctor."

"Still in the library," Murray called out.

As Mary, S.R., and Murray had tried to help heal the wound in Candy's emotional heart, which had not healed one little bit, they had managed to convince her to let the doctor look at the wound near her physical heart. Candy had changed into a skirt and a blouse that she could open at the front, so the doctor could look at the scar that had been healing for a few weeks.

As a slave with proper respect, Abraham walked to Mr. Strong with his eyes looking at the floor. "Thank you for allowing me into your home, sir."

"See if there is anything you can do for Mrs. Daniels, then I'll take you to Mrs. Knapp. She and her husband would like you to check her wounds."

"Yes, sir." Abraham turned to the woman. "Edwin tells me you were shot and are having some troubles. Where is the injury, ma'am?"

She touched the left side of her chest just above the breast. She pulled her shirt slightly to the side to reveal the wound.

Abraham instructed her, "We'll go out into the hall. Take your arm out of your shirtsleeve then bring the sleeve under your arm and across your front. If you have a pin, pin it at your other armpit."

Edwin, S.R., Abraham, and Murray left the room. Mary helped Candy get her clothes arranged as instructed. Candy notified the others, "I'm ready."

Murray wasn't leaving Candy alone with a man

they barely knew and went back into the room with Abraham. Abraham looked at the wound, then checked her back. "It didn't go all the way through?"

"It went all the way through my husband and into me." Tears filled her eyes and threatened to overflow onto her cheeks again.

"I'm sorry, Mrs. Daniels. I didn't mean to upset you. I didn't know."

Candy told Abraham how she felt, "I don't really want to try to get better. I can't believe he's gone."

Abraham felt the wound. "Tell me when it hurts." He raised her arm, gently moved her arm toward the back and then over her head. He noted where the muscles and tissues pulled.

"Everything you're doing hurts."

"Scar tissue has adhered under your skin and made a connection where it shouldn't. It's limiting your range of motion. You have three choices: do nothing and live with it, do exercises to stretch the tissues, which will help some, or I can open the wound and remove the adhesion. Then, you have to do the exercises as it heals, so it doesn't form an adhesion again."

"I don't know how good of a doctor you are."

"I performed a very similar procedure just a few weeks ago, and the patient is doing very well."

"If I did want you to remove the adhesion, when and where would you do it?"

Even though it wasn't really his business, Murray asked, "Do you have a reference?"

"Edwin is one. You could go to Little Rock and ask Mr. and Mrs. Harrow, or Mrs. Hall, plus any number of other people, but I won't be here that long. I can't stay in town. I'd have to perform the procedure here in this house right now and then leave."

"Go see what you can do for Esther while I think about it." Candy remembered what her sister had told her when she had been in Little Rock.

"Yes, ma'am." Abraham turned. Murray led him to the room where Mrs. Knapp was laying on her side in the bed. Getting dressed, going down the stairs, sitting in the dining room, and then getting back up the stairs had caused her wounds to bleed slightly. She wore her husband's shirt again just as she had the day Edwin had cared for her.

As Abraham looked at the bullet hole, Mr. Knapp said, "I told her she shouldn't get out of bed."

"This should have stitches, Mrs. Knapp. May I see your back?"

"My whole back hurts." Esther rolled onto her stomach, so Abraham could look.

Mr. Knapp saw a look of sheer anger pass across Abraham's face as he assessed the damage. "I can stitch this. However, you need to have a skin graft and reconstructive surgery. You shouldn't travel. You should have a surgeon come to you."

Mr. Knapp asked, "Where would we get somebody?"

"You would have to go east to a big city like Richmond, Philadelphia, or New York to find a good enough doctor, and it's going to cost a lot to get him to come out here."

"I'm in terrible pain. What can you do to help now?"

"I can give you a sedative that will put you to sleep. When you're asleep, you won't feel pain, but you will when you're awake, to eat and such. I can stitch some of this muscle damage and close the skin. I can give you an antiseptic wash. You don't want an infection to set in."

"Put me to leep, and do what you can."

"Please come into the hall." Mr. Knapp motioned to Abraham.

Esther told her husband, "You will say whatever you have to say right here in front of me."

"Yes, dear." Before allowing him to perform surgery on his wife, Horatio questioned the man they didn't know. "Have you ever done this before?"

Abraham told the truth, except that he didn't mention the fact that the patient had been a mule. He figured it didn't really matter since the procedure would be the same. "I've done this once before with a large amount of her body severely injured like this. The patient is doing very well. She is almost completely healed and doesn't even need any pain medication. Her skin will never be as it was before. I'm not going to be able to make this look pretty."

"Horatio, will you love me if my back is a horror?"

"Of course, I'll love you no matter what."

Esther pointed out their major constraint with doctor selection. "He's done this before, and Abraham is the only one here."

Horatio agreed, "Do your best."

"I can give you the sedative now, so you can go to sleep and not be in pain."

"Please do that for me. I can barely stand it."

"I'll be back soon." He stepped into the hall. "Edwin, I'll need your help. I know you're tired. Can you do it?"

"Let me talk with my folks." Edwin went to find out if they had to leave right away. He returned to the kitchen with both his parents.

S.R. spoke up, "We can stay. Let us help too."

"Show your folks how to make the sedative and make a lot of it. We may be performing surgery twice." Candy came into the kitchen. Abraham asked her, "Did you decide?"

Candy had a question. "You wouldn't happen to know Dr. Luke Smith, would you?" Edwin and S.R. didn't know if they should run or what. Murray and Mary only heard a casual conversation with a woman trying to make small alk, instead of a difficult decision.

"How do you know about Dr. Smith?"

"My sister Pearl told me how he helped her son."

Abraham wasn't going to confess to anything, but he needed to know what kind of situation he was facing. "How do you feel about your sister?"

"I love her dearly, and I'm ever so grateful. We'll never be able to thank him enough. Ansel is a happy boy, instead of the boy who wished for death every night."

"I'm very happy to hear that. Was it milk?"

"Yes, it was. I've decided. I want you to fix me, but I won't be able to take the pain."

Edwin and S.R. let out the breath they had been holding. Abraham did too. "I can put you to sleep."

Mr. Strong was standing next to Candace, so

Abraham asked, "This is your house. If I do this surgery, these people are going to be in your house and under your care for months."

"I don't mind them being here, but I'll need help to cook and clean." He looked at Mary. She looked at S.R.

"I need her to cook for me," S.R. informed them.

Candy had decided that she didn't want to spend the rest of her life not being able to move her arm, and she believed Abraham was the man to fix her. "If Mr. Strong will let all three of you stay here, I'll pay you for your help, and I'll pay for your keep."

"I have enough rooms, but it's going to take a long time for these women to heal. You'll have to live here the whole time."

"I need to take Mr. Harrow back his horses and the plants, and I'll need to take care of a few things before I come back. Mary and Edwin can stay here if they want."

Mary instructed her husband, "Bring all our clothes and my tatting, and take the chickens to Mr. Lull."

Candace wanted to look at attractively clothed people, but she didn't want to be insulting. "I'll buy you new clothes. Just make arrangements for your chickens."

Edwin brought up their other animals. "We have two horses to stable here in Maumelle."

Candace negotiated, "Mr. Strong, if you'll let them keep their horses in your stable, I'll pay for their feed."

S.R. knew that meant Edwin had gotten all the belongings of Roy Butterfield. "I'll be back as soon as I can." He left the house and headed to the stable to get the Harrow's horses and his own, so he could get to Little Rock and back.

344

Fifty Four

"Edwin, maybe you should bring your new possessions here. They'll be safer in Mr. Strong's house. There wouldn't be any complications if you did; the others have already left." Edwin nodded his head and left with his father. He wanted to show him everything, anyway.

Abraham got started. "Mary, please help me. We'll need a tarp and towels for each woman to protect the beds."

Candy asked, "Abraham, how much will I owe you?"

"Would you buy me some of the books I saw in Mr. Strong's library?"

"I don't know if he'll sell them. Which books do you want?"

"Any medical or law books that he'll sell, up to what you want to pay me, and the book Edwin has been telling me about. I want to give it to him."

"I'll go ask and see what he has while you get ready."

Edwin announced his return when he got back, "It's Edwin."

Murray yelled from the library, "You have to just come and go if you're going to live here."

Edwin walked into the library. Books were off the

shelves, on the floor, and stacked on the desk. "Where shall I put my things?"

"I'll show you your rooms." Murray took Edwin to a small room by the kitchen. He opened the door of a larger room beside it. "This one is for your parents."

"Thank you. I put my horse in the stable and gave all of them hay and water. Can I bring my other things in through this door back here?"

Murray pulled open a small drawer in the hall table and handed over a key. "I keep the key in here." Edwin unlocked the back door but then went out the front. He took the small cart with all the things he now owned to the back door.

Abraham and Mary had the sedative ready, so they followed Murray and Candy up the stairs. Murray led them to the room across the hall from Mr. and Mrs. Knapp. "This will be your room, Mrs. Daniels." Murray opened the door.

She walked into the room. "Thank you. It's a beautiful room. I'm sure I'll be as comfortable as a woman who's been shot can be."

"Mrs. Daniels, I'm going to give you this sedative and fix your shoulder first because it will take a long time for me to help Mrs. Knapp. Mary and Mr. Strong will stay in the room with us while you're asleep. We can get Mr. Knapp as well if you'd like."

"You and Mary are enough." She glanced at Murray out of the corner of her eye.

Murray took the other cup of the concoction Abraham had cooked up to Mrs. Knapp across the hall. Candy took her cup and drank the sedative. She sat on the bed with pillows behind her back and talked about Ansel until she was asleep. Abraham cut the wound open then cut away the scar tissue that was causing the problem. He moved her arm up, back, and around. She had full range of motion. He stitched the wound as neatly as possible. It was much smaller than the previous scar. Abraham made it look like a crescent moon surrounded by stars instead of the previous jagged mess made by the doctor who was trying to get to Jasper quickly. He explained to Mary how Candy was to move her arm several times a day, so the tissues would remain free as they healed. "Watch over her. Mr. Knapp will be in the room with me and his wife."

When Abraham crossed the hall, Mrs. Knapp was already asleep. "Are you ready for me to start?"

Since his wife could not hear, Mr. Knapp gave permission, but he added a warning. "You may start, but you'd better make her better, not worse."

"I understand." Abraham wanted to do his best for both women. Not only for the women but also for himself. They should have executed Gus, Roy, and Ben in Harmony, or done as Ben had done when he had rid the world of Gus. They would have protected everybody the man had harmed since then.

Maybe it was to give Ben the opportunity to repent that God had led the people of Harmony to request that the sentence be executed in Little Rock. He didn't really know why. However, the result was that Jasper, Candace, and Esther had suffered terrible consequences because his family had tried to take the men to justice in Little Rock and had unintentionally let Roy escape.

Abraham stitched Esther's stomach, starting with the muscles and then her skin. He made the scar as beautiful as he could, exactly as he had done for Candy. He put a bandage on the injury with more yarrow and shepherd's purse. "Help me turn her over."

While Esther slept flat on her stomach, Abraham searched the tissues carefully for internal injuries to essential organs. Her organs looked unscathed. He carefully found the correct pieces of muscles and tissues to attach together, just as he had with Beauty. For hours, he meticulously put Esther back together.

When he got to the skin, he cut small pieces from places where he could stretch the skin together and used that skin to fill in places where the skin was gone. Mr. Knapp saw that Abraham was doing his best to make Esther's back beautiful.

When he had finally finished, Abraham said, "You should still take her to get a skin graft."

"I don't know about that, Abraham. I think your patchwork is beautiful, and I watched your face. If I didn't know that you aren't connected to this, I would have sworn that putting her together was more than just a job."

"I hope both of them heal well. I hope they never feel that they're not beautiful because they are beautiful women. Don't let your wife ever wonder whether or not you find her beautiful."

"I won't. Tell me what to do for her to heal well."

Abraham explained how to use the sedative to help with the pain while the women healed and how to use the antiseptic wash to prevent infection. He decided not to tell him about using maggots if they got an infection. Abraham knew Edwin would know about the maggots if it became necessary. Last, he explained how to use a honey and warm milk rub to minimize the scars.

Abraham left the room and went down the stairs. Mary was cooking in the kitchen, wearing her new dress and new slippers. Edwin smelled like roses as he slept on the bed in his very own room at Mr. Strong's house. Candace and Esther both slept with their bodies and lives forever altered by Roy Butterfield. At the least, both women had their bodies put back together by a slave named Abraham.

As Abraham packed his first aid kit, Murray informed him, "I was asked by Mrs. Daniels to allow you to select books and to give this one to Edwin. I don't know how many you can carry. Mr. Knapp said to see to it that you have the means to transport the books. This is a letter to the owner of the stable. It instructs him to give you, from those he has for sale, the animal of your choice. The letter also states that Mr. Knapp will pay him later. In addition, I added a letter of assurance of payment because the stable owner knows me, but not Mr. Knapp. I also want to thank you for what you've done for my sister, Esther. Is there something else I can do for you?"

Abraham looked at the books. He read the preface of the Edgar Allen Poe book that Edwin wanted. "I can see why Edwin wants to read this. I'm grateful that he'll be educated. Edwin is very important to me and to my family. I thank God for allowing me to have known him. I believe you'll enjoy him. What I would like is for you to be sure he is treated respectfully, and that he gets the best education he can. I think he has the potential to be a great man."

Murray assured him, "That is our intention. We'll all see to that."

From Murray Strong's library, Abraham picked: the two volumes of Bouvier's Law Dictionary, The Theory of Presumptive Proof or an inquiry into the Nature of Circumstantial Evidence: Including an examination of the evidence on the Trial of Captain Donnellan by W. Clarke; The Anatomy of Humane Bodies by William Cowper; Domestic Medicine: or a treatise on the prevention and cure of diseases by regimen and simple medicine by William Buchan; All three volumes of Practical System of Surgery, Elements of Surgery by Darcy and the three volumes of Medical Essays.

"Would it be too much to ask for something sweet for the sweetness in my life, the woman who is my wife?"

Upon hearing the poetry of Abraham's request, Murray immediately thought of the proper book. He walked across the room and retrieved Hours of Idleness by Lord Byron. "I think this sweet woman of yours will like this."

Abraham flipped to a page and silently read. "I think this will be perfect. I'll be back soon to pick up these books. Do you have a string or something I can use to tie all those letters together?"

Murray retrieved a ball of string from the desk. They walked to the stack of letters that sat on the table beside the first aid kit. Abraham unrolled some string, laid it across the letters, picked up the stack, and flipped it upside down. Something clattered when it hit the floor. Both men looked down at the key that lay on the floor. Abraham picked it up and put it in his pocket, thinking, "I know what this fits. Edwin must have the box in his room."

Through the open door, Edwin had heard the sound of the key landing on the wooden floorboards. He knew what he thought had made that sound. He looked into the hall. Abraham and Mr. Strong stood by the medicine box, tying a string around the letters.

"I believe you want to help me pick out a horse." Abraham needed to tell Edwin he had found the key, and he wanted to spend as much time with Edwin as possible. Every time they parted, Abraham believed it would be the last time. This time, however, he was certain that would be true. They would move on to Harmony as soon as he got back to Fletcher Creek.

Edwin put on his new shoes again. "I'll give them another round of breaking in."

"The key was in one of the letters. We should see what's in the box before you say anything to anybody. It may not be anything important, but we don't know."

"I can't wait to look. What a person keeps in a locked box would probably be special items." They walked to the stable. Abraham picked a mare that was young and appeared to be well bred. He also got a new saddle, bridle, and a large packsaddle that could carry all his books.

"What kind of stories are in those books you want?" Edwin was curious about what Abraham would find in a book that was worth what he had done for Mrs. Daniels.

"They are books about medicine and law, except one for my wife, Lily, which has poems." They put Abraham's new mare into the stable at Mr. Strong's home, so they could go in and look in the box.

Being a person who did as he was told, Edwin did not announce that they were back when they entered through the back door and went into his room. The locked box sat at the foot of the bed. Edwin knelt beside the box, inserted the key, and turned it. The key rotated. He looked at Abraham, then opened the lid. Inside was what they believed to be Roy's spare clothes, or maybe it would have been better described as Roy's original clothes.

Edwin dropped from the heights of anticipation and excitement to the pit of disappointment. "I guess it's nothing important."

Abraham picked up a piece of clothes with the tips of his fingers. "There must be at least some of the booty from his robberies." They saw a silk bag with the monogram J.D.

"That must be the moneybag of Jasper Daniels." Edwin picked it up. It was empty.

"I guess that's why he tried to rob Horatio and Esther. It didn't take long for him to spend the money he stole from Candace and Jasper."

The two of them gingerly removed the clothes that looked like they had not been cleaned for a very long time. Underneath them, they found the booty. They removed items one at a time and lay them on the floor.

There were several wallets and moneybags. All of which contained no money.

"I sure hope he didn't kill all these people," Edwin remarked with dismay.

"I do too. I told you, I knew he was a bad man."

Edwin took out a beautiful necklace of red stones. The pendant was a large red stone shaped like a heart. He stroked the heart. "It's beautiful. You think it's something good?"

"I'm not qualified to figure that out. It's very nice, no matter if it is or not." Abraham exclaimed, "It can't be," then gently removed a music box from the trunk. There was the hole where the bullet from the Butterfield Gang had ruined its ability to play.

Edwin remarked, "I thought it was something like that because you wanted to punish that man."

"It's important that nobody knows who I am, and it's best for you if you don't know anything. Your letter from Mr. Sweeting gives you all the possessions of Roy Butterfield, except items known to be stolen if you can identify the owner. This belongs to my family."

"I guess I have to give it all to Mr. Sweeting." Edwin started putting things back into the box.

"I don't know how you'll be able to find out who owns any particular item, but you should take it all to Mr. Sweeting. If nobody claims anything, it will go back to you eventually."

"I'll help him with it." Murray walked into the room. "What's in there?" he asked.

Abraham informed Murray, "Clothes and other items. At least some of them are stolen. This belongs to my family."

"So that's why you care so much about these women. You were a victim of Mr. Butterfield as well."

Edwin picked up the cloth bag with the initials J.D. "This probably belongs to Mrs. Daniels. I think this proves the man was as guilty as sin."

With assurance, Abraham stated, "He was," then stood up. "Come with me, Edwin. I have something for you."

The three of them walked back to the library. "This is for you. Learn to read and enjoy it. Make getting that education your priority. Promise me that you won't allow yourself to be pulled away from learning."

"I won't. I promise to learn as much as I can."

Abraham stated his sincere appreciation to Murray, "Thank you for letting me have your books, Mr. Strong. They will help me quite a lot."

"All they'll do here is take up space on the shelf. I'm glad for you to put them to practical use. Thank you again for your help. Are you sure there's nothing else we can do for you?"

"I can't think of anything."

"I'll pray life will be good to you." Murray went upstairs to check on the two women who were now long-term guests in his house. He thought about the blue-eyed, educated slave who hadn't asked for money.

"Help me pack the books, Edwin."

Edwin helped Abraham carry the books and pack them into the packsaddle. "Will you take something to Nancy?"

"Of course."

"It's something from the box."

"Those are supposed to go back to the owners."

"We'll never be able to get them back to their owners, and I won't be able to give it to her later." He ran into the house and came back with the necklace of red stones. "I don't know if it's any good, but it's pretty, and this big one shaped like a heart reminds me of her lips. I never got to kiss them." He kissed the ruby heart then dropped it into a green velvet moneybag. "If she ever needs a kiss, there's one right here for her."

"I'll let her know. Goodbye, my good friend. Take care of yourself and everybody here."

"Goodbye, my good friend. I promise to go to school."

Abraham led his new mare, laden with his new books, toward Eyanosa. Edwin watched until Abraham was out of sight.

When Abraham rode away from Maumelle, he was five hours behind the others. He followed their trail at a trot. Morris and Matt had walked to Maumelle. Abraham figured they would go home together. Therefore, they would be walking and probably be around ten miles ahead. If he rode at a trot, he would travel four times what he thought was the speed of those ahead. He would catch up in two hours and be about two miles from home. Then he could make a wide berth around them and still beat them home by half an hour.

Fifty Five

In the woods, the morning of the same day, Lily left before anybody else was up. She checked for travelers before she rode Shaggy to the beehive to wait for Abraham. Everybody of Fletcher Creek would think the two of them went looking for travelers and either took them to the next stop or were spending the rest of the day alone. They wouldn't know that Abraham had left the night before and spent the day in Maumelle.

At seven thirty in the evening, Abraham rode over the ridge from the north. He looked down toward the beehive and saw Lily lying on a blanket. When Abraham got close, he called out, "My wife!"

Lily looked in the direction of her husband. She stood up and waved. "My husband, I'm so glad you're back. You have another horse. What happened?"

When Abraham got to her, he jumped down and hugged her tight. "I'll tell you as we go. I'm not far ahead, and I need to hide our new horse someplace safe. We need to leave Fletcher Creek tomorrow and pick her up on our way out."

"She's got a big bag. Should we get her close, so we can get the load into the wagon tonight?"

"Good idea. She's been trotting a long time with that bag. I'm sure she's tired."

They left the mare tied in a nearby grassy clearing.

All the people who had remained at home were in their cabins when Abraham and Lily arrived and put Eyanosa and Shaggy into the newly built corral. Abraham carried a bundle over his shoulder as he entered the tent.

"I have something very important to tell you, and I want everybody to be together."

Suddenly, Lily was afraid. Abraham took the bundle off his shoulder and laid it in the middle of the tent. By the light of their two lanterns, his family watched him open the bundle.

"That looks just like Mama's music box." Nancy picked it up. "How can this be?" She examined the bullet hole and knew that it was the music box that had been in their home in Harmony.

Abraham took out the boots, pulled out the clothes, laid them out, and then removed the shiv from its hiding place. "You shot Ben?" Marie asked with horror.

"No. It wasn't Ben, and it wasn't me." Abraham handed Lily the bundle of letters address to Hank Butterfield.

"Roy was in Ben's clothes?" Lily guessed.

"I don't know how he came to be in Ben's clothes, but Roy was wearing them when Matt, Morris, and Edwin saw him attempting to rob a man and his wife in an alley. They tackled him. The gun went off and shot the woman. The gun slid over to her. She picked it up and shot Roy nineteen times before she collapsed. Roy Butterfield is very dead. The sheriff locked up Matt, Morris, and Edwin until after the investigation. That's why they didn't come home. They'll be here soon, and you can hear all the details from them. Roy robbed a different couple a month ago. He killed that man and almost killed his wife. After the others left, I fixed the wounds of the two women. That's why I have the books in the saddlebag. The same way I did with Beauty, I repaired a large amount of damage to the back of the woman who shot Roy. That's why I have the mare. I'm hiding it because I don't want the people here to know that I followed them. Justin asked me not to go with them. It's time for us to leave anyway. If everybody agrees, can we leave tomorrow? We can tell them tonight because now they know they're capable of caring for themselves."

James said, "I'm healed enough to travel. I'm ready to go."

"As long as it won't hurt James, then it's fine with me," Marie told them.

Nancy knew Justin was no longer interested in her, and she didn't want to watch him court Carmen. "I have no reason to stay here."

Lily answered, "It fine with me."

Now that he had told his family what he thought they needed to know, Abraham asked, "Is there any food we can eat quickly?" Theo retrieved some easily accessible food from the wagon. Abraham and Lily ate the only meal either had eaten since the night before.

When Justin, George, and Will triumphantly escorted Matt and Morris home, everybody gathered outside to listen to the stories. Matilda sat on Matt's lap and listened with fascination to everything that happens to the body of a dead person. "Paw, you're so brave."

Abraham also listened to every detail of the stories to determine if they had any idea that anybody had intervened along the way. It was evident to him that they had no idea. He hadn't done much anyway. He had only made sure that scared and worried people hadn't done anything rash. Matt and Morris, along with Edwin, were the real heroes, and now the people of Fletcher Creek would receive an education.

The unsung hero was Katie, who had made the decision to bring home travelers in The Underground Railroad. After the men had reported all the happenings in Maumelle, Abraham announced their decision. "We're leaving in the morning."

Katie spoke up, "Let us make a wonderful farewell breakfast for you before you go."

Marie accepted, "That would be nice."

They were ready to move on, but they were glad they had stopped. Because they had been there, the people of Fletcher Creek had everything they needed to survive and thrive. Abraham believed the people who had become their friends would never again be desperate. The people of Fletcher Creek knew it as well.

In addition, Theo, Abraham, Lily, James, Marie, and Nancy had completely restocked their supplies.

Later that night, Abraham brought his mare to the wagon and unloaded all the books, then put the mare in the corral where she would be safe for the night. Before anybody was up the next morning, he moved her to the exit path.

As the people of Fletcher Creek prepared a farewell breakfast, Abraham and his family divided and balanced their possessions between the two wagons. The wagon with the removable back and side, now also had a removable wooden center divider in the wagon box. To the center divider, they had secured their India rubber tarp that had been damaged in the blizzard early that spring. They had pulled it up and attached it to the wagon bows at the top. It created a barrier that protected the items stored in the front from the rear section where they could carry the goats.

Justin came over. "Nancy, may I talk with you for a minute?"

They walked a short distance away. Justin reached out to hold Nancy's hands. "I want to apologize for behaving the way I have recently. You're a wonderful and beautiful woman, but my family needs me here. I can't leave them to go with you, and I don't think I would be able to live up to your expectations for life. Besides, you can do everything. You don't need me, Carmen does, and she doesn't have any expectations for how I should live. I'm sorry for making you think I would go with you."

"Don't be sorry. I enjoyed what we shared for a while, and I understand completely how much a family means to a person. I made the same choice. I think you're right that Carmen needs you, but don't believe that she has no expectations about how you should live. It might be best for both of you if you talk about what both of you want out of life and marriage. I hope you will have happy lives. I hope everybody here will."

"May I kiss you goodbye?" Justin asked.

Nancy stepped into Justin's arms. "I will always remember you." She raised her lips to his.

After a long kiss, he replied, "I'll remember you too." They walked back to join the others.

The meal was excellent and full of warm companionship. All of them were grateful to have known each other. As the people leaving harnessed their mules, Katie told them, "I would have been happy if you had stayed and become part of our community, but I understand that you have reasons to move on. I can never tell you how much I appreciate all of you. You saved us."

"I only wish we had gotten here sooner and had saved Ann as well," Lily replied.

"May she look down on you from Heaven and protect you." Katie truly appreciated the comfort Lily had given her about her daughter.

Except for Mule 4, that would always have a slight vision loss in its right eye, and Beauty that was well on its way to full health but still healing from the extensive damage to its side, they had fully recovered animals when they drove away. The six mules they owned that had previously belonged to Russell and Arnold now had patchwork skin on their right sides. That was what identified them as the mules of the Williams family. So that the two-month-old baby goats could keep pace with their mothers, they progressed slowly as they followed the creek to the crossing. When they picked up the new mare, they had thirty-five animals, two fully stocked wagons, and six happy people.

Acknowledgements

Hristo Argirov Kovatliev is the creator of the cover.
I am
the creator of this story. God is the creator of
everything.

Did you like this story?
Please write a review!

https://www.amazon.com/dp/B078HHNQR2/

Chance and Choices Adventures
by Lisa Gay

Pray for Justice
Choose Your Consequences
No Remorse
Means of Escape
Torn Hearts

62088772R00221

Made in the USA
Columbia, SC
02 July 2019